Killers Countdown

(A DI Shona McKenzie Mystery)

Wendy H. Jones

Published by Scott and Lawson

Copyright © Wendy H. Jones, 2014

www.wendyhjones.com

Cover Design by Cathy Helms of Avalon Graphics LLC

ISBN: 978-0-9930677-1-6

DEDICATION

To the memory of my mother, Catherine Jones who fostered my love of reading

To my aunt Moyra McDermott who encouraged me every step of the way

To my nieces Hope and Freya McDermott who kept asking when the book would be published. Well here it is girls

To the memory of Chick Buick who spent many hours advising me about crime fiction

Thank you to all of the above, without whom this book would not be here today

ACKNOWLEDGMENTS

I would like to thank the following people who have helped me every step of the way.

Megan Appleton, Liz Strachan and Betty Doe for their tireless work with editing.

Fellow crime author Chris Longmuir, for all her help and support throughout the process of bringing the book to completion.

Karen Wilson of Ginger Snap Images, Dundee for the professional author photograph.

Nathan Gevers for all his hard work and enthusiasm building the website to go with the book.

Joseph Wilson for producing the video to go with the book.

Police Scotland for their patience in answering myriad questions about the nuts and bolts of policing. Particular thanks must go to my local police sergeant who has never failed to answer any of my questions with good humour and has supported me in my endeavor.

The members of the Angus Writers Circle for their valuable advice, feedback and support

.

Prologue

As I stared down the barrel of that gun I had a feeling, deep inside, that this would not end well. How did I find myself here, deep in the bowels of a frozen Scottish wood, eye to eye with the business end of a Browning Pistol? As I stood, motionless, adrenalin heightened my senses. The rough bark of the tree was cold against my skin as sweat froze on my neck. Acid bile rose in my throat, burning, threatening to erupt. I swallowed against this lava flow of vomit. I could see the gunman's face with startling clarity, lit by the cool winter sun. Blue eyes. Devoid of any emotion. This was a killer's mask. The hand, holding the gun, was unwavering. This was a hand that was strong, with only one purpose in mind. The chase ended here. Before the day was out, one of the two participants in this chilling game of cat and mouse would be dead. Of this I was certain.

1

February 1998

The sound of laughter rang around the house competing with the raucous thump of music. It was difficult to tell which was loudest in that cacophony of noise. I stood and watched my new friends, teenagers, dancing, screaming, drinking, and having fun. I drank it in greedily; imagining this was an echo of all such parties gone before. Never previously invited, I wasn't sure. The cacophony of sound was exhilarating, a devil's dance bouncing on my eardrums. Breathing deeply, I inhaled the overpowering scent of expensive perfume, mingled with the stale smell of cheap alcohol. I didn't care. To me this was headier than the most powerful drug. This was the party to end all parties, the one that everyone who mattered, should be, and was, at. Anyone not here was a nobody. Everyone knew that. As I watched them party, with the increasing abandon that unites teenagers worldwide, I could hardly believe I was one of the elite. What did I care if the beer was cheap and the smell in the room overpowering? I was here, a girl from one of the worst housing schemes in Dundee, partying with the chosen ones. I shook myself. I needed to make sure it wasn't a dream from which I would awaken to a world of disappointment. I finally knew, in the midst of my miserable life, true happiness. That feeling deep inside me that caused my heart to soar and set my emotions singing.

Raising the beer bottle to my lips I drank a cold mouthful whilst taking in more of the scene around me.

Jostled by a drunken teenager the beer poured down my top. "Watch out you prat," but it was said without rancour. I really didn't care. Swearing, he stumbled on.

"We need more beer and wine. Where've you got it hidden?"

"Didn't you bring your own booze you tight fisted git?"

"This is meant to be a party. There should be enough booze."

"Drew, you're that stingy you'd ask Scrooge for a loan."

"I'll knock your ..."

Beer and spirits appeared, to loud shouts and cheers. The threatening fight was avoided. The party continued.

In the dim lights, through a dense fug of smoke, I could make out vibrant flashes of colour, moving to the wild thump of the bass. I watched the writhing bodies carefully, eager to know the rules of this group. I didn't want to do anything to break the fragile bond between us. What were they wearing? What were they doing? What was normal for this crowd? Both sexes were dolled up and dressed to impress. The lipstick was liberally bright and the make-up thick. Short skirts and long legs melded with tousled hair and cut-offs. Teenage hormones oozed from every pore and mixed with the smell of pot, causing an almost palpable blend. The air was thick with it. These particular teenagers owned the world and didn't care who knew it. I soaked up the experience like a druggie in an opium den.

Suddenly, the music stopped. The hubbub slowly died. Silence descended. I turned, as did everyone else, to find out why. Why, I wondered, was each face aglow with expectation? They obviously knew something I didn't. I listened carefully. Not wanting to miss anything. A few moments of expectant hush before the leader of the group shouted, "I've an announcement to make." A murmur moved around the room, reaching a crescendo before dying again. Everyone wanted to hear what was being said. I was listening intently and moved as she beckoned me forward.

"You've been a part of the group now for a few weeks so it would be the right time to officially welcome you as one of us."

My heart swelled as I listened to her. I could hear it beating loudly in my chest, a drumbeat accompaniment to the words, which were being spoken. What was said next changed my life. It was then it fell apart. The emotional pain pierced me with the force of a sword strike.

"As I say it would be the right time," she paused, "if you were the right person, but you're not. What makes you think someone like you could ever be one of us? You're nothing and no one. You're nothing but a tink. We've been stringing you along for our own amusement for weeks. This little game was all planned. You assumed you were as good as us just because you have a few brains. Well, that means nothing. You thought you could scuttle your way out of the sinkhole you call home. Wrong. You'll never make it, and you'll never be anybody so crawl back in your hole and die. We don't need you or want you."

As I heard those cruel and taunting words my long dreamt of new life came crashing down. As laughter exploded, grew louder and echoed around the room, I felt humiliation and shame wash over me, filling my chest and spilling over. I tried to blink back tears but it was futile. They poured down my cheeks as I fled from the room; away from those I called my friends. My anguished heart was filled with utter despair. How could mere words be so powerful – cut so deeply?

I wished I could die.

2

November 2012

Stumbling down the steep bank of the Law Hill, slippery with wet leaves, Detective Inspector Shona McKenzie wondered why it was always raining when she was called out to a murder scene. On second thoughts it was a stupid question; it was *always* raining in Dundee.

She had moved here only a year ago following her now ex-husband up from Oxford. "You'll love it there," he said. "It's a great opportunity for us. Property prices are better as well so we'll make money on the move. The Dundee police will snap you up. It will be a whole new start."

What he had failed to tell her was that the new start meant him moving in with a new woman and divorcing her. She could still picture the scene perfectly. After a week in the new job, returning home from a long shift, her husband, as always, was waiting.

Dropping her bag she said, "It's been a day and a half that's for sure. I've not had a minute for thinking never mind eating. Do you fancy a take away? Is curry OK?"

He remained silent, which was strange. She was expecting his usual witty comeback. "What's up? Have you lost your voice?" Then she stopped short in the kitchen as she realised that he was dressed in his winter coat with a couple of Louis Vuitton suitcases at his feet.

Before she could properly take it in, or open her mouth to ask what was going on, he said, "I'm leaving.

5

We're over. I love someone else and have done for months. I'm sorry but that's the way it is." With that he picked up the suitcases and walked calmly out of the door, giving her no time to reply. Not that her brain could formulate a response. The only thought she could muster was where did he get the Louis Vuittons? Searching the flat she realised all he had left behind was a lingering scent of spicy aftershave, his keys, and her with an inability to trust men. It turned out that his insistence she should go with him to Dundee was merely a money saving ploy. The police were paying for the move.

This left her in a job in a city which, to her surprise, was growing on her. Yes, it rained most of the time, but people were much friendlier here than down south. They cared about and looked out for each other, something Shona appreciated. These were tough, hard-working people, their characters chiselled by history, formed on the decks of whaling ships, in jute mills and shipyards. Nothing could kill their spirit, not even years of growing unemployment and social disadvantage. They were proud and generous, loud and yet caring. Despite being born in Dundee she had lived in England most of her life, but that didn't matter to them. She was a Dundonian, so one of them, and they welcomed her back with open arms.

As she slipped down the hillside inane thoughts crowded her head. Why are bodies always discovered on a Saturday night? What is it about winter that brings out the madmen and killers? It stopped her thinking too closely about what lay ahead. The dank, musty scent of wet earth, mixed with the sweet, metallic smell of freshly spilt blood, assaulted her senses as she continued down the dark bank. It was an early indication of what she faced.

Arriving at the crime scene her wandering thoughts were replaced by keen professionalism as she assessed the scene before her. It was a horrific sight. In amongst the tall Scottish pine, their branches dripping dismally, lay a young woman, perhaps in her early thirties. Her throat had been cut with such ferocity that her head hung from her body. Her trachea was open to the elements. Even without a decent light Shona could tell that much. Spilt blood, mixed with the sodden bracken and leaves, pooled around her. She lay like she had been hurriedly tossed aside. One of the strange things about dead bodies, Shona mused, is that they looked as if they had become part of the ground. The woman was wearing running clothes, now stained with copious amounts of her own blood. Moonlight, filtering through the trees lent a spectral glow to the sight. It reminded Shona of a scene from a black and white movie.

With the number of officers milling around, it seemed like every man and his uncle was at the crime scene. They looked like ghosts as their faces flickered in the blue flashing lights from the police cars on the road above, ghosts with heavy feet who were most likely contaminating her crime scene. "Nina, get everyone out of the way," she barked at her newest DS, Nina Chakrabarti. "How am I supposed to process a crime scene with half of Tayside's finest having a Saturday night stroll in there? We might as well get a carry out and let them have a picnic."

"Yes Ma'am." Nina jumped to it. "Move it you lot. You're cluttering the place up."

Looking round she added, "that means you," to a young PC who had a belligerent look in his eye. "What makes you special?"

To mutterings of "Typical CID. Come in here and start ordering us all about," or "We can process a crime scene you know," everyone moved hurriedly back up the road. They didn't want to get on the wrong side of the DI as she wasn't famed for her patience, especially with young coppers who couldn't do what they were told. Brilliant she may be, but she didn't get to that rank by tolerating idiots.

Once most people had disappeared, Shona recognised Peter Johnston, her other DS, who was looking his usual miserable self. "Coming down in stair rods and cold enough to freeze your assets," he muttered as she approached. "Do you ken how many words there are for rain in Scotland? Well I can trot out at least 28 and I'm no' really trying." His voice softened as he said, "and this poor lassie's lying out in it, but she'll no' be worrying about the rain any more."

"I actually understood every word you said there," Shona said somewhat amazed. Following a Dundonian in full flow could be difficult for someone brought up in Oxford.

"Aye, I'm glad. My native tongue can be hard to get to grips with," Peter responded good naturedly. Despite being able to moan for Scotland, Peter took ragging about his accent in good humour.

"Much as I'd love to talk accents with you all night, Peter, what's your first impression?" She nodded towards the body. "Anything spring to mind whilst you've been standing here?"

"Difficult to say without lights," he answered, "We're just waiting for them to arrive. That man over there behind the crime scene tape, with the dog, is the poor bloke who found her. His name's Jock Morrison. Nobody's had a word with him yet."

"I'll speak to him in a minute. I want to take a closer look," she said, pulling blue plastic covers over her feet and producing a torch from her pocket. She proceeded cautiously towards the body. It looked even more macabre close up. She shone the torch on the neck wound. There was something not quite right but Shona couldn't put her finger on what it was. There might be bits of fibre in that wound, or maybe it was just congealed blood. Iain, their crime scene expert, would figure it out once he had a look. She shone the torch around the body and the general area. Nothing leapt out at her as being out of the ordinary. She noticed a couple of snapped tree branches that might have happened during a struggle. But this could have happened before the murder took place.

Shona left the scene and approached Jock Morrison. "Mr. Morrison, I'm Detective Inspector McKenzie, I believe you found the body?"

"Call me Jock lassie. Aye, I did. I don't mind telling you it's been a shock." Shona could well believe it. Jock had the look of a man who was going to be meeting his tea again soon.

"Would you like to sit down in one of the squad cars?" Shona didn't need a vomiting pensioner to deal with, on top of a corpse.

"No. You don't need to worry about me. I'm fine lassie."

"Jock, do you mind telling me what happened and how you found her? I know it must be difficult but every little detail could help."

"I was taking Hector here for his evening walk," he said, pointing to the Alsatian lying quietly at his feet, "when he ran away. I kept calling but he wouldn't come back. Hector's a good dog and he always comes when I call, so I knew something was wrong. When I went after him he was standing by the lassie, whining as though he wanted to protect her. It was easy to see she was past help so I called the polis. That bobby over there came very fast and moved me over here."

"Did you touch her, or touch anything else?" Shona enquired.

"No, I'm a great fan o' those crime programmes on the telly, so I knew not to touch her and to stay out of the way."

For once in her life Shona was grateful for "CSI" which usually made her job more difficult. The general public now thought the police should solve the crime in an hour. She was also thankful for a witness who, although shaken, seemed articulate and able to answer questions sensibly. "Did you see or hear anything else suspicious?" she asked. "Anyone else around, sounds of running, anything?"

"No, nothing until the dog disappeared. I saw one other dog walker about an hour ago but nothing else."

"Do you know the other dog walker?"

"I've seen him and his arthritic collie a few times but I don't know him. We just nod to each other in passing. He's older than me. Must be 90 if he's a day and no' much more sprightly than his dog. I think he'd have difficulty cutting up his sausages never mind that poor wee lassie."

"Thanks Jock. You've been a great help. Come with me and I'll get someone to take you to Hilltown Station to give a statement. It will be a bit more comfortable there." She let her thoughts drift longingly to the warm station and a cup of boiling hot coffee. She was frozen through.

"Of course, lassie. I hope you get it all sorted and find out who did it. It's usually pretty quiet around here. I've never seen such a thing since I was in the war. Courting couples is all you usually see around here."

As she handed Jock over to a young PC the Council arrived with the lights and proceeded to set them up. She could hear Nina Chakrabarti saying, "Don't get too close to the body but make sure the

10

lights shine on her." Knowing how good she was at bossing people around, Shona left her to it. The men from the council didn't stand a chance.

Turning to walk away she banged into the Police Surgeon, Larry Briar. "Evening Shona, the Procurator Fiscal is on his way as well," he said as he passed her to examine the body. Since coming back to Scotland, Shona had come to realise the importance of the Procurator Fiscal. The PF was responsible for investigating all sudden and suspicious deaths in Scotland, amongst many other things. They often turned up at the scene of a crime to get an initial view of the situation. The one in Dundee was a conscientious chap who was liked by all who worked with him.

Shona heaved a sigh of relief. "Hallelujah," she said as an aside to Peter. "There's been far too much hurry up and wait on this case already. I'll be glad to get on with it."

Two minutes later the surgeon was back, "Definitely dead and you won't be surprised to know the likely cause. Her throat's been cut with a sharp object. From the state of the body I'd say she's been dead about three hours. I can't be certain until the post mortem though. Mary should be able to give you a better idea of time." Mary was the Pathologist for Dundee.

"Thanks Larry. Appreciated." Shona spoke to his disappearing back as he hurried to the warmth of his car.

"How are you holding up with the cold?" Peter asked, knowing her preference for all things warm.

"I'm fine. I can't actually feel anything anymore, so nothing to worry about." Truth be told she felt a bit like a nudist at the North Pole. Its best friend, a bone chilling wind, accompanied the lashing rain. Together they produced the type of cold that laughed at your clothes as it whipped right through them and seeped into your marrow.

"Right, let's get to it. If the photo and fingerprint guys are finished I'll see if I can find any identification. Iain, how far along are you with the photographs?" she shouted across to DC Barrow.

"Just doing the last one now, Ma'am. Fingerprints are a washout." He grinned, Shona groaned. "Sorry Ma'am, couldn't resist. Seriously though we'll get nothing in this rain so I'm done."

The snap of elastic was heard as she pulled on a pair of vile blue rubber gloves. "These gloves are enough to make you lose the contents of your stomach. They're worse than the dead body."

"Apart from the obvious gaping neck wound there's also a wound on her wrist. Could be defensive. Although from the bits of greenery adhering to it she could have scraped it on a branch while struggling." Shona reached in the victim's pocket and pulled out a purse. Rifling through it she said, "Looks like we've identified our victim as Megan Mackie. She's got business cards in that name. It would seem she's a solicitor in town. There's a University ID card with the victim's photo as well. Looks like she does some work up there." Shona's stomach churned. No matter how much experience she got, Shona still felt a churning in the pit of her stomach at the thought of someone being killed and discarded like yesterday's rubbish.

She was pulled out of her reverie by the simultaneous arrival of the Procurator Fiscal and the team to take the body to the mortuary. After checking that all the SOCOs were finished and the Police Official Licensed Search Advisor (POLSA) was happy, she nodded that they could take the body away. Business-like she briefed the Procurator Fiscal, Douglas Lawson. "Not much so far. The dead woman is Megan Mackie, found by a dog walker, throat cut by a sharp object, been dead about three hours."

"Thanks Shona. Short and to the point as always." A smile lit up his eyes. "I'll pop in and see you on Monday and you can bring me up to date with any new developments."

"Sure. See you then," but she was already turning away. She called over the officers who remained at the scene. "You, you and you," she indicated three PC's "search the area for anything suspicious. We need to find the murder weapon."

Returning to her team she said, "Nina and Roy go house to house and ask anyone in the area if they saw or heard anything out of the ordinary. Also, find out if they know anyone who usually frequents the area."

"Peter, you're in charge. Make sure every inch of this area is gone over with a fine toothcomb. I'm off back to Bell Street to update the Chief. I'll see you and the others back there."

"Oh, he'll be in a good mood having his Saturday night wi' the missus disturbed."

"Sod his Saturday night, I've a murder to solve and we're all working. If he gets a row from the missus then so be it."

"Fighting talk Ma'am. I like it."

Shona turned and trudged back to the car, the thought of heating and hot coffee motivating every step.

3

November 2012

I know I look like any other idiot, out for an early evening run, moving through the gloomy streets of Dundee. Who in their right minds goes running on a day such as this? The grey stone of the buildings, dripping with rain, form a drab background to my movements. With breathing even, and steps smooth, I cover the distance to the place where I am staying. Despite the time of day I pass few people. The dreich night keeps everyone in his or her house, warm and safe from the elements. Reaching Tullideph Road I take the slope in my stride. The imposing red brick of the Friary appears menacingly at my side. Even in the gloom it casts the eerie shadow of centuries looming in my path. I pay it no heed. The ghosts of long dead monks do not bother me. Pounding the cracked, uneven pavements, I pass shuttered and abandoned shops. This place is a broken down microcosm of this decrepit city. They say Dundee has reinvented itself. That it's a place of art and beauty. That's not my impression. I see only misery. The only life is in the packed chippies and the smokers huddling miserably outside the pubs. It is nothing more than another dreary Saturday night in Dundee. Avoiding the multitude of narrow streets that characterise this city, my route follows the wider ones. There is less chance of being noticed if I do the same as any other runner. I am fluid, casual, my pace measured. Nothing to draw attention, I am hiding in plain sight.

Notwithstanding the apparent ease, I am alert to

everything around me and the few people I pass. Immersed in their own worlds, huddled against the cold and rain, they seem oblivious of me. Except, as I pass the one bright streetlamp, a shabbily dressed man, or it could be a woman, calls out. "Canny believe you're running in this. You must be a right bampot."

Paying him/her no heed I continue to pound the pavements. No one else looks up or appears to see me. I am an expert at blending into the background and not being noticed. I can instantly make myself a nonentity.

As I run, I rehearse in my mind every detail of my next move. With only twelve hours to prepare and plan I need to be certain of each minute detail. Precision and order could make the difference between success and failure.

Once past the dingy flats, and where no one can see, I stop. Pulling a tightly sealed bag from my backpack, I drop it deep inside a rubbish bin. No one will think to search this far. Scanning the area for movement, I satisfy myself there was no one around to see me and continue my run.

Entering my temporary abode, I quickly strip out of my Gore-Tex outer top and trousers and pull on some warm clothes. The cold doesn't bother me; I have been in colder and more desolate places than this. The weather merely exists to be mastered and provide a dark backdrop to my plans. Dropping my now empty backpack on the ground, I gather together everything I will need in just a few short hours. Taking each pristine piece of the rifle out of the bag in which it is temporarily stored, I place it gently on the bed. Precisely. Each piece in its place and accounted for. I swiftly click the pieces together and then dismantle them. Over and over, the repetition is monotonously soothing. Once I am satisfied that everything is as it should be, I lovingly polish each already gleaming piece before placing it in my backpack. This rifle is one of my most precious possessions, almost an extension of not only my body but also, my personality. Each piece is placed exactly, chosen to ensure protection but also maximum speed when reassembling. It is only then I climb into bed fully clothed, secure in the fact that no one knows where I am, or what I am doing. There is nothing and no one to bother me. My internal world and my plan, the focus of my life, are the only things that matter. Satisfied that all is well with my world, I fall into a deep, untroubled sleep. The yawning darkness of my emotional world is once more at peace, if only for a few snatched hours.

4

November 2012

Stopping only to grab a mug of the thick sludge the station called coffee, Shona moved to her office. Every time she went through the door she wished the bloke that did this job before her would stop lurking in the shadows like some dim spectre. This proved to be difficult. His physical presence was in the ring marks on the scarred wooden desk, left there by his mug. As a neat freak, these made Shona shiver. He seemed to follow her to every crime scene and hung about like an uninvited guest at the wedding feast. She always felt like she was walking in a dead man's shoes. He wasn't literally dead of course, just figuratively. She was beside herself trying to work out why he had been thrown off the force in disgrace. In a place with so many people this seemed to be a very well-kept secret. The police are usually like a bunch of fishwives around each other, but not in this case. She couldn't help feeling that everyone was waiting for her to screw up as well. It was the main thing driving her to crack this case. She was going to prove the whole damn lot of them wrong. So she told her stalking spectre to sod off back to whence he came.

Pulling herself out of her reverie, she picked up the phone and dialled the home number of the Chief Inspector. He picked up on the first ring. "Reynolds."

"Sir, it's DI McKenzie," she answered.

"What have you got for me?" he snapped, "and you'd better make it quick. My wife isn't going to be very happy if you waste much more of her Saturday night." The inspector was definitely under the wife's thumb.

"Not much at the moment Sir. The body of a young woman was found at the top of the Law with her throat cut. Looks like she's a lawyer by the name of Megan Mackie but I need to get someone to identify her properly. The team are out there now combing the crime scene and the area. I can give you more when they return."

"Don't ring me until Monday," he replied. "No use me wasting my weekend. Unless of course you manage to solve the case before then."

Shona was left listening to the dialling tone.

He's his usual cheery and helpful self, Shona thought. Perish the thought she should waste any of his precious weekend for something as unimportant as a murder. Shoving aside thoughts of recreating the murder, with her boss as the central character, she dialled the number on the victim's business card. She was soon speaking to James Dennis, Megan's partner in the law firm.

"Mr Dennis, this is Detective Inspector Shona McKenzie from the Tayside police."

"How may I help you Inspector? Have you got a client for me?"

"I'm afraid it's more serious than that. I believe Megan Mackie works in your firm."

"Yes. She's my partner. What's wrong? Surely she's not in trouble with the police. Not Megan. She's never put a foot wrong in her life."

"I'm sorry to have to tell you that it looks like Megan is dead."

"What... Megan?" There was a pause. "How? What happened? Was she murdered?"

Shona thought that he had jumped to that

conclusion a bit too fast.

"I'm sure, being a solicitor, you'll appreciate I can't go into that Mr Dennis."

"Yes. Sorry. I'm a bit shocked."

"I'm sure you are. We need the contact details of Megan's next of kin and her home address. Have you got them?"

"Sure. I'll go into the office and get them. I'll ring you with them."

"Someone will have to escort you to her office. I'll send someone round now if you give me your address."

"I'm perfectly capable of getting them myself."

"I am sure you are but someone still needs to escort you."

He reluctantly gave his address and hung up. "This is getting to be a habit," Shona said to the dialling tone. "God spare me from solicitors. In fact God spare me from all men. Ignorant, dirty lying cheats, the lot of them."

She picked up the phone and rang Peter. "Have you got any spare officers?"

"Aye. Iain's finished and about to join you in Bell St."

Shona rattled off the address. "Get him to pick up James Dennis and take him to his offices. Tell Iain to keep a close eye on him. I don't want him tampering with possible evidence. He's to seal the offices until we can search Megan's files. Our Mr Dennis seemed a bit put out that we were escorting him. He also jumped to the conclusion that she was murdered more speedily than I would have liked. He might have something to hide."

Switching on her computer she started a case file. Someone would update HOLMES (Home Office Large or Major Enquiry System) later. She let her mind picture the crime scene and examine it critically. Nothing stood out as being unusual. It was as if the body just appeared there without anyone or anything else involved. There was no one around except a couple of dog walkers but that appeared to be well after the time of death. Not that she'd expect much else on such a miserable night. Even Dundonians, used to endless rain, had more sense than to drag themselves out tonight. She pictured the ground, the trees, the body, the surrounding area and still nothing niggled her. This was not something she was used to. She pictured previous murder scenes to see if they would jog her memory. Nothing. She was used to finding blood splatter, but there was none in this case. That in itself is significant, she mused. How would the murderer prevent blood spatter, even with this heavy rain? One thing in particular seemed strange to her. A runner wouldn't have left the path willingly, especially in filthy weather. The ground was treacherously slippery. She must have gone there against her will. But why were there no signs that she'd been dragged or signs of a struggle. Maybe she'd walked down there with a knife at her neck. If she'd been killed on the road, why was there no blood there? Even with heavy rain Shona would still expect to find some blood. Why was there only blood on her clothes and not on the ground? This is getting me nowhere she said to herself. She hoped the others had come up with something.

She was still sitting with her head in her hands when Peter blew through the doors of her office, accompanied by a sound like her six year old nephew's attempts on the violin. She reminded herself to get the hinges of her office door oiled.

"We're all back Ma'am."

"So I heard. Grab the others and come to the briefing room. We need to pool notes."

In the still pristine briefing room she picked up a whiteboard pen and wrote the victim's name and the date. The name on the otherwise blank board, was a stark reminder of their grisly task. "What have we got so far?" she asked before realising her mistake. A cacophony of sound erupted.

"Shut up," she shouted. "One at a time. Peter, you start."

"Every inch of the area's been searched and we found nothing. No footprints, no sign of a struggle, nothing. We searched all the bins in the area and no murder weapon or discarded claes to be found. The only unusual thing was this wee gold chain caught on a branch." He pulled an evidence bag from his pocket. "If you were asking me to hedge my bets I'd say this could be the victim's."

"I'm not asking you to hedge any bets, I'm asking for the facts," Shona snapped. "For all we know it could belong to some teenager who crawled in the bushes for a quickie with her boyfriend." Any vestige of patience had long deserted her.

"Well, I would say it looks like it broke on a branch when she was carried to the place we found her," Peter said huffily. "Unlikely to be the killer's as my gut feeling is that he was a man."

"What makes you say that?"

"Well I don't mean to be sexist, but I doubt any lassie would have the strength to do this, and carry her down the hill like that without dragging her."

Shona reserved judgment on this. Choose your battles she reminded herself.

"Hang on. Why are you carting possible evidence around in your pocket? That should be firmly in the hands of the POLSA and on its way to the evidence room."

"I looked for him but couldn't find him. I thought it

would be better if I brought it back."

"You call that an excuse?"

"It's no' an excuse. It's a well put together, well formed, reason."

"So is a bullet and right now I'm tempted to shoot you with one. You should have looked harder. You're going to be joining Megan Mackie in the morgue when the POLSA finds out. Get it down to evidence now and get it logged in."

"Was there blood anywhere else?" Shona asked. "If you think she was carried there then where from?"

"Blood around the body, as you well know, but none anywhere else. Mind you, that's no' surprising given the amount o' rain. Any blood would be washed away. There might be traces but we'd be hard pushed to find them tonight." With this Peter departed to put the evidence in the right hands.

"Who's next? What about fingerprints?"

DC Iain Barrow, the team's fingerprint expert was looking decidedly fed up. "Not a print to be found anywhere. If there were any they've been washed away by this b... blasted rain," he continued, seeing the DI's sharp gaze focussed on him. "Not even a partial or a latent. Complete waste of time if you ask me, the only DNA we've got is probably the victim's blood. I did manage to get fingerprints from the victim though."

"I decide whether something is a waste of time or not," Shona countered. "One thing we do know so far, our killer, be they male or female," she said, glancing at Peter, who had returned from the evidence room, "is extremely good at covering their tracks. Ah! Peter, welcome back. From the look on your face I'd say the POLSA wasn't best pleased."

"Ye'd be right there," Peter answered.

"At least you're still alive to tell the tale." Lips twitching Shona asked, "Nina and Roy, what did the house to house dig up?"

"Absolutely nothing. Everyone we interviewed was indoors eating their Saturday night take away and watching the telly. Several people complained they had seen some youngsters up there smoking what looked and smelt like pot a couple of times. Also there was mention of possible drug dealers hanging about the top of the Law. We'll pass that on to uniform. It should keep the locals happy that we're doing something about it if nothing else."

"She could have interrupted a drug deal and this was an attempt to stop her talking," Shona added. "It's worth looking into. Dig into it a bit deeper, Nina."

Roy chipped in, "All those takeaways and there's not one of them works for a living. They're all on the take and a criminal in every house."

"That's enough, Roy," Shona remonstrated.

"It's true Ma'am there's even a song about it. We're the lads fae the tap o' the hill, never worked and never will."

"Roy I'm warning you, you're a hair's breadth from returning to uniform. Shut up and keep your stupid opinions to yourself."

Shona's mobile rang. "DI Shona McKenzie," she left the room.

"It's James Dennis. They've sealed my offices. How am I meant to get any work done? What right have you got to treat me like this? This is not good enough."

Shona's tone was placatory but firm. "As a solicitor you will appreciate that this is standard procedure. I will make sure that by Monday you are able to use your office but Megan's will remain sealed." She abruptly hung up, giving the pompous git a taste of his own medicine.

While she was gone Peter turned on Roy. "You

ignorant little sod, you don't even know what you're talking about. The area we're canvassing isn't even the top of the hill and, even if it was, you shouldn't be talking rubbish. Get your facts right before you make stupid comments. Are you trying to piss off the DI? For someone with a university degree you can be a right bampot."

"I was just saying."

"Well don't say. We're not interested."

Returning, Shona was brisk. "We need to move on this. Peter, you and I are going to break the news to Megan's parents. We'll get some photos of her. Nina and Iain, go round to Megan's house and see if the neighbours can tell you anything. Here are some keys. They were in her pocket. I'm sure one of them will open her door. Roy, follow us with another car, it might be needed."

5

February 1998

As I travelled to school I couldn't make up my mind whether to think about what I'd left behind at home, or what was in front of me. My mother was comatose on the sofa, a result of cheap vodka and drugs the night before. Could even have been this morning. Who knows? My stomach rumbled. No food in the house so my breakfast was non-existent. As had been tea last night. Why would anyone use money to buy food when fags, drugs and drink were more of a necessity? The man my mother had dragged home last night was still asleep. Rifling through the pockets of his scruffy jeans I'd pulled out a tenner. He woke and saw me, his swearing following as I ran both from him and the house. Still, I wanted the journey to last forever, dreading what a day at school would bring. Things were bad enough at home, but I usually managed to get some measure of respite at school. I knew intuitively that this was about to change.

The taunts follow me up the corridor all day. There's never a moment's peace. The peeling corridor walls were of sudden interest to me. It was like each flaking piece of paint would somehow turn out to be my saviour, or each crack holds all the mysteries of the world.

"Loser."

"Little Miss Clever Clogs."

"No friends. No life. No good."

"Nothing but a tink."

Not too bad individually, but in a persistent barrage they are like a dripping tap in a torture scene. Designed to drive one mad. Sometimes gestures replace the words. These are easier to ignore.

Some things I don't want to repeat, not even in my mind. Not that I haven't heard them all before from my degenerate mother. Mother love is a joke. She doesn't know the meaning of the word love, never mind put it in to practice.

In the way that schools have always worked, everyone seems to know about my humiliation the previous night. How did it get round so quickly.

"Why are you doing this? What have I done to any of you to deserve any of this? Lay off me. Please go away," I cried.

No direct answer. Merely derision. Whispers, followed by laughter, accompany me as I go to my locker to get the latest Jonathan Kellerman novel. I will find a quiet corner and escape in the only way I know, in the pages of a book. Opening my locker I scream. There is a sheep's heart lying on the book, its blood staining the covers. Stolen from that morning's biology class. My head spinning, I can hear the sound of laughter. It seems to come from somewhere far away. Thoughts swarm around my head, the main one being; I wish this were a nightmare from which I could wake. I have the dreaded certainty that this would not happen. This was my life.

6

November 2012

The streetlights, partially hidden by wind-blown trees, send spectral shadows dancing against the walls as Shona and Peter approached the newly painted front door. They were glad to see lights on in the house. Shona hated this part of her job. The only good thing was that she could be one step closer to finding the killer. Peter rang the bell and, within a few seconds, the door was answered. An elderly man stood in the light from the hallway. "Mr Mackie?" Shona asked.

"Yes," he said warily. Holding up her ID she explained who they were and asked if they could come in. Fear flickered in his eyes as he moved aside to let them enter. The police knocking your door at this time on a Saturday night couldn't be a good omen.

The house had the stale, lingering smell of Chinese takeaway; curry and sweet and sour of some description, if Shona had to guess. This was just another normal Saturday night, in a well-kept council house, in not so Bonnie Dundee. Normal was about to explode in front of this elderly couple.

The woman in the living room rose as they entered. "The police are here to see us love," her husband explained.

There was a flash of alarm in her eyes but Mrs Mackie said, "Can I get you a cup of tea?"

Shona, always surprised by how hospitable Dundonians were, said, "We're fine thank you." No one was as polite as this in Oxford. Not wishing to prolong things she asked, "Do you have a daughter called Megan who is a solicitor in town?"

"Yes. Yes we do. What's happened?" Mr Mackie forced out, his face suddenly pale.

Shona said as gently as she could, "I am sorry to have to tell you that Megan is dead. It looks like she has been murdered."

They both aged before Shona's eyes, their skin now visibly grey and crumpled. Tears spilled down Mrs Mackie's cheeks. "Nooo," she wailed, "This can't be happening." As her mascara trickled down her cheeks her husband held her hand and asked in a weak voice, "Are you sure?"

"We will need you to come and identify the body but yes we're sure." Shona, as always, felt sick at the fact she would still have to ask so many questions of the grieving couple. Despite the necessity for this task, it only made the family's pain deeper. As if she was dissecting them at the single most difficult moment of their lives. She waited a few seconds for them to take this in and then asked, "When did you last see Megan?"

"She came for her tea last night. We had fish and chips."

Shona wondered, yet again, if everyone in Dundee lived on takeaways. Pushing the thought aside she said, "Did Megan seem all right to you lately?"

"Aye. She was in a good mood. Said she'd just taken on a big case," said her father and then he fell silent.

"Did she say anything about it?"

"No. She never told us anything about what she was doing." Mrs Mackie managed to pull herself together enough to join the conversation.

"Do you know anyone who could have held a grudge against her?" Shona enquired. "Has she spoken to you of any cases where things may not have turned out the way she wanted?"

"No. Everyone loved her. She was always a good girl. She had a lot of friends. She was always looking after her father and me. Came to see us every week and often took us out to lunch. Nobody would want to hurt her."

"She sounds like a lovely daughter Mrs Mackie and I am sure she did have a lot of friends. We will need to speak to them to see if they know anything that could help us. It would be useful if you could give us a list of their names. Also where they live if you know. Did Megan have a boyfriend?"

"She split up with her boyfriend, not long ago. I don't think she's going out with anyone at the moment."

"What was her boyfriend's name?"

"Gage Washington. He was American."

"Thank you Mr. Mackie. Why did they split up?"

"Megan didn't say too much. As far as I can gather he was wanting to get more serious but Megan didn't think they had a future together. She wasn't ready to get married," Mrs Mackie answered.

"Do you know anything more that could help us find him?"

"He was a lecturer at the University. I think she said it was something to do with America."

"We will need to speak to Megan's friends. They might be able to give us more information. Did she have any particular friends?"

"Not really. She didn't keep in touch with any of her school friends. She made some good friends in Edinburgh at University, Louise Smith and Blossom somebody. She was African. I think her surname was Nwosu. It sounded like that anyway."

"Thanks Mr and Mrs Mackie You've been really helpful. I just need to speak to my colleague for a moment."

Pulling Peter aside she said, "Could you take them to the mortuary to identify their daughter? I'm going round to Megan's house to see if they've found anything. Chat to them and see if it throws anything up. You also need to write down a couple of names of girls who were friends with her. We'll get in touch and see if there was anything troubling her."

Returning to the sitting room she said, "Mr and Mrs Mackie, I am going to leave you with DS Johnson. He'll look after you. Once again, I am sorry for your loss. I assure you we are going to do everything we can to catch Megan's killer." With that she returned to Roy and the waiting car.

Nina and Iain had made little headway. Everything seemed to be in place in her house, everything neat, tidy and in order. "Looks like she was a bit of a neat freak," said Nina. "I've found her address book in the desk in the office and her mobile phone. That may give us something to go on. I'll bring her laptop in as well."

Iain chipped in, "A few sets of prints most of which are more than likely Megan's but another two or three different ones. Not only was she neat but she also had a passion for cleaning. Not sanitised as if done deliberately to hide traces though. Just fanatically clean."

"OK, if you're finished here I think it's time we all knocked off for the night and came back to this fresh, in the morning. I know it's Sunday but if we could all be in by nine, a.m. that is," she added knowing Roy's ability to twist the rules to suit himself.

"9 a.m. on a Sunday. That's the middle of the night." Roy proved her point.

"I'd be happy to let you stay on tonight. You can find Megan's boyfriend and bring him in for questioning. Then you can come in at 09.30 tomorrow."

"No. 9 is fine Ma'am. I'll be there." Shona was left looking at his receding back as he flew from the room. She thought that would clarify things for the lazy little git. The corners of her lips lifted into a grin. There were times when she loved her job.

Shona returned to her flat in Broughty Ferry. Walking in her door, she threw her keys on the antique hall table. Donated by her mother, it reminded her of home. "Shakespeare mind where you're going." She had almost fallen over the purring body of her cat as it wound around her ankles. He was expressing his pleasure in seeing her. He could just as easily be in a huff because she had been gone all day. Definitely a cat of many moods was Shakespeare. After feeding him, exhaustion took over and she fell into bed and a dreamless sleep.

7

November 2012

Slipping quietly from my bed, and dressing warmly, I creep into the still dark morning. Wearing black I blend into the shadows. A small backpack carries everything I need. As I break into a jog I am just another dedicated runner out in the early morning; a fanatic or someone training for a marathon. There are very few people around; it is still too early for most. The chink of milk bottles alerts me to the presence of a milkman. Turning up a side street, I avoid him. Measured paces take me through Charleston, a depressing housing scheme of grey harling and spiked, iron railings. This is not a place in which one wants to linger. A weary cleaner, loaded with the tools of her trade, forces another change of direction. I do this with practiced ease. I know these streets like the back of my hand. This unforgiving, godforsaken city is the place of my birth. A place I had roamed at will since the age of five. No one to care I was out alone or even out at all. These streets were my childhood playgrounds. An almost imperceptible quickening of my breathing is accompanied by a slight stumble. These are the only signs I am nearing a certain house. I force myself to relax.

"Steady, your time will come." My childhood home held nothing but demons. Thrown out of the house each night so my mother could lead her own life, one which didn't include a whining brat, as she had so often told me. Still, it meant I was away from the wandering hands of my mother's visitors. Male, female, it didn't matter to her, so long as they had a pulse and a purse full of money. Not all from my childhood was lost. My circumstances then gave me an added edge now, given my current mission. There were some things to be thankful for. Every crack, in every worn paving stone, was as familiar as life itself.

Each practiced, easy footstep had a corresponding step in my mind as I put my rifle together. Picturing my victim, I line up the scope and take the shot in my mind. Then I go through it all again as I feel the reassuring weight of the rifle on my back.

Reaching my destination I am quickly in place. My rifle is put together even more swiftly than my virtual practices whilst I run. Every piece locked in place and I am at the ready. Waiting. Patient. Still. This is a shot I have wanted to take for years. This is a deliberate choice of weapon. I never want to be close to this woman again. I need the distance this firearm brings. Daylight arrives. Hesitant. As though wishing to put off its day's work.

As night turns to day I see my victim arrive and step from the car. Her movements are arrogant, as though she owns all around her. In her mind she probably does. I wait until she is in that sweet spot for my shot. I pull the trigger, disassemble the rifle, and leave. I had seen her fall. Intuitively, I know that my bullet will have hit just where it was intended. I do not look back. I know where my next steps into the future will take me.

8

November 2012

Shona woke to the shrill sound of her phone. Shakespeare was draped across her chest sleeping soundly and oblivious to the noise. Pushing him off and picking up the phone, she glanced at the clock showing 7 a.m. She knew this could not be a good sign. "DI McKenzie."

"It's the duty sergeant Ma'am. There's been another suspicious death."

Shona managed to force a word out through a tongue cleaving to the roof of her mouth, "Where?"

"Ninewells hospital car park."

"Which one. They've got more than one up there."

"Of course Ma'am. Number three."

Struggling from her bed, forcing one leaden foot in front of the other, Shona started the coffee maker then had the quickest and coldest shower in the history of human existence. The boiler was on the blink again and the repairman couldn't come until Wednesday. Shona wondered what it was with British tradesmen. They all seemed to respond with the speed of a striking snail. In the meantime the poor unsuspecting public froze their innards, waiting. If she were in charge of the country she'd force every single tradesman from British Gas or any other company to take a cold shower in a Dundee winter. That would speed up their response times - the lazy sods. Dressing in jeans and a leather jacket, she pulled a brush through still damp blonde hair. Stopping only to gulp down the scalding coffee and feed the cat, she was out the door in minutes. The scene of the crime was at the other side of the city, which gave her thirty minutes to get there. As she settled in the car Meatloaf blared from the speakers, a combination of the iPod in her pocket and a stereo system that had cost almost as much as the car "Just the ticket," she said to the empty car. "That should waken me up nicely and get me in the mood for a tussle with a crime scene."

Driving, with some difficulty, past a number of irate staff being denied access to the hospital staff car park, Shona pulled up at the now raised barrier of Car Park 3. There seemed to be a minor argument going on between a young police officer and a sartorially dressed young man.

"I'm a doctor. Do you know how many people could die if I don't get in to work?"

"I appreciate that your job is important Sir but so is mine. No one is coming into this car park. Now if you follow the orders of my colleagues your car will be in another car park in no time."

"You can't speak to me like that."

Shona interjected, "Yes he can. He was a lot more polite than I would have been. Now if you don't shut up I'll have you arrested for interfering in an investigation." Turning from the astonished Doctor, Shona smiled and showed her ID to the young police officer standing guard. This was more of a formality than anything. Everyone in the Dundee force knew Shona. Her reputation went before her. He still looked grim, but his lips twitched, as he waved her through. Probably due to the amount of abuse the poor sod has taken about parking she thought. Deny any member of the British public a car parking space and they turn into maniacs. I'm surprised the victim isn't the PC himself Shona thought, but then corrected herself. This was no time for levity. She parked and moved quickly to the crime scene at the other end of the car park, where a feeling of déjà vu overcame her. Here were the same cast of characters, minus DS Johnston, who had gone straight to the station at her request. A crowd of emergency personnel milled around the body. This appeared to have a variety of tubes protruding from it. There goes the crime scene Shona thought, though in fairness, the hospital staff had been trying to save the victim's life.

Although physically different, Shona noticed that this new victim was of a similar age to the previous one. This wasn't a complete surprise as young women tend to be the victim of choice for a serial killer. Were they dealing with one? Shoving the thought to the back of her mind she reminded herself that in any investigation facts came before speculation. She concentrated on the body, dressed in a cream winter coat, which now had a large crimson stain adorning it. Blood covered her face and her open staring eyes. She lay in a pool of blood and at first glance it looked like she'd either been shot or stabbed in the chest. Shona's immediate thought was that cream was a pretty stupid colour for a filthy Dundee winter. The coat would spend more time at the dry cleaners than on the owner's back. Cars were parked either side of the body and these were now also adorned with blood spatter as was the wall beyond. Iain was busy taking pictures of the crime scene. Emergency personnel hung around outside the tape.

Alert, eyes scanning the body, Shona couldn't see much for congealing blood. Not a lot to tell from initial inspection. The scene was littered with emergency equipment with bloody footprints everywhere. This was a crime scene investigator's worst nightmare. "You're going to have your work cut out here, Iain."

"Don't I know it Ma'am. Still there's nothing like a challenge to get you going in the morning." Iain loved his work and the messier the crime scene the more he loved it. Shona was thankful to have him on her team.

"Any clues as to what might have happened here?" she asked the assembled police officers. One young PC piped up "She looks like she's been shot by sniper fire." Shona swivelled to face him. "Sniper fire?" she rattled out, "This is Dundee not the battlegrounds of Syria." The PC held his ground, "That may be the case Ma'am, but I did a tour of duty in Afghanistan with the TA before joining the police, and that definitely looks like sniper fire to me."

Shona was stunned into silence. At last she spoke, more to herself than to the others "What in the world is going on here? We barely have a murder from one year's end to the next in Dundee, and now two in less than 24 hours, different methods and completely different areas." Coming out of her reverie she said, "Nina, do we know anything about the victim?"

Nina answered, "Her handbag is here but we didn't want to touch anything until you arrived." Shona nodded and Roy searched the woman's bag pulling something out and handing it to Shona. "Hospital staff ID in the name of Dr Jennifer Brown, definitely her from the picture."

A ringing sound came from the handbag. Shona took the bag from Roy, rummaged, pulled out the mobile and answered "Hello," she said.

"Is that Dr Brown?" came the disembodied voice from the phone.

"No it's Detective Inspector McKenzie. Who's speaking?"

"Why are you answering her phone? This is her House Officer, Cameron Lewis, she's needed on the ward urgently."

"Well Dr Lewis, Dr Brown won't be coming in and one of my officers will be coming to speak to you. Where can she find you?"

"Ward 19. What's wrong? Where is she? We need her."

"If it's that urgent you'd better find yourself another doctor. My officer will explain everything."

"But..." Shona clicked to end the call. "Good grief. I've better things to do than hold cosy wee chats with house officers who can't seem to find themselves a spare doctor. Who does he think I am – Consultants R Us? The flaming hospital must be crawling with senior doctors he can call on," she said to the gathered crowd. They looked puzzled but no one said anything.

Dispatching Nina in the direction of the ward she said, "Interview the staff on duty and see if you can find any reason why anyone would want to kill her. See if anyone knows anything, saw anything. Oh and we'll need details of next of kin."

Despite there being a plethora of doctors around, the police surgeon appeared to certify the woman dead. If he was turning out to a hospital on a Sunday then he must need the overtime, Shona thought. It smacked of coals to Newcastle but, as it wasn't coming out of her budget, she kept her council. "Morning Larry. What brings you out so early in the morning on a Sunday?"

"I'm helping an old pal of mine with some research and we'd arranged to meet this morning. It's a bit difficult during the week. Thought I might as well kill two birds with one stone."

Larry sounded very cheery for someone who was about to examine a dead body. Shona supposed it came with the territory. "The body's already certified, Larry, but thanks for coming anyway."

"No bother, Shona. I'll away and get a full cooked and a nice strong cuppie in the staff canteen. I need sustenance to deal with research. Especially with Gregory, he's a lovely chap but a bit long winded."

Shona turned to a couple of very upset and green looking witnesses standing beside the wall, both nurses who had arrived early for their shift. Shona thought they'd be a bit less shaken given the job they did. Still, she gave them the benefit of the doubt - most of their dead bodies would be wrapped up nice and neatly in their pyjamas. It's not exactly the way to start a Sunday morning shift, with a consultant's chest exploding in front of you. Tends to put a dampener on things.

Flashing her badge again Shona said, "DI Shona McKenzie. Can you tell me what happened?"

"We'd just got out of the car. I gave Gemma a ride into work. We were walking from our cars to work when we heard what sounded like a firework and Dr. Brown collapsed."

Gemma took over from the nurse whose name Shona hadn't yet found out. "Instinct kicked in and we both dived behind cars. I waited a few minutes then started to creep out. We were scared. We had to..." she pulled herself together, "but we had to do something. There were no more gunshots so I dashed to try and help Dr. Brown. Lily phoned A&E then came to help me."

Ah Lily, that was the other nurse's name. Although both were covered in blood from trying to help, they basically knew nothing.

"Gemma, Lily, we'll need to get statements from you both."

"What about work. We're already late," said Gemma.

"Does your ward know what's happened?"

"Yeh. Someone took a message."

"Then I'm sure they'll understand. The night shift will just have to hang on."

"They wont be happy."

"I understand but I need to get your statements. The minute we've got them you can be on your way. What ward are you on in case we need anything else?"

"I'm on ward 14 and Lily is on ITU."

"Thanks. Can you give the info again to DC MacGregor who will take your statement? You've been very helpful."

Turning, Shona spoke to Roy, "Can you get statements from all the medical personnel involved in this then tell them they're free to go to work. Start with Lily and Gemma here." Shona wanted the interviews done promptly. All she needed were was a bunch of medics saying the police had compromised patient care by holding up their staff. She could see where they were coming from, though.

Roy moved towards the rather pretty young nurses with a glint in his eye.

"Hoy. Casanova. No flirting on the job."

Roy turned and grinned at her.

She wondered what on earth she was doing sending Roy to interview a couple of bonny young women.

The Procurator Fiscal had appeared and was walking towards her. Shona was glad to see him again. Having Douglas Lawson around always made her feel better. He smiled, showing off the twinkle in his deep brown eyes, and said, "We really need to stop meeting in these circumstances. A cup of coffee together would be much easier." Shona smiled and felt a familiar flutter in her stomach, something she never thought she would feel again after the departure of her husband. She told her stomach sternly to stop it. She didn't have time for fluttering stomachs.

"What have you got for me?" he asked. She briefed him, finishing with, "Looks like it could be sniper fire."

"Sniper fire? In Dundee? I know we have our fair

share of nut jobs but a sniper's a new one even for us. Maybe they're copying all the snipers in America. There seems to be a lot of that in the good old US of A at the moment."

"I know. I couldn't believe it either, but one of our PC's is an ex soldier. He seems pretty convinced. Would you like to come with me whilst I speak to him."

"Sure. This is something I've got to hear." Douglas said with a smile in his voice.

Leaving her team to take photographs and salvage what they could of the crime scene, Shona turned to the soldier turned PC. "OK soldier boy, I need your expertise. What's your name?"

"PC. Jason Roberts Ma'am."

"For now, I'll go with your sniper idea. Seen as you seem to have some knowledge of these things would you like to hazard a guess as to where the shot came from?"

PC Robert's thought for a few minutes. "It could have come from the windows or the roof. More likely it was the roof. All these windows are to offices or the wards. The roof would be more secluded and would make for easier retreat. It's likely the gunman would have entry and exit routes pretty well thought out in advance. Given that it's Sunday they could have used an office but entry to Outpatients is through doors just off the main entrance and would be locked. It would be difficult for anyone to get in without being seen. So, as I say, the roof's your best bet."

"How come you know so much about the layout of the hospital?"

"I worked here as a cleaner while I was at Uni."

"You seem to be extremely au fait with all the facts of this murder," Shona said testily. "Where were you all night?"

"Night duty Ma'am and my partner can testify to

that."

"I'll be asking him. You can be certain of that. Go and find out if Iain's free and go with him to search the roof. I suppose I ought to be thankful that you've got a bit of nounce."

She pulled out her phone to call the Chief Inspector. To say he was not amused would have been testing the great British art of the understatement to its limits.

"I told you to solve the murder not find more bodies," he snapped. "How am I going to tell the Superintendent, and the Lord Provost, that Dundee is littered with murder victims despite the best efforts of Dundee's finest? I'll see you back at the station. We're going to have to call a press conference, which means I'll have to come in." With that he slammed the phone down. She was sick of being the butt of his temper. How did he expect them to solve a murder overnight? They were the best team in the UK, but seriously! She wondered if she could write a book, 'DI Shona's Guide to Killing Your Boss in 7 Million Unique Ways and Not Get Found Out'. She was sure it would outsell *Harry Potter* and *50 Shades* put together.

Ringing Peter at the station she said, "The Chief's on his way in and not in the best of moods. You'd better put that *Sunday Post* down and look like you're doing some work."

"The big cheese! Working on a Sunday! Things must be bad. Don't you worry Shona, I'll be a hive of industry, just like I always am." Shona was almost lost for words.

9

November 2012

Trudging out of the back door of the hospital, my backpack snug on my shoulders, I start to run. I look like just another staff member returning home after a long shift. As I pick up the pace I feel a long forgotten thrill. Like God, I saw what I had done and it was good. Like God, I deserve a day off after all my efforts but there is no time. God might have that luxury but I don't. I can, however, replay the steps in my mind. I can picture it all perfectly. The scene replays over and over in my mind, in all its Technicolor brilliance. Oblivious to the cold I had waited patiently. This is a woman driven to succeed so I know she will be at work regardless of the day or the time. She is not someone who will let family get in the way of what she wants. All I have to do is wait until she arrives. In my mind I see her stepping from the car and slamming the door. All this time I was watching. I was aware of every movement in the vicinity. I saw her. As she turned I squeezed the trigger. The shot was sweet, reaching its target, true and straight. I had watched as she tumbled to the ground. Each step in perfect formation, precise, just as it was meant to be. I play the movie again.

I allow myself a moment to feel unfamiliar pleasure. I had turned the tap off to this particular emotion many years before.

Approaching the centre of the City I slow to a walk. I am now another harassed shopper, out to beat the early morning crowds, eager to do my Christmas shopping. I look in festive shop windows, as I stroll down the Perth Road, giving the appearance of someone searching for the perfect present. In reality I see nothing. My mind is focussed on what I will be doing next. I buy a paper. I enter an early morning coffee shop. "A grande pumpkin spiced latte and a cheese and ham Panini." I grab a packet of festively wrapped coffee. "This as well. It will make a good present for my dad." I play the part to perfection. Picking up my order from the slack jawed server, who doesn't care what I'm buying, I settle on a comfortable sofa. Seemingly relaxed I pick up the paper and use it as a shield. In reality my mind is on my next move, going over every step in minute detail. With ease born of repetition I rehearse what could go wrong and what I could do to change the situation if it did. My expression blank, I slowly chew my sandwich but taste nothing.

10

November 2012

As Shona drove back to the station the clouds parted and the sun made an appearance. The river Tay sparkled like a million perfect diamonds. With the bridges and spires of Dundee in the distance and the Kingdom of Fife on the opposite shore it was a beautiful sight. Shona felt glad to be alive. The feeling disappeared rapidly as she approached the station with its grim concrete façade. It wasn't any better when she entered and had to wade through all the human detritus found only in the reception of a Scottish police station. The punters sat slumped in hard chairs, their faces masks of resignation. They had been through this routine far too many times already.

Entering the squad room she saw Peter resting, his feet on his battered metal desk, reading back copies of the Dundee Courier. "Did you know Scotland is one o' the fattest nations in the world?" he informed her. "Mind you seeing the sizes of some of the women we get in here that doesn't surprise me. They're the size o' whales and no' strangers to a peh or two."

Shona translated the local word for pie. Looking at the Sergeant she was lost for words. He wasn't exactly svelte himself. "I'm glad tolerance is alive and well and living in the Tayside Police Force," she replied.

As an afterthought, "I thought I told you to look busy. Is the Chief here yet?"

"You can relax lassie. He's not appeared. He's probably tucking in to a full Scottish, cooked by the beloved Mrs Chief Inspector, before he tips up here."

Shona mused, "I've been thinking. Considering part of our jobs as Officers was traditionally the preservation of public tranquillity, we don't seem to be making a very good fist of it." She leapt into action to bang Peter's back as he choked on his tea. "Public tranquillity," he spluttered, "We're more likely to have public riots with all these dead bodies we have. There are a lot of things you can say about Dundee but tranquil isn't one of them. You lived too long in Oxford lassie."

Saying, "Oxford isn't as quiet as you think," Shona left him to ponder the failings, or otherwise, of Dundee as a city. "Get rid of those papers before the Chief gets here," she threw over her shoulder. "I need you to get in touch with the team and find out where they are in the investigation. See if they've managed to get the next of kin details yet. Send someone to interview James Dennis," she added. "Let's see if we can dig anything up there."

Writing up her notes Shona was interrupted by Peter. "The latest victim's married with two kids. Lives in the Perth Road."

"OK. Go and pick Roy up from the hospital and go and see her husband. By the way, I've been meaning to ask, why does everyone call him Roy when his name's Alasdair?"

"Because o' his surname MacGregor. You know Rob Roy MacGregor."

Shona was none the wiser. "Who's he?"

"Who's he," Peter bristled. "Only one of the greatest folk heroes in Scottish history," and with that he turned and left, displeasure showing in every step.

"How the heck am I meant to know that?" she said to his retreating back.

"You were born here. You should know." There was no arguing with a Scot who thought he was right.

Shona needed to arrange a press conference urgently if she wanted to avoid the Chief Inspector's wrath. Two murders in 24 hours was news even for Dundee, the murder capital of Scotland. She rang all the major players, local and national, arranging it for 4 pm. That would give her sufficient time to get all the info for the Chief. He, of course, would be doing the briefing. The Big Chief liked his five minutes in the limelight. Not that she envied him. It was not a job she was hankering after. If she could do her job without ever speaking to a member of the press she would be a very happy detective Inspector indeed.

As the team returned they gathered for the briefing along with a bag of doughnuts, a selection of cakes and some of the aforementioned peh's. This Dundee delicacy was shortcrust pastry filled with spicy mince and enough grease to keep the wheels of a shipyard running. It also permeated the room with a smell which made you think you had died and gone to heaven. To Shona, the food was as manna from heaven but, actually, it was straight from Wallace's bakery. The long hours involved in doing her job meant that meals were often missed; so all food offerings were gratefully received. "I'm glad you lot found time to stop and do a spot of shopping. Never mind the investigation." Her smile took any sting from the words. "What have we got?"

"A couple of cream horns, four apple tarts, a...."

"Roy. I meant what have we got with the investigation you stupid sod. Have you forgotten we're here to work?"

"Whoops. Sorry Ma'am."

Iain gave the floor to PC Roberts. "You deserve

your moment of glory seeing as you led us there."

"We found a partial footprint on the roof. It looks like a man's trainer but Iain will need to do some forensics to get a match."

"I've also done some swabs for cartridge discharge residue in the surrounding area. When the lab's had a chance to get it under the electron microscope we'll know if a rifle's been fired in the vicinity," Iain added.

Well I never, it looks like soldier boy may be right. She needed to consider him for a transfer to CID. It was always worth keeping the good ones close.

"Nina, did you get anything from the staff on the ward?"

"No one has seen or heard anything suspicious or anyone around that shouldn't be. It was interesting though. Usually people don't want to speak ill of the dead but in this case everyone was falling over themselves to say what a complete basket she was. No one had a good thing to say about her and she appeared to be universally disliked. One nurse said, and I quote, 'She was only happy when demeaning someone - or make that everyone. Just a couple of days ago she was screaming at a student doctor, reducing her to tears, in front of all the patients." Nina looked up from her notebook. "She's being sued by a couple of patients as well. I would say your suspects include the entire staff of Ninewells and a large number of the population of Dundee," she said, delivering the gloomy news in her usual upbeat and cheerful manner. Nina could always make a disaster sound like a celebration.

Peter added, "I went to inform the husband she was dead. He was obviously upset, but he said up front everything wasn't perfect at home. She wasn't the easiest person to live with. When she was there that is. They were always arguing particularly about the fact she was never there to see their 5 year old twins."

"Look into that," said Shona. "See if he was mad enough to hire someone to shoot her. Not really likely in Dundee I know, but one thing I've learnt in this city, is never assume anything."

"I think he's being a wee bit too up front if you ask me. Sounds like he's trying to throw us off guard."

"You're probably right, Peter. Keep him in the frame. Nina and Iain, what did you find out from James Dennis, Megan's partner?"

Iain replied, "He said exactly the same as Megan's parents. She was well liked, a good solicitor and pleasant to everyone. Did the job to the very best of her ability and usually won her cases. There was an exception where a couple of her clients were sent down for a seven and twenty year stretch respectively when they both felt they should have got off. He thought they could have been angry enough to find someone to take her out."

"Has she got a boyfriend?" Shona enquired.

"She recently split up with her boyfriend but they parted on good terms and still occasionally see each other as friends," said Nina.

"The clients are worth looking into but that would fit the sniper scenario better than cutting her throat. The boyfriend bears looking at as well." None of this was making any sense and Shona's usually rosy outlook on life was slipping fast. "Find out the names of the disgruntled clients, find out where they're being held and arrange to interview them. Arrange to get the boyfriend in as well." Shona paused. "Why are you all still here? Get on with your jobs," she barked, to an immediate flurry of activity.

Picking up the phone, Shona dialled the pathologist. "Mary, it's Shona, have you had a chance to do the post mortem on Megan Mackie yet?"

"Hi Shona, you're having a tough time over there

at the moment that's for sure. I know we're the murder capital of Scotland but two in a couple of days is a record even for us. As you suspected, your victim died after having had her throat cut with a sharp blade. Someone right handed I would say. There are two other things that are interesting though. She also sustained a blow to the head, not hard enough to kill her, but to knock her out. There were also fibres in the neck wound that look like those from a towel. I'd say she was knocked out, carried to where she was killed and then somehow a towel was used to stop the blood spraying everywhere. I looked up incidences of this and it's rare but is sometimes used by mercenaries. I'll email all my findings through to you now."

"Thanks Mary." Shona hung up. She gazed out of the window at the grey buildings opposite. For a place like Dundee these murders were bizarre. The more information she got the less sense it all made. It looked like Peter was right. It must have been a man. How could a woman have the strength to do all that?

A very cold and miserable looking Chief Inspector came through the door of her office. "I want to see you in my office in five minutes and bring me a cup of tea." With that his six foot, four inch bulk lumbered off to his office. Bemused, Shona went off to be the Chief's tea girl. It was a good job she had a sense of humour. Anyway, she needed to butter him up as this case needed manpower. Maybe a couple of chocolate biscuits and a doughnut would do the trick.

Peter came up behind her. "Good luck with that."

"How do you know what I'm doing?"

"Lassie, anybody taking that much care with a pot of tea and a few cakes is after a favour. It doesn't take the brains of Einstein to work out you want something."

Taking the tea and assorted sweet treats into the

Inspector's office she smiled at this new definition of the term 'honey trap'. She gave him a summary of where they were so far. "I've also written an outline of a press statement Sir. Once we've spoken to the press I'll put requests for information on Facebook and Twitter."

"Facebook and Twitter! For goodness sake put it anywhere you like as long as we get information. I can't be doing with all this modern technological malarkey. What happened to good old-fashioned police work? Go and get some work done." The Chief huffed.

Shona took a deep breath. "While I'm here we really need extra bodies on this one. Lack of manpower's holding us back and I'd like to get moving on this as quickly as possible." To Shona's amazement the Chief readily agreed. "Get on to uniform and tell them to give you as many men as you need. Borrow from other forces if necessary and we'll pay overtime." Shona was stunned. She wondered who might be putting the pressure on, or calling in favours, over these cases.

"Well?" asked Peter as she returned to the Squad room.

"He agreed to everything. We can have as many officers as we want." Shona felt like whipping out her iPhone and taking a picture of Peter's face. It was the first time she'd ever seen him looking astonished.

"Well I'll be jiggered," he said eventually.

Shona wandered down to Uniform and broke the news, which didn't go down well until she mentioned overtime. The duty sergeant, a taciturn man, was unusually ebullient. "I'll call in some o' the lads Ma'am. I'm sure they'd be happy to help you and your team."

This was nothing to do with their vastly inflated pay packets of course. Shona was cynical. "Thanks Jeff.

Send them to me the minute they arrive." She could play the game as well as anyone else.

The local press were assembled and ready for the conference. She went to find the Chief who rose from his walnut desk. He was a picture of sartorial elegance his number one uniform pressed to within an inch of its life. Next to him she felt like Auld Jock, Dundee's man of the road, on one of his worse days. Asking Shona to join him, the Chief Inspector stepped up to the microphone and began.

"In the last twenty four hours two young women have been found murdered in Dundee. These were in the Law area and Ninewells Hospital respectively. They would appear to be two separate crimes. There is no need for the general public to panic, but we would urge young women to take extra care. The police are dealing with the crimes effectively and efficiently. A number of leads are being followed up but I cannot tell you what these are at the moment. I am sure you will understand that doing so would interfere with our ongoing investigation. I would like to assure you that these murders are being taken very seriously, and all available manpower is now being deployed to work on these cases. We will not rest until the perpetrators are found and we can bring closure for the families. The victims' relatives have already been notified, so we can therefore confirm their identities as Megan Mackie and Jennifer Brown. If any member of the public has information which would be useful to us, we would ask them to go into any police station or phone the senior investigation Officer on 0300 572 8761."

The Chief turned and walked away leaving Shona to deal with questions.

"What leads are you following up?"

"Have the victims got anything in common?"

"Could this be the start of a murder spree?"

One enterprising reporter, who identified himself as John Laird from the Dundee Evening Telegraph, said, "What makes you say that they are two different crimes? Both victims are women of a similar age. Surely there could be a link there?"

Shona replied, "At present these would appear to be unrelated crimes. We have no evidence to suggest otherwise. Another press conference will be held as soon as we have more information."

Back inside the station Shona noticed there were several extra officers waiting to be briefed. She updated them quickly and split them in to two teams.

"Team one, get yourself into pairs. I want you to go and interview friends and neighbours of the victims. Find out anything you can about them."

There was general movement before she addressed the second team. "Again I want you in pairs, interview all the hospital staff coming on or going off duty at the time. Admin are expecting you and have held the night staff. Find out if anyone saw anyone or anything suspicious. Iain, brief the teams on what's expected."

Calling on Peter, she asked him to join her in her office. "Ask Megan's business partner and Jennifer's husband to come in so we can interview them. We can do it together."

As he went off to sort it out, she went to find Nina. "What have you found out about the clients?"

"One went down for 5 counts of GBH and assault with a deadly weapon," replied Nina. "The other was serious fraud, a bank manager who embezzled a large amount of the customers' money. I think we should focus on the GBH guy as it's unlikely our embezzler would be into revenge killing. More likely that someone would be out to kill him."

"OK, set up an interview with him soonest. Is he anywhere near here?"

"Yes, Perth prison. I'll give them a ring. Do you want me to go and interview him?"

"Thanks." She added almost as an afterthought. "Take Roy. It will do him good to see how a proper interview should be done. He might also come in useful. You never know."

"Roy come in useful?" Nina was incredulous.

"Just take him, Nina."

Peter popped his head around her office door, "Alexander Jenkins will be here soon. Don't you think it's a bit odd that they have different surnames?"

"Some Doctors keep their maiden name for professional purposes. Maybe it's that." Shona then asked one of the PCs to get a room ready for the interviews. Forty minutes later the front desk Sergeant ushered in Jennifer's husband. "It's good of you to come so quickly," said Shona, shaking his hand. "Can I get you a drink?"

"Coffee would be good," he replied.

Shona, looking at his shaking hands, thought he looked wired enough already without adding caffeine to the mix. Still, who was she to judge?

Shona spoke to a passing PC. "Can you bring two coffees and a tea?" Showing the door of the interview room to Alexander Jenkins, she said, "If you would like to come in and take a seat."

As they sat down Peter switched on the digital recorder and Shona began. "Interview with Mr Alexander Jenkins on Sunday 4th November 2012 at 5 pm. Detective Inspector Shona McKenzie and Detective Sergeant Peter Johnston in attendance."

"Mr Jenkins, firstly I want to say how sorry I am for the loss of your wife and I want to assure you that we are doing everything we can to find her killer. I know this must be difficult for you but I am sure you will understand that we need to ask you these questions as part of the investigation."

"I understand. I don't mind anything as long as you find my wife's killer."

"How has your wife seemed lately? Has she acted differently in any way or has anything been bothering her?"

"No, nothing seemed different. Jennifer was in the same mood as usual which isn't saying much. She is..." he faltered, "was always in a bad mood, finding fault with everyone and everything. It started even before we were married when she refused to take my name. She said the name Jenkins didn't have enough clout for her. Her father was a big name around town and she wanted to ride on his coat tails. So I should really have known. Today it was the usual litany of the house being a mess, the twins were getting in her way, stopping her getting out to her important job at the hospital, and I was doing nothing about it. The twins are hyperactive and barely sleep. What can I do if they are up at an ungodly hour and running around?" He sounded bitter. Shona was taken aback. They didn't usually get this much information so quickly.

The door opened and she said for the benefit of the recording "PC Blair has entered the room with refreshments." As he left, she continued. "I take it from what you are saying that you and your wife were having difficulties?"

"Having difficulties? That's an understatement. We were heading for divorce. We only got married because she was pregnant with the twins. Jennifer really didn't like people. She only wanted to exert power and control over them. She hated me, she thought I was weak and not exactly the person she would have chosen to marry. I'm an accountant," he explained. "She really didn't like the kids and saw them as a nuisance. They're lively five year olds and haven't yet learnt it's best to keep out of Mummy's way. We had another argument this morning. I'm going to be honest with you and say I felt a small measure of relief when they said she was dead. But I didn't kill her and was home with the girls at the time. Did I have her killed? No, I wouldn't leave Olivia and Charlie without a mother no matter how rotten she was. I could still see flashes of the woman I first met."

The small room was getting warm and the smell of Alexander's aftershave was overpowering. Peter wrinkled his nose in distaste. What man takes the time to groom himself when he's just had the news about his wife's murder, even if their marriage was in trouble?

"It's obvious there was no love lost between you and your wife but was there anyone else who may have wanted to do her harm?" asked Peter.

Mr Jenkins gave a cynical laugh. "Everyone she ever came into contact with," he said. "People were drawn to Jennifer like moths to a flame but soon disappeared when they got burnt. At first they would find her magnetic but she was only using them for her own ends. Everything Jennifer did or said was for her own advantage. If you're going to interview everyone who ever held a grudge against her then you're going to be at it a long time."

Shona didn't think it was going to be useful to prolong the interview any longer. "Thank you for your time, Mr Jenkins, and for being so frank. Interview terminated at 5.30 pm."

"There's something not right about him, I think he warrants looking at," Peter informed Shona, after Alexander Jenkins had left.

"I agree. See what you can dig up. What time is Megan's partner coming in?"

He should be here soon. I'll give you a call when uniform bring him up."

Grabbing a coffee, Shona slumped into her office chair and groaned. This had been a very long day. It felt like she had the entire drum section of the Police Pipes and Drums band banging in her head. Rummaging through her drawer she found a couple of Paracetamol that looked as old as time itself. Not caring, she swallowed them and went to think. A bacon roll in the canteen would help to aid the thinking process. As she hurried to pay Doreen in the canteen a visit she wondered what would happen next.

11

February 1998

With both my home and school life now playing out like a scene from The Haunting of Hell House, I feel like I have nowhere to turn. Home, if that were possible, is worse than school. My mother would either be missing or drunk. There is only one thing I know which would bring me some measure of comfort. I would bury myself in study. Knee deep in research I could put everything to the back of my mind and focus on my upcoming exams. Doing well in my exams is my ticket out of this hellhole of a city, and my equally hellish hole of a life. I can't tell the teachers as this can only go one way. My bullies will increase the pressure and I am not sure I can take more pressure than I'm already under. Something would explode in a way which I didn't even want to imagine.

During a free period I settle in the library ready to immerse myself in my books. Reaching into my bag I notice everything is wet. My English books and notes are dripping, rivulets of what looks and smells like beer running down them. I thought there was an odd smell of beer on my short walk here but I'd put it down to the scum at this school drinking where they shouldn't. Never for one minute did I think it would be me. I stare in horror as the drips slowly reach the floor. How had I not noticed this before I arrived in the library? I see the figure of the librarian bearing down on me.

"Look at the mess you're making. You need to get

that rubbish out of here. It's smelling the place out."

The librarian liked me so her tone was kind, but she was right. It was a mess. Everything was ruined, all my notes, my coursework, my crib notes. Everything. How would I ever be able to salvage anything from this? The year's work lay in front of me taunting me, asking if I could ever make anything of myself now. Would this torment ever end? Steeling myself not to cry I wondered yet again what I had done to deserve any of this.

Seeing my obvious distress the librarian reached out to help me in any way she could. Unused to such kindness, it almost broke me.

12

November 2012

Back in her office, Shona didn't have to wonder for long. Iain knocked at her door and said "Uniform have been on the phone. It looks like there's been another suspicious death."

"This is spiralling out of control," Shona responded. "We're not getting time to investigate one murder before the next one's hit. What is it this time?"

"There's been another suspicious death. A woman, by the name of name of Amanda Carter, who was fully fit and healthy, according to her husband. She was found collapsed in the hallway when he came in from his work. He did a bit of amateur CPR and called for the paramedics but they could do nothing. Normally they wouldn't call CID if this was a one off but she's a woman the same age as the others. Also the paramedics thought it looked like her neck was broken, so uniform thought they'd better call it in."

"Find the others and tell them to come with us. What's the address?"

"Grange Road in Monifieth."

"Monifieth! That's the other side of the city from Ninewells. We're all over the place. What on earth can be linking them? If anything. Could be completely unrelated. I could understand if some nutter was out to murder women who looked like his dead wife or something, but they're all different. We need to look into whether the women knew each other. This can't be a coincidence. Hey, wait a minute. Monifieth isn't in our area it belongs to Angus."

"That's right but they've requested we pick it up in case it's part of our investigation."

Shona didn't even have the energy to complain. She grabbed another doughnut in an attempt to keep body and soul together and rang Nina. "How are things going?"

"They're just taking him into a visitor's room and we're going in now. From what the guards are saying he's a model prisoner. He's found religion or something and turned over a new leaf. In fact, he's waiting for a transfer to Castle Huntly open prison. It's not looking promising."

"Well he wouldn't be the first prisoner to put on a front to get less time so make sure you question him every which way. We're all off to another suspicious death. See you back at the station."

Before leaving Shona put in a call to Mary to warn her there might be another on the way. Mary was philosophical. "You're keeping me busy that's for sure. It's going to be tomorrow before I can get to it though. Even a hardnose like me needs some sleep now and again. The good news is I've done the post mortem on Jennifer Brown. It was a shooting through the heart. I'd say rifle fire probably from a .338 Lapua Magnum and you're looking for a .388 bullet."

"You seem to know a lot about guns and bullets," said Shona.

"Guns and shooting are a hobby of mine. I'm a member of a rifle club. Plus it's my job to know these things."

Well you never really know people thought Shona. Mind you we haven't had much call to talk about things. Even Dundee's usual murder quota didn't give rise to talk about shooting. "Much as I'd love to chat I have to go to another crime scene. I'll give you a ring later and pick your brains."

Driving to Monifieth Shona found herself with Peter, which suited her, despite his moans. "What gave somebody the idea it would be a good crack to merge all the wee forces into one big Scottish wide force? Word on the street is they're only doing this to save money. Never mind us poor sods down at the coalface who'll probably have fewer people to do the same job. You see they'll no' sack any Chiefs. You mark my words."

Shona thought, this subject is getting old. It had been going on for weeks now. Changing the topic, she asked, "How are your wife and kids?"

"They're fine. Angus is having his 18ᵗʰ birthday party next week. Jean and I have, of course, been told we've to go out for the night. He's been warned. One foot out of line and the local polis can have him. The boys in Tayport have agreed to keep a quiet eye on the situation. No that he's meant to know that of course but I'm sure he does."

Fishing in his pocket he opened a KitKat and passed half of it to her. She accepted it gratefully. For a few minutes they munched in companionable silence until Shona said "I read crime novels and none of them ever seem to have as many bodies stacking up as this. The police always seem to know what they're doing."

"Crime novels are a complete waste o' time," he retorted, "But if you're talking about the case then you're right, it does seem to be a wee bit convoluted. In twenty-seven years on the Force I've never come across anything like this. Dundee has its fair share o' murders but never so many in so short a time. If this turns out to be a murder then it's really beginning to look like one killer. Someone's certainly got it in for the women o' Dundee, but why so spaced out, why the different methods? It's a rum do this one."

"You've a cheek decrying crime novels with all the rubbish you read."

Laughing, Peter said, "I reckon we're even then."

13

I stroll up the quiet terrace, bottle of wine in hand. Unhurried, I am relaxed and blend into the suburban surroundings. I'd made sure the unsuspecting husband would be at work and there would be no one around to disturb me. Only the tinny squawking of multiple televisions disturbs the silence. Sunday night is for television drama, not the drama that is about to unfold in this gentle slice of suburbia. Knocking on the door I wait for it to be answered.

My hostess says warmly, "Hi. Come in."

Stepping in to a spacious hallway she closes the door behind me. The door to a comfortable living room is open, ready to receive me as a guest. "It's so good to see you. I'm looking forward to our catch up," says my hostess.

She has changed and yet not changed. Her face more angular, more refined, and yet still with the striking looks of a film star. The look in her blue eyes says she is at peace with herself and with the world. Not for much longer though. Death has brought her calling card into this refined hallway.

"It's certainly been a long time. Too long. I'm looking forward to catching up with all your news," I reply, forcing some warmth into my voice. In reality I find the inane chatter repulsive. "I've brought a nice bottle of wine. We can share it while we blether." My hostess takes it with a smile that lights up the room, and parks it next to the phone on an expensive looking hall table. Obviously not strapped for cash in this household.

"Let me take your coat. It's Baltic out there but I've got it nice and cosy in here."

Shrugging it off, another forced smile, and I hand it to my hostess who turns to the coat rack. Then I carry out my assault. A precise blow to the back of the neck with my booted foot Her neck breaks instantly. My hostess falls to the ground, knocking over the coat rack on her way. Unable to breath she can utter no sound. I want to see her face, to savour this moment of triumph. I can see the pleading in her eyes and watch the life drain from them. Once I am certain she is dead I pick up my coat and turn to leave. Stopping, I complete one last piece of business and then finally walk out of the door. I don't want to look at this woman any longer. She is part of the past. Firmly closing the door behind me, back I go into the still quiet street, a lone figure on a wintry night. My plan is moving along nicely and I have those fools at the police station running around like mice in a maze. Not knowing where to go or how to get out. It's time to stir things up a bit more. I smile. This is my first true smile in many years. If anyone could see it, they would be very afraid.

14

November 2012

The same characters were assembled like the cast in a long running play. Despite all the activity, the street remained quiet, but Shona could see a few people peering furtively through miniscule gaps in the curtains. Obviously an area where people kept themselves to themselves, Shona noted. Unless, of course, when the emergency services turn up and then everyone suddenly turns into peeping Toms, ready to fuel the latest social media gossip mill. There was never a convenient witness who could tell them everything. Still, she supposed the job would be boring if this were the case. Flashing ID badges and nodding to the young policeman on guard, Shona and Peter entered the house. A young woman lay to the side of the stairs, an overturned coat stand behind her. She was on her back, left there after the resuscitation attempt. Once again there were a lot of people milling around the crime scene, making Shona wonder if they'd started selling tickets. Why were there always so many people at a crime scene? Despite having been in the force for many years this still mystified Shona. At least most of them had moved into the living room and away from the body. One man looked as though his life had come to an end. He had a pallor that could not be faked. That must be the husband.

Someone had already phoned Larry Briar, the Police Surgeon, and he arrived to examine the body.

"Evening Shona. Two in one day must be a

Dundee record. You seem to be attracting dead bodies like they attract flies."

"You're not kidding Larry. I feel like the grim reaper."

"The grim reaper could take lessons from you, lass." Larry bent to examine the body.

"Looks like she's had her neck broken, but whether from the fall or deliberately would be hard to say. Another one for Mary to cut open. I've certified her dead so you can start your investigation." At that he left, a bit player, albeit a rather important one, in the whole drama.

The woman was lying with her head and neck at a distinctly unnatural angle. "If I were a betting woman I'd bet on Larry's diagnosis being 100% correct," Shona said to Peter. "One for the Procurator Fiscal."

As if he had read her mind, Douglas appeared by her side. "We meet again. Twice in one day. People will talk. We should arrange that coffee we were talking about. You must think Dundee's a right mess with dead bodies cluttering up the highways and byways?"

"Well there do seem to be rather a lot of them, I agree. I'm sure we can't blame the city for that though."

Smiling, he wandered off to talk to the other officers and the dead woman's husband. That was a first for Shona, arranging a date over a dead body. She knew there had been a rash of corpses recently, but seriously that was weird. Shoving her swiftly beating heart back into her chest, from where it had leapt into her throat, she turned back to the business in hand. She examined the area carefully, voicing her findings for the benefit of the recorder on her mobile phone. "No sign of forced entry. Looks like the victim let her killer in. Could be someone she knew. An overturned coat stand behind the victim. Victim's head lying at an unnatural angle. Likely broken neck."

She suddenly had a feeling she was being watched and turned round to see a wee boy of about nine standing beside her. His piercing blue eyes were friendly and enquiring. He took in the scene around him and didn't seem put off by the dead body lying at his feet.

"What the ..." She paused and started again. "Hello there. Who are you and where have you come from?" she asked, deliberately keeping her voice low and friendly. He might belong to the house and she didn't want to upset him any further. Mind you he didn't look very upset. Quite the opposite in fact, he looked positively cheerful.

"I'm Rory Strachan Lawson," he announced with relish, "and I've come from my dad's car. He's the Procurator Fiscal you know. He comes to lots of murders. He told me to stay in the car but I thought the police could do with some help. Who are you?"

Shona's heart sank and she felt sick. How could Douglas have been flirting with her when he was a married man? Were all men complete baskets looking for something, or someone, outside their marriage?

"I'm Shona McKenzie, the Detective Inspector in charge of all this," she answered. "I think you should come with me." Taking a willing Rory by the hand she led him through to his father who was just leaving the sitting room. Shona thought Douglas looked rather displeased. "You seem to have misplaced something," she said.

"What are you doing here, Rory? I told you to stay in the car. Come on I'm taking you home," Douglas said sharply. He turned to Shona and said, "I'm sorry about this. I'll ring you later and we can talk"

"Not if I see you first," she said, "I'm swearing off men for life, they're too much trouble."

Douglas looked puzzled but Shona had turned

away. "Bye Shona," Rory said over his shoulder. "It was nice meeting you," as his father pulled him towards the door.

"Come on Rory. You're in serious trouble, young man." Rory didn't look too worried.

I don't know how he turned out so well when his father is obviously vermin thought Shona, feeling utterly miserable. This was panning out to be a grim weekend in far too many different ways.

As they left, Shona moved outside to speak to the PC guarding the crime scene.

"What do you mean by letting stray kids wander through the door. That boy's just seen a dead body."

"What boy?"

"The Procurator Fiscal's son. He's been standing in the hallway having a cosy chat with me right beside the body."

"He..." the young policeman cleared his throat as his face flushed. "He must have got in whilst I was talking to Constable Seymour."

"You're not here to have tête-à-tête's with your mates, you're here to guard a crime scene. I'm reporting this to your Sergeant and you'll be lucky if you've a career left."

"Yes Ma'am." There was a slight tremor in his voice. She didn't care if he was young and upset. The stupid sod needed to do his job and do it well. Now she'd had a 9 year old messing up her crime scene and trailing muddy shoes all over the evidence. She silently begged God to spare her from incompetent dolts.

Stiffening her back and shoulders, she returned to the task in hand. She called in the forensics team and asked them to process the body, take fingerprints and dust for prints.

She had noticed an expensive bottle of wine sitting on a small table in the hallway. It looked completely out of place. It was time to speak to the husband, she thought, moving into the sitting room. It was a bit quieter in there now with the team off looking for evidence. Mr Carter was sitting staring at the floor, looking no better than he had when she arrived. She introduced herself, speaking softly, "Detective Inspector Shona McKenzie."

"Craig Carter," he replied with dull eyes not really registering anything. "I'm Mandy's hu... hu... husband. We've only been married three months." He started to cry, great sobs, which rattled his slight frame.

Shona handed him a tissue and asked, "Can I get you anything? A glass of water? A cup of tea?"

Through chattering teeth, Craig managed to force out some words. "I need a whisky. There's a bottle and some glasses in the kitchen. Do you want one?" Dundonian's were certainly hospitable. Whatever was going on, they always offered you a beverage of some sort.

"Not for me. We're not allowed to drink on the job. I'll have some water."

Returning from the kitchen she handed him a generous measure of Glenfiddich and sat down. He drank it in one go. It seemed to restore him, as he looked slightly better.

"I noticed a bottle of red wine on the hall table. Did you put it there when you came in and found your wife."

"No. Mandy couldn't drink red wine. It gave her migraine. She's a strictly white wine person. She loves..." he paused. Swallowed. "Loved a glass of chilled Pinot Grigio."

"What about yourself?"

"I'm a beer and whisky man. What's this got to do with her being dead? She wasn't a drunk you know."

"I don't mean to imply she was. We just need to

cover all angles. Do you know where the bottle of wine in the hallway came from?"

"What bottle of wine? I didn't see anything."

"Was your wife expecting any visitors today?"

"No. Not that I'm aware of. Why are you asking all these stupid questions? You should be out there finding the monster who killed my wife not, sitting in here interrogating me about things that have absolutely nothing to do with you."

He started to sob again. Shona handed him the box of tissues and, giving him time to collect himself, said, "I'll be back in a few minutes." She went to talk to the team. "Nina, put that bottle in an evidence bag and get it logged in. We'll need to get it dusted for prints."

Returning to the sitting room she saw that Craig had calmed down a bit. "I'm sorry I know this is difficult but I need to ask you a few more questions. When you came in was there anything unusual or out of place?"

"No I came in from work about six thirty. The door was on the snib. I opened it, put on the light, and saw Mandy lying there beside our coat stand. We only got it from Ikea last week. I phoned an ambulance and the police and they both came straight away. They must have come from the Ferry."

"Is there anyone you think would want to do your wife any harm?"

"Not that I'm aware of but as I say we were only married three months and had only been going out for six months before that. What don't I know? There could be anything. What do I know about her, it seems like not very much."

"Where did your wife work?"

"She did work as a researcher for the University, on something so top secret even I don't know what it was. She never spoke about her work so I suppose it could be something to do with that. Do you think that could be it? That must be it." His emotion-choked voice cracked.

"We'll look into that," Shona replied. "Is there anyone I can call to come and be with you?"

His eyes filled up with tears again but he managed to stay calm "It's OK. I'll have to call my parents and Mandy's parents." She left him looking bereft at the thought, a man suddenly alone.

As she was leaving the room she turned back to Craig "Did your wife have any friends called Megan Mackie or Jennifer Brown?"

"Not that I'm aware of. She never mentioned them and they weren't at the wedding. I know that because we only had a small wedding." She thanked him and turned away again.

The team had finished so they returned to the cars. "Roy, call in a pizza order, just get several extra-large. Any dislikes?" No one shouted out so she told him to get a couple of vegetarian and the same again but meat feast. They could fight it out at the station. With a bit of luck the pizzas would arrive at the same time as them.

While Peter drove, she rang the Chief Inspector with an update. He was apoplectic "There are women dropping around the streets of Dundee like flies and you and your team seem to be clueless as to how you're going to find the people or person responsible. I've given you enough officers to police a small country. They're being paid extravagant amounts of money in overtime but you're not one step further forward. I have the Lord Provost leaning on me to get a quick resolution on this so we need to come up with something – and fast. Am I making myself clear? I'll speak to you in the morning." The dialling tone made its usual appearance. There were habits, and there were habits. This was one she could really do without.

Arriving back at the station they made short work of the pizzas. They were about to recap the situation to date but, just as Shona opened her mouth to speak, she was pulled out of the room by a very disgruntled desk Sergeant. He had a well-dressed young man in tow who was looking distinctly unhappy. "This is Mr James Dennis." The sergeant had no sooner got the words out than Mr Dennis started on Shona.

"I've been here three hours waiting for you to ask me questions. If this is the way you treat everyone then I can see myself having a lot of business coming my way."

Shona groaned inwardly. This was all she needed, a lawyer with a grudge against the police in general and her department in particular. Of all the people to forget about she had to choose a lawyer.

"I am sorry that you have been kept waiting so long Mr Dennis. I agree it is completely unacceptable and the only excuse I can offer is that we were called out on another case. I can assure you that we want to catch Megan's killer and it's important we speak to you. You will probably agree that it would be better if we waited until tomorrow, when we've all had some sleep. Now I know it's a business day so what time would be best for you?" she proffered.

"That's not good enough. You could at least have let me know. I've better things to do with my Sunday than hang around this dump." He consulted his iPhone. "Eleven a.m. as I have clients before and after."

Whilst secretly agreeing with him about the station Shona merely said, "That's fine. The forensics team have finished with your office although Megan's room is still sealed. I am sure you'll realise why it's out of bounds."

Returning to the briefing room Shona said, "I know it's been a long day but there's still work to be done, so let's get on with it. What about the latest murder?"

"We've collected a bit more evidence this time but not much," Nina said. "A neighbour who was out walking his dog saw someone go into the house at about half past 6. Could have been a man or a woman from the way they were dressed. The individual was about five foot ten and completely dressed in black including a black hat. That's pretty standard dress for this time of year in Dundee, so it's unlikely anyone would remember seeing him or her. It just so happens our neighbour is a retired police officer so noticed more than the average."

Iain, looking slightly more cheerful than he had with the other two murders, interjected, "That would tie in with the footprint we found outside. Looks like a man's boot with a square heel. I'd say about a size 9 but I'll measure it and find out. I'll be able to give you a bit more then."

"Does anyone know what size shoe Craig Carter wore?" No one being any the wiser Iain went off to ring the husband to find out.

"He'll be happy. He already thinks we're a bunch of useless wasters who keep asking daft questions instead of getting on with the investigation. This question will just about confirm it for him. Right, your thoughts so far?" Shona continued.

Peter summarised it for everyone. "We've got a murderer or murderers. They could be men, women or a mixture of both. We don't know anything about them. The murders are all over the place. From what we know so far I'd say we're stuffed. How on God's good earth are we ever going to solve this?"

"Don't be so gloomy Peter. Of course we'll solve

it. We're Tayside Police's secret weapons. Nina, how did you get on with interviewing the prisoner in Perth?"

"The guards were right, he is a changed man, or seems that way anyway. He's going to church, studying the bible and he's completely altered his behaviour towards other prisoners. He said he has no interest in revenge as being put away was actually the turning point for him. He doesn't want to jeopardise his transfer to Castle Huntly as it will be easier for his wife and kids to visit him. He seemed genuine enough so I think it's a dead end."

The atmosphere in the room had the feel of Perth Prison in a snowstorm. Everyone looked exhausted and miserable. Some good news was needed to give their get up and go a jolt. Iain returned, smiling. "I was right. It is a size nine man's boot and Craig Carter wears a seven. The victim wore a size four so it's definitely not hers.. The husband says they haven't had visitors in weeks. They've been too busy and too wrapped up in each other being newlyweds. So it's looking increasingly likely the shoe belongs to our large footed male murderer. Maybe it's a woman with a fetish for men's boots. "

Laughter broke out and relieved some of the tension. However, they all looked exhausted. "It's time to knock off. I'll see you here at 0800 sharp. There might be something we've missed and sleep will sharpen our brilliant minds." It was only a glimmer of good news but Shona was ready to take anything she could get.

Returning to feed a very disgruntled Shakespeare with gourmet chicken cat food, Shona found some brie, stilton and a few crackers for herself. She poured a large glass of Talisker as an accompaniment. She considered this the perfect comfort food. Sighing she settled on to the sofa to eat the repast. A replete Shakespeare was now more amenable and curled up on her lap whilst she watched a recording of Downton Abbey. However, she found it difficult to concentrate. Why were these murders so difficult to solve? What were they missing? What did the women have in common except their age? At first glance there was absolutely nothing. One was a tall, slim, blonde, one a rather plump redhead and the last a petite brunette. Not a serial killer targeting a certain type of woman then. One was universally liked, another universally loathed, and the third was married to someone who seemed to know virtually nothing about her, apart from her taste in wine. She made a mental note to get someone to check in the morning if the women knew each other. She felt like she was wading through ever shifting sand. This case was seriously depressing her.

She focused on the programme again realising that she'd missed about 10 minutes. The plot had moved on to Lady Mary and Matthew who were obviously very much in love. This set her thinking again about how improbable these programmes were. In real life nothing went to plan. Her track record included a cheating ex-husband, and a flirting Procurator Fiscal who turned out to be married. Even the most optimistic person would have to agree this was not good. Despite the fact nothing had happened, she still felt there was something special between her and Douglas. A certain little something in the air each time they spoke. His turning out to be married had definitely put a damper on that. He seemed so nice she thought and not the type to cheat on his wife. Mind you, that was what she had thought about her husband and look what happened there. It was a good thing she had found out now and not after something had happened. She was puzzled though as she didn't recall seeing a wedding ring. Not that she had actively looked. She had other things on her mind, like solving murders, every time she met him. "Why do all men treat women so badly?" Shona asked the cat. He just blinked and threw her a look which seemed to say, excuse me, I'm a man and I think I'm doing a jolly fine job of sticking by you.

"You're right Shakespeare. You're the only man I need in my life. Stuff the lot of them. We're doing all right you and me."

15

So far the day has been quiet. As I walk around the echoing hallways of the old school, everyone is totally ignoring me. This is actually worse than the usual torment. Something has to happen. I had heard of a theme park ride called The Tower of Terror. You never knew when that lift was going to fall. I could feel the tension as an almost palpable presence deep inside my soul just as I would on that ride. I can't take much more of this. Running around the hockey field, with each and every one of my self-appointed tormentors, I wait for them to catch me "accidently" with a stick. It's the last period of the day and they all seem remarkably well behaved. As the whistle blows for the end of the match, I heave a sigh of relief that I had survived the day unscathed. Perhaps they had got fed up with me and would leave me alone. Maybe they had moved on to some other poor victim. I hoped so. My sympathy, for anyone else suffering, was deleted by relief. Hurrying to the changing room I go to get changed. I stop short. Where are my clothes? My bag is there, with everything else in it, but no school clothes. I search the room looking for where they have been stashed but they are nowhere to be found. "Where are my clothes? What have you done with them? You've got to give me them now." There is only silence. A couple of people are hanging their head but do not speak. "Please, give them to me now." The last girl to leave throws a taunting look behind her as she shoots out of the door. I will have to go home like this in a T-Shirt and shorts in subzero temperatures. Wandering about the now frosty streets, I shiver violently. A few people look but no one speaks. I can almost hear them thinking 'just another stupid underdressed teenager.' I leave it until after 9 pm to go home hoping my mother's latest man, Robbo, if I had got the name right, would have fallen into a drunken stupor and ignore me. Blue with the cold and shivering, I go in the front door only to realise he is not only still fully compos mentis, but also roaring drunk. This is a worse combination than the school bullies and my clothes. "Where've you been," he snarls, "and where's your school uniform." Without giving me a chance to answer his fists fly, beating me anywhere he can land a punch. Thankfully he is so drunk his blows are mostly missing their mark and the alcohol has taken some of the power from them. Still every blow sends a million pain signals whizzing to my brain. Every punch intensifies the resolve that I am not going to be a victim. I am stronger than that. When he finishes I drag myself to bed, my body screaming with the agony I cannot vocalise. I am not going to cry. I'm better than all of this. I am not going to cry. No one will see how much this world is hurting me. I am alone. I can do nothing about the present. I can do something to change my future, and I will.

16

November 2012

The next morning Shona woke early with a feeling that she'd missed something. It was disconcerting. Then she realised, no ringing phone. That had to be a good sign, she thought as she prepared to go for a run. Going down to the waterfront, she ran along the prom, her blonde ponytail swinging with every step. She breathed in the salty smell of the sea air with every invigorating pace. The castle made an imposing backdrop to her run. She ran for a couple of miles and, turning back, watched the sun rise over the road and rail bridges with the church steeples in the distance. She might moan about Dundee but it really was a beautiful city. It didn't deserve its bad name. One past judge had described it as a sinkhole of atrocity. Despite this, she'd actually found the people to be, on the whole, pleasant, friendly, and helpful, excepting of course any low life she had met in the course of her work.

Dressing in her usual casual fashion, she tickled Shakespeare under the chin, and drove to work. Passing Sainsbury's she dropped in to buy cakes for the troops. The fastest way to a police officer's heart was always through his stomach. At the front of the store the newspaper headlines shouted the most recent news:

"Killers Stalk the Streets of Dundee: No Woman Safe."

"Ex-Lord Provost George Brown's Daughter Dead."

"George Brown lambasts police. What are you

doing to find my daughter's killer?"

These were the more anodyne of the selection on offer. That should make the women of Dundee sleep more easily in their beds, and reinforce their confidence in the Police. You have to love the press. Always willing to help the police out and make their job easier. Not. Jennifer was emblazoned across all the headlines with no mention of the other poor woman. Surely her life was just as important, but no. It had to be all about George Brown's daughter and his grief. Shona bought a copy of the Courier and the Scotsman. She'd give the Courier to Peter once she'd read the highlights. That should cheer him up and give him plenty to moan about all day. Peter could whinge for Scotland and perhaps with a bit of England and Wales thrown in for good measure. The local paper was always great fodder for his moan fest. She passed the journey to work entertaining pleasant thoughts of rounding up all reporters and dumping their very dead bodies in the deepest part of the river Tay. She decided against it, reasoning that the press were so poisonous their rotting corpses might kill all the salmon.

Entering the squad room silence reigned. They were all there, but chewing on the sort of heart attack breakfast that Scots worldwide dream about, huge rolls slathered with butter, filled with fried sausage, bacon and egg and dripping with grease. The aroma of greasy food made her mouth water. Give the officer who thought of this an OBE, she thought. "Ths rrs," Peter mumbled as he pushed a greasy bag towards her. Putting aside thoughts of a looming heart attack she gratefully tucked in.

Fortified by breakfast and strong mugs of builders brew, they pronounced themselves ready and raring to go.

"We're a much more cheerful bunch this morning,"

Shona said. "It's amazing what a decent night's sleep and a full belly can do for the spirit."

She gazed around amazed, yet again, by the assorted bunch. Nina, Roy and Iain were dressed head to toe in designer gear. No Matalan for them. Peter, in a suit, still managed to look like he'd just fallen out of bed and into the station. Still, they were individuals with their own unique gifts they brought to the team. Except for Roy that was. She was still trying to figure out what his talents were, unique or otherwise.

Feeling like she ought to give Roy a chance to prove himself, she asked him to go and look into Alexander Jenkins's background. He looked positively perky at the thought and trotted off with a determined glint in his eye. That was the first time anything seemed to have flicked Roy's switch. Shona was still going to reserve judgement though. It was going to take a lot for her to believe someone like Roy has a good side.

Iain said, "We've had the swab results back. The ones I took on Ninewells' roof. Soldier boy was right. They confirm a gun had been fired in the vicinity."

"So it was a rifle. Unless the medical staff are doing clay pigeon shooting in their breaks. Thanks Iain. It gives us somewhere to start."

"Peter, have a word with all the local gun clubs and see if there are any suspicious characters in their midst."

"Nina, could you have a butchers at Craig Carter? See if you can find anything there. Peter, talk to Mandy Carter's parents. The husband seems clueless as to her past or even her present. Iain, find out more about the research project she was on."

Excusing herself, Shona went to find the Chief Inspector. Knocking, she was asked to enter and found the Lord Provost sitting in a chair. "Lord Provost, Chief

Inspector," she greeted them formally.

"Come in and sit down, Shona." The Chief Inspector had obviously had a chance to calm down since last night. "I'd like you to brief the Lord Provost on what we've got so far."

"As I am sure you already know, three women have been murdered over the weekend. It is difficult to say if the cases are connected but we suspect that at least one of the murders was carried out by a woman. No motives as yet but we're looking into the backgrounds of all the women and also the background of Jennifer Brown's husband. There was a lot of strife in their marriage and he himself says he is relieved that she is dead. Detective Sergeant Chakrabarti and I are going to speak to Megan Mackie's business partner. We need to tread carefully with him as he's a lawyer and had a bit of a run around from us last night."

"Well, try and keep him happy, but don't let it interfere with our investigation. Just because he's a lawyer doesn't mean he didn't kill her," replied the Chief Inspector.

"I'll be sure to keep an open mind Sir." Privately she was thinking, Stupid sod. Doesn't he think I already know that?

"Shona," the Lord Provost said, "I'm obviously interested in all the cases but it is particularly important that we solve this one quickly. Jennifer Brown's father used to be the Lord Provost of Dundee, so the media are going to be on this like vultures round a rotting corpse. Today is just the start."

"I can assure you, Lord Provost, that we are taking *all* these murders extremely seriously and doing everything we can to solve them quickly."

"I am sure you are, Shona," replied the Lord Provost. "I have every faith in you and your team. Tayside Police has never let us down yet."

"Thank you Sir."

She was dismissed. "Thanks Shona. Keep me updated with any new developments. Immediately," said the Chief.

"Of course, Sir." Three bags full, Sir. How was she meant to solve a murder with every official in the city breathing down her neck?

Returning to the squad room she found everyone had dispersed. Only Peter was at his desk, rereading the case files.

"Looking for inspiration are you?" Shona said "Well good luck with that. I'm going to take Nina with me to interview the lawyer. I'd like you to delve into his background, see what you come up with. He might be a big shot lawyer but I'm sure you have learnt to trust no one in this job. Keep an eye on Roy. He can be a bit slapdash. We can't afford for him not to pull his weight."

"No problem. I'll keep the work shy little toerag on the straight and narrow. That laddie's either going to have to shape up or ship out," he said. "He's no use to anybody at the moment. Who knows where his head's at?"

"Let's see how it goes today," said Shona "and if needs be I'll have a stern word with him tomorrow. I'm off to get Nina and we'll have a team briefing when we get back."

Just as she was leaving the phone rang. It was Mary with the results of the latest post mortem that of Mandy Carter. "I'll be quick," she said, "as my backlog of bodies is beginning to remind me of the inner sanctum of hell. Don't even think about dropping any more dead bodies on my doorstep until I get through the routine stuff. Anyway, as you suspected she died of a broken neck. I'd say one blow from a blunt object. Could have been anything but I'd say that whoever did it had the strength and ferocity of a rabid animal. She did have a slight cut on her neck, which looks like the edge of something, but I've no idea what. Not much help I know but it's all I've got."

Shona thanked her and hung up. They were no further forwards. Shona wondered what it was they weren't getting.

Nina was in a very good mood as they drove to the lawyer's office. She'd met a new fella.

"He's very good looking. Looks a bit like Justin Bieber only taller and older. He runs a night club in Perth."

Shona was thinking that the whole world seemed to have a better love life than her. "There's a match made in heaven, a nightclub manager and a police officer. With the hours you keep when do you actually get to see Justin Bieber senior?" Shona asked.

"Oh, I go to his club most nights and we get to see each other then." The likelihood of that relationship lasting wasn't high. Mind you the likelihood of any of Nina's relationships lasting wasn't high. She seemed to have an endless stream of men after her.

"You're up half the night clubbing and then come to work. When do you sleep?"

"I don't need much sleep. It's a good thing really."

"If your sleep deprivation ever causes a problem with my investigations, you're dead."

"Stop worrying Shona. When have I ever let you down?" Nina's smile took the edge off the words and Shona couldn't help smiling back.

James Dennis was not looking any happier than he had the previous evening. "I hope you lot aren't going to waste much more of my time. Make it quick, I've another appointment in an hour and I had to cut my last one short." Shona had a sudden urge to kick him in the teeth.

"If we could sit down, we need to ask you a few questions in case there is anything you know which could help us? We would like to record this interview if that's all right with you? As I am sure you are aware this would be the case in all murder investigations."

"Fine, just get on with it."

"What sort of person was Megan? How did she relate to other business associates or her clients?"

"This is a small practice so there was only Megan and I. We had a good business relationship. We occasionally had a drink outside of work but that was it. We share a secretary and she is always waxing lyrical about how nice Megan was. Dundee is a small city so Megan had dealings with most other solicitors. As far as I know they liked and respected her."

"And her clients?"

"As I said on Saturday night, most of her clients were happy with her work. She's a good lawyer and managed to settle a lot of cases without going to court. I gave you the names of a couple of likely suspects on Saturday. No one else has come to mind. Why are you asking me all the same questions?"

Shona stayed calm despite a rising feeling that she'd like to bump off the one remaining partner. "Now that you've had a bit more time to think is there anyone else who may have wanted to harm Megan?"

"I've been racking my brains. My secretary has gone through her files and there's nothing there apart from the two names I gave you. Oh. Actually, there is one other person I can think of. When we were at University there was another student who had a thing for Megan. It started out friendly and then, when she told him she wasn't interested in anything else, he turned out to be a bit of a pest. Kept texting, phoning and turning up on her doorstep. Eventually she took out a restraining order against him. That was in Edinburgh though and, as far as I know, she'd heard nothing from or about him since."

"Do you have a name?"

"Yes it was William Berry. He was a politics student. I'm surprised he's not running the country by now. Politicians are a load of useless tossers."

Shona had to agree with his evaluation of the Government, especially the ones in Westminster, but kept her counsel. It wasn't a good look for the police to slag off the duly elected Government of the country. "Can you tell us where you were on the night of Megan's murder?"

He stiffened, "I was at home watching a DVD with only the dog and a bottle of whisky for company, so no alibi. There's nothing I can do to prove I was at home but I didn't kill Megan. Your time would be better spent looking for the real murderer."

Shona gazed at him with practiced eyes and her ears tuned for any sign of discord. He was either telling the truth or a very good liar.

"Did you notice any changes in Megan's character or demeanour recently?"

"No. She was as cheerful as ever. Nothing she did set any bells ringing."

Shona rose. "Thank you for your time Mr Dennis. We'll look into Mr Berry and be in touch if we have any more questions. In the meantime you'll need to stay in Dundee just in case."

Nina rang the station to let them know they were on their way. By the time they arrived everyone was in the briefing room, various beverages in hand, waiting for them. If there were ever a world tea and coffee crisis the whole British police system would collapse. An

Army might march on its stomach, but the machine that was the police force was definitely oiled by caffeine. Shona noticed Peter wasn't there. He was at his desk looking intently at the computer. "Hey," she said, "are you coming through for the briefing?"

"I was just coming," he replied. "I've found some interesting stuff here about our boy James Dennis. Needed a bit of a hand from Roy though to get me on the right track."

Roy, thought Shona? I would never in a million years have imagined Roy would be able to help Peter.

"Great you can fill us all in. How has the morning gone with Roy?"

"He's worked hard the whole time. I popped in a couple of times and he seemed to be productive. He was certainly intense and didn't seem to take his eyes off the computer screen. Maybe he's been captured by aliens and replaced by a newer model." He grinned.

"You read too much trash. The *Daily Record* isn't good for your intellect you know," she joked.

"The *Daily Record's* a great paper. All the news you could ever want and then some."

"It's the 'then some' I'm worried about Peter."

Shona was brisk as they arrived in the meeting room. "Nina, summarise where we are and feed back to everyone about the interview with James Dennis."

Nina gave a precise but succinct briefing.

Peter followed, "I've some interesting information about our Mr Dennis. Despite his very healthy salary as a partner in the firm, he has been living hand to mouth waiting for the next pay cheque. There are a lot of withdrawals from his account. His credit cards are also maxed out. I'm not sure where his money is going but there are some suspicious transactions we need to look at. I'd like to know what happens to the business in the event of the death of one of the partners. My bet is it passes to the remaining partner."

"Good catch," Shona said.

"What about the gun clubs. Anything crawl out from there?"

"Not a thing," said Peter. "I know most o' the blokes running the clubs. I've had dealings wi' them all at one time or another. They all said they would have let me know if there were any potential crazies. I believe them. The clubs around here run a tight ship. Most of the members are ex military."

"Would that not mean they are better at hiding their tracks."

"It could do. Yes. I still think that most of the club chairmen are astute enough to sniff something out. They've all said they'll keep an extra close watch and let me know. I believe them."

"Ok, we'll go with your intuition and set it aside for now. Keep a close eye on the situation though."

"Aye, you can trust me."

Roy was looking as eager as a cocker spaniel on speed so she asked him to go next. "I've been looking into Alexander Jenkins. It turns out his marriage was a lot worse than he was letting on. His wife could be very volatile and has thumped him on more than one occasion. Empty wine bottles seem to play a large part in the damage. She thought he was useless and was threatening to divorce him. She, of course, being a doctor, earned much more than him and the house was in her name. She was also threatening to take the kids saying that he wasn't fit to look after them. He had recently taken out an insurance policy which meant he got £2,000,000 in the event of her death."

Shona looked stunned. "How on earth did you find all that out?" she asked him.

"Oh it's easy on the internet. You can find out just about anything about anybody if you know how."

"Was all of this information found legally?" she said sharply "We can't use if it's not."

"Of course it was Ma'am. I'm not a hacker. It was all freely available information on the net. You'd be amazed what people put about themselves on places like Facebook and Twitter thinking it's secure, when it's actually open to everyone. Most of the Social Media using public are as thick as mince."

Thank goodness for that, she thought, making a mental note to watch what she put on Facebook. Well, well they seemed to have unearthed Rob Roy MacGregors' hidden talent. Maybe he had some of his ancestors' hero genes in him after all. She still wasn't convinced about his future in the CID though.

"Two million quid," said Peter. "Did you actually say two million quid?"

"Yep. I most certainly did."

"I agree Peter, it's a bit sus that she's insured for so much. Not even a doctor could be worth that much. Not unless they were plastic surgeons to Hollywood's rich and famous. Nice little earner for the recently widowed Mr Jenkins. Nice work Roy," said Shona.

"Thanks, Ma'am. I agree. She might be some top notch surgeon but that would pay her salary for an awful long time," said Roy.

"Iain, what have you found?" Shona changed direction.

"Nothing much new. I've looked at the photos from the crime scene of Jennifer Brown. The blood spatter appears to be small droplets sprayed in a mist like pattern. Also there's a lot of forward spatter against the wall and back spatter down the victim's body. Her car's in the crime scene garage and I still need to look properly at that."

"Thanks Iain. It's good to know we're probably on the right track. Get on it the minute we're finished here.

What about the Carters? What did you find out about them?"

Iain grimaced. "I was stonewalled by the University. Seems the research is top secret. They were quite snooty when they told me that it would be detrimental to the ongoing development of the project to help us with our enquires."

"We'll see about that. It'll be detrimental to their ongoing good health if they stonewall me. I'm handing this one over to the Chief and he can sort it out."

Nina added, "Craig Carter seems squeaky clean. He's a physiotherapist up at Ninewells and he's well respected. No previous convictions and nothing to suggest he was up to no good. Mandy's father says they were deeply in love. It will be difficult to speak to the victim's parents at the moment as the father is distraught and the mother under heavy sedation. I also checked out the bottle of wine. Iain says there were fingerprints all over it. That's to be expected given it was in a shop. And you were right about the price tag. It's one of the more expensive bottles. La Croix de Beaucaillou 2007 St. Julien comes in at £30 a bottle and that's when buying it by the case online. The offies will be selling it at a much higher mark up. Could be 50 or 60 quid. There can't be many places around here that sell wine that retails at that price, and if they do, they won't sell many.

Almost as an afterthought she said, "There seems to be something that might link these murders. Two of the victims, Megan and Mandy, worked at the University. I wonder if Jennifer has any links to the University?"

"Good thinking, Nina," said Shona "Follow that up. Get uniform on to checking out the off licences and wine stores as well."

"Anything else to add?" she asked. No one

responded. She sent the uniforms to speak to friends of all the victims. "Peter and Roy, look into the suspicious activities on Mr Dennis' account. Nina, get Alexander Jenkins in to speak to us. We need to lean on him a bit harder and see what we can squeeze out."

Sitting in her office writing notes, Shona suddenly realised there was someone in the room. She looked up to see young Rory Lawson standing just inside the door. Much as she liked him her heart sank. Shona knew that if Rory was there then his father could not be far behind. Still it wasn't the boy's fault his father was an accomplished liar and a cheat. "Hi Rory, nice to see you again, what brings you here?" she said.

"My dad's been called in. Someone important needs to speak to him," he said. "I'm not allowed in the room when they're talking so I thought I'd come and see you. Have you had any more dead bodies? Do you need help? I'm going to do your job one day," he said matter of factly.

Shona was tempted to give it to him now. He couldn't do a worse job than the entire Tayside Police Force at present. "Would you like something to drink? There might even be some cake left."

"Have you got any coke please?" he asked. "And if you've got a cream cake they're my favourite. Éclairs are the best."

"I'll see what we can do but they're gannets around here and there might not be much left." Rory followed her to the squad room. Luckily she managed to find an éclair and a slice of homemade fruit cake which Iain's mother had made. Rory would probably be sick from all the cake but it served his father right for bringing him in here and leaving him to his own devices.

"Can I take a piece home for my little sister?" Rory asked.

Shona's head was reeling. Little sister. How many kids did this man have and why wasn't Rory's mother looking after him instead of his father dragging him around at work?

The ability to appear from nowhere seemed to be a Lawson family trait as the man himself appeared beside them. "Afternoon Shona. Rory I hope you haven't been bothering the Detective Inspector." The cheek of the man Shona thought. Does he have no shame? Standing here chatting like everything's normal.

"Would you like to join us for some lunch?" Douglas enquired.

"No I would not," she said coolly. "Anyway your son's just had two cakes so I doubt he'll need much lunch." She turned away and walked back to the office.

They both looked after her with puzzlement. "Did you do anything to upset her?" Douglas asked.

"No, I did not," Rory said vehemently. "I was well behaved like you told me to be. Anyway she was all right until you turned up." None the wiser they turned and left the building.

Nina had asked Alexander Jenkins to come in and he was now waiting in an interview room. His stiff back and folded arms did not indicate a man willing to talk frankly. "For goodness sake what do you want now? I've got twins to look after and a funeral to arrange. I haven't got time to trail down here and speak to you every time you have a whim."

Shona remained placid although her gaze was steely. "I'm sure you'll find it is more than a whim. Need I remind you we are trying to solve your wife's murder? Detective Sergeant Chakrabarti we are ready to start." Nina switched on the recording equipment.

"Interview with Mr Alexander Jenkins, husband of the victim Jennifer Brown. DI Shona McKenzie and DS

Nina Chakrabarti in attendance. Monday 5th November at 3 p.m. Mr. Jenkins I know you said that your marriage was in difficulties, but can you give us a few more details?"

"What details do you want? I've told you everything you need to know. We didn't get on. Everybody knew that. Jennifer was a difficult woman with a quick temper. If there was anything wrong in her world she took it out on me."

"We've heard there was a bit more to it than that. You and your wife were having serious problems and your wife was about to divorce you."

Alexander blanched, "Where did you hear that. Things weren't that bad. Yes we had our problems like any other couple, maybe more in fact but we were working through them."

"That's interesting. In our previous interview you said you were heading for divorce. What's changed? So it's not true that your wife was about to kick you out of the marital home and sue you for custody of your daughters?"

Sweating, Alexander replied, "Well she did ask for a divorce but it was in the heat of the moment. She didn't really mean it. She needed me to look after the girls and make sure everything was all right at home."

"Did your wife physically attack you, Mr Jenkins?"

"She did occasionally lash out but it was just temper. She soon calmed down. She never meant anything by it and she didn't hurt me. How do you know all of this?"

"Never mind how we know," said Shona "We ask the questions. It would appear that you recently took out an insurance policy on your wife's life. You're now a very rich man Mr Jenkins. No wonder you were relieved at Jennifer's death – an end to all the turmoil and a millionaire to boot."

His body tense, Alexander asked, "Do you think I murdered my wife?"

"I don't know," said Shona "but you certainly seem to have several motives for getting her out of the way. You tell me, did you murder her?"

Alexander clammed up. "I am not saying anything else until I speak to my lawyer. Am I free to go?"

"We have a few more questions to ask you but we'll wait until your lawyer gets here."

Leaving the room she turned back, "Oh, just one question and it won't incriminate you, was your wife a student at the University or did she ever work there?"

Alexander looked a bit puzzled. "Yes. She went to medical school there and did the odd visiting lecture to medical students."

"Thank you," said Shona. "Interview ended at 16.42."

"Nina, could you take Mr Jenkins to make his phone call and then find him somewhere to wait until his lawyer arrives?" A couple of hours cooling his heels in the cells should focus his mind and make him a little more desperate to get out of the station. This might loosen his tongue, Shona thought.

17

November 2012

I take a quick walk through the streets of Dundee, just another person in a hurry to get to their destination. The salty tang of the sea announces I am close. The river Tay, gunmetal grey, plays hide and seek through the buildings. Now you see it, now you don't. Long strides eat up the ancient, narrow streets of Broughty Ferry. Like a cheetah after game I am stalking my next victim. It is time to shake things up and really give those fools, trying to find me, something to think about. It's been too easy for them so far. A change of direction will keep them on their toes and far from my scent.

The peeling door of the ugly, postmodern building is heavy in my hand as I enter. The strong smell of paint assaults my brain as I move quickly to avoid tripping over a discarded ladder and half open tins of coloured paints. I call out and a man appears. "Can I help you?" he asks. This is the person I am looking for. Time not having changed him I recognise him instantly. I knew he would be here. I know his every movement.

"I'm interested in hiring your decorators. Can I speak to one of them?"

"They're not here. They'll be back tomorrow to pick up...."

His words are cut off as I step back, pull a knife from my coat and throw it at his chest. It meets its mark spot on, as though in the middle of a perfect bullseye. I see a brief flicker of fear in his eyes but there is no time for him to defend himself or shout out. Not that there is anyone to hear him in this place at the moment. His body drops to the wood floor. Blood erases the paint spatters on the torn lino and spurts up the freshly painted walls. I watch it drip, decorating the wall a macabre shade of red. It darkens as it congeals. I contemplate the newly painted pattern, knowing I have plenty of time before anyone else comes along. My research, thorough in the extreme, always serves me well. No chance encounter, this meeting, in this place.

While he lies dying I go to the toilet. Washing the blood from my face, I change my clothes. I look around then, taking face wipes from my bag, clean up some spatters of blood. Taking a syringe from my pocket I remove the seal from the end and spray some blood in the sink before washing it away. This little trick will have them up all night puzzling. They have met their match in me. Going back to the main room, although giving the body and the blood a wide berth, I make certain he is now dead. Leaving the building I melt into the streets of Broughty Ferry, the latest kill forgotten and the plot of the next one taking root in my mind. There's no time for thinking of what is past. I need to concentrate on the future. There is no time for anything else. Everything's going according to plan. Not long now and it will all be over and I can start my new life of freedom. Walking briskly, I make my way to Caird Park a few miles away, and drop the bag with my clothes into a rubbish bin. They will never look here. Nothing left to chance. Everything in its place.

18

November 2012

Pondering the University angle Shona picked up the phone to give said institution a call. Nina's appearance led to a hurried dropping back in the cradle. "We've just had word from uniform that there's been another suspicious death, an elderly man this time."

Shona's furrowed brow signalled her internal thoughts. More work. It wasn't likely that this killing was related to the other murders but they still had to pick it up and investigate it. "As if we haven't got enough on our hands without this. Don't get me wrong, I'm as eager to investigate a murder as anyone else in the building, but this is ridiculous. Let the team know we're on our way again." Sighing, she pulled herself from her chair and followed Nina out of the door.

This time they were heading to the Broughty Castle Bowling Club in the Ferry. Beyond the perfectly manicured lawns lay a clubhouse that looked in need of some serious TLC. The battered front door was open. Beyond the crime scene tape a lone policeman was guarding the entrance. Shona stopped, showed her ID card, and peered inside. It looked like a scene from *Friday the Thirteenth Parts 1-4* all rolled into one. An elderly man lay on the floor in a gelatinous pool of blood. His open eyes stared upwards in death. Blood spattered the walls which, judging by the strong smell of paint, and the shoved aside paint pots, had been recently decorated.

"Do we have a name?" Shona asked. One of the uniforms piped up "Stuart McKay. He's the President of the Bowling Club. One of the elderly members found him and called it in. She came in to help him clear up as the club has just been redecorated. She's in a right state Ma'am, so I sat her on a chair in the next room. Her name's Mrs O'Brien if you want to speak to her."

Shona went into the next room and immediately called for help. The woman looked dreadful and was clutching her chest and struggling for breath. "My chest," she gasped.

"It's all right Mrs O'Brien I'm a police officer and I'm going to get help." She called louder, "I need help in here." Nina appeared. "Call an ambulance. Suspected heart attack."

As Nina pulled out her mobile to make the call the police surgeon arrived to certify the body. "Larry we need help here," Shona said, "I think she's having a heart attack." As Larry took over Shona hovered, not knowing what to do for the best. "Is there anything I can do to help?"

"Get someone to fetch my bag from the car."

Within a few minutes she could hear the sound of the Sirens and a bevvy of paramedics flew through the door. Monitors were attached, oxygen applied and Mrs O'Brien was stretchered off in the back of the waiting ambulance. Larry stopped long enough to certify the victim dead, and say, "Mrs O'Brien's going to be fine," before he disappeared out of the door.

"Roy, we still need to interview her so could you follow them up to the hospital. As soon as she's in a fit state get a statement. Try not to kill the poor woman though." Roy's face said it all. She added, "Get a grip Roy. I'm not saying you'll do anything. I'm just pointing out she might be a bit fragile so we need to be gentle. We don't want another death on our hands."

Roy left still with a face like a slapped bum. Shona was tempted to whack him. He was getting on every nerve she possessed. Shona had thought CID in Dundee was going to be a quiet affair. She was beginning to realise how wrong she had been. Nothing much for a year and now a body count she could barely keep track of. Add to that a collapsing witness and things were getting very interesting. She was thinking of applying for the post of grim reaper. He seemed to have less work than she did.

When Shona returned to the scene of the murder the Procurator Fiscal was there. "Hello," he said, "Here we are again."

"You seem to come to a lot of murders," she said frostily. "You don't have to come to them all you know."

"Ah, but if I do, it gives me a chance to see you."

She ignored the comment. "No kids tonight then?"

"No they've gone to stay with their gran for a few days. I can't seem to trust Rory to stay where I park him. He's fascinated by all of this and wants to do your job. He's taken quite a shine to you."

She blushed slightly and said, "He told me when he visited me in my office. I'm thinking of drafting him in. We need all the help we can get." She wondered why she was being so chatty with the lying swine. He didn't deserve a civil conversation.

He laughed and her stomach flipped. She told herself to get a grip. She couldn't go falling in love with a married man. "I've work to do," she said and moved away. Douglas followed her. Can't the man take a hint she thought? "Is there something you wanted?" she asked. That smile was back as he replied, "Some information about the murder would be good."

All this stomach flipping was making her head spin. She quickly briefed him.

"Thanks Shona." He then left. Shona felt somewhat bereft at his leaving, but at the same time, relieved. She had a job to do and she couldn't do it with her stomach flip-flopping and her heart dancing a highland fling in her chest.

"What have we found?" she asked the collected officers. She felt like she spoke to them more than her parents. She made a mental note to ring her parents that night.

Iain was speaking. "Sorry Iain I missed that. Could you repeat it?"

"From the blood pattern around the walls and the few spots I can see on the ceiling, I'd say whatever wound he's got, it punctured his lungs, or his heart, or both. The blood is everywhere which means it was probably mixed with exhaled air as he breathed his last."

"That was my first impression as well Iain."

"We've also found some blood in the changing room, just a few spots which are smudged, more like transfer. It also looks like the hand basin has been used, so I applied luminol, which showed up a lovely bright blue. It made my day. There was definitely blood in the basin. We've taken swabs to find out if it's the victim's or belongs to someone else."

"Good job," Shona said, making Nina smile.

"You've been watching too many American programmes Ma'am."

Shona grinned "Yep. NCIS is my favourite. Not. Keep going. See what else you can find. Looks like our killer might be getting sloppy."

Just then an elderly woman ran into the clubhouse, noticed the body on the floor and screamed. She rushed towards the corpse and a couple of officers caught her.

"How did she get in here? What is it with the uniforms? They can't seem to keep people away from a crime scene," Shona said.

A young PC appeared. "Not you again. You seriously need to get a grip on this or stop guarding the entrance to my crime scenes," said Shona.

"She pushed me Ma'am. I couldn't stop her."

"She must be 70 if she's a day. Surely you could have grabbed her. I can't believe you were beaten by a pensioner."

"She's stronger than she looks Ma'am. I did try."

The woman was sobbing hysterically and trying to pull away, but the bobbies held their grip. "What's happened? What's wrong?" From her reaction she must be someone very close to the victim, Shona thought. The woman stopped struggling and went limp as though all the fight had gone out of her, tears streaming down her face.

Shona turned back to the young PC and pulled him away from the others. "You might be right about her strength. However, I don't intend to have any more little chats with you about stray relatives strolling around my crime scenes. Either get your act together or don't come back. Do I make myself clear? Now go back to your post and guard this scene as though it's personal."

"Yes Ma'am. I'm sorry."

Leaving the chastened PC to his misery Shona took the woman's arm and led her from the hallway into the lounge. "Could someone bring a glass of water please?" she called back out of the door. Sitting the woman down she said, "I'm sorry Madam but can I ask who you are?"

"Elsie," she said her voice trembling "Elsie McKay. That's Stuart, my husband." She started sobbing again. Shona handed her the glass of water and waited for her to calm down. It wasn't the best way for Elsie to find out about her husband's demise. Shona was going to serve that blasted PC's brains up on a platter.

Elsie sobs subsided, "He only came in to tidy up. Why would anyone do this to him? He's never done anything to anybody. He doesn't deserve this. He's a good man. He goes to church. He likes a beer and a game of bowls. He's never done anything wrong. Why? Why?" She started to rock back and forward.

Shona's heart contracted, feeling some of the agony that this poor woman was going through. She gave her a few moments and then said, "I don't mean to make things harder for you but I really need to ask you some questions. Do you think you are up to that?"

Elsie nodded.

"How did your husband seem recently, had he changed in any way?"

Elsie seemed to pull herself together. "No, he was happy. He retired a couple of years ago and was really enjoying his retirement. After 40 years in schools he'd had enough. He loved his bowls and he'd recently been made president of the club so he was the happiest I'd ever seen him. Tomorrow was our wedding anniversary so he'd booked a table at the Ship Inn." The sobbing restarted.

Shona handed her a tissue and waited. "Was there anyone you can think of who would want to do your husband any harm, Mrs McKay?"

"No. We've a lot of good friends. Everyone at the club liked him and he never said a bad word to anyone. There's nobody would want to hurt Stuart. He's a good man," she said as she started to sob again.

"Do you know if the club was having any difficulties?"

"I don't think so. Stuart never said. It's mainly retired people who play."

"Would there have been any money on the

premises?"

"No. As you can see it's been shut for a couple of weeks. All the money went into the bank before then."

"Have you anyone we could ring to meet you at home?" Shona asked.

"My daughter lives in Balumbie, she'll come. How am I going to tell our kids that their father has been murdered? We were only made grandparents four weeks ago, now the poor wean won't know her granddad."

"Have you got your daughters number and I'll ring her?" Moving from the room she rang the number she'd been given. "Is that Jenna Scarrat?" When the woman answered in the affirmative she continued. "This is Detective Inspector McKenzie. I'm afraid I have some bad news. Your father is dead and it looks like he has been murdered." There was a gasp and then silence.

"Mrs Scarrat are you OK?"

"What, what, no. My mum. Does she know?"

"Unfortunately your mother turned up at the crime scene and is quite distressed. One of my officers will take her home and stay with her until you get there. I'm sorry for your loss."

That was now six grieving relatives she had spoken to in three days. She was sure this had to be some sort of force record. Even the spectre of her predecessor wasn't laying claim to a higher body count. She asked a young female PC to take Mrs McKay home and, once she had gone, pulled out her phone to ring the Chief Inspector.

"For goodness sake woman, when I said keep me up to date with new developments I didn't mean bring me news of yet another dead body. I appreciate it's not your fault but we need to be clearing up the murders not adding more." His voice was tinged with worry not his usual bluster. "Have you got any leads at all? Throw me a bone here."

"I wish I could Sir, but we've nothing. There's a tenuous link to the university but nothing concrete. I'm going to ring them later."

"What's happening to this city, it's getting worse by the day? We've got a body count higher than New York at its peak and we've only got 150,000 residents. You'd better arrange another press conference for tomorrow morning."

Shona didn't quite know what to say to that. Muttering, "I'll keep you abreast with developments, Sir," she hung up.

Then, shouting out to the others that she was off to Bell Street to arrange a press conference, she disappeared swiftly out of the door.

19

March 1998

I've tried to take it, I've really tried. I said all along that I wouldn't be a tell tale but I have to tell. Fear dances along each of my nerves every minute of the day. I can feel it prickling along my skin and keeping adrenaline pumping through my veins. I can't do this any more. I need to be free. Exams are coming up. My grades have to be high otherwise I will never get out of here. How am I going to keep it together? Despite utter exhaustion, fear keeps me awake, alert. I'll go to the teachers again. Surely they'll help this time. I've got to do it or I'll go insane. I told a teacher and her only response was to ignore them and they'd stop. I've done that. They haven't stopped. Things are getting worse. No. I'm going to the headmaster. His secretary goes into his office. Coming out she says, "He'll see you now." I knock and enter.

"Sir, I'm being bullied." The whole sorry tale comes tumbling from my mouth. I relax for the first time in months. A feeling of relief washes over me.

His response takes my breath away.

"You need to man up and get tougher. A bit of roughhousing never hurt anyone and it will make you a stronger person in the long run. You'll see when you're older."

Roughhousing! They'd broken my arm! I stiffened my spine,

"Thank you Sir. I'll do that."

Right that's it. Nothing anyone can do or say is

going to hurt me again. I'm out of this miserable hellhole the minute my exam results are through. I'll play their vicious little game. I'll be the perfect pupil until my real life begins.

20

Shona picked up the phone and started arranging the next day's press conference. By the time she'd finished everyone, including Peter and Roy, were gathered over a cup of tea and the remainder of the cakes. Picking up a huge piece of fruitcake Shona said, "Can everyone report back? Nina and Iain you start." She concentrated hard on listening to what they had to say rather than devouring the fruitcake.

Iain led off. "We thought there might be a print on the taps or around the basin, but nothing. Well, when I say nothing, I mean there were hundreds of prints. Being a public club they have a constant stream of traffic, which means too many prints to make anything useful. We did find a long auburn hair down the side of the washbasin but it could be anyone's. We've bagged it for evidence. I sprayed the floor of the changing room with luminol and got a partial print. Looks like someone attempted to clean it up. I'll give you more when I've examined it."

Shona, sufficiently through her cake to respond, said, "Fingerprint all club members and any guests from the past 2 weeks. We'll need the painters as well. I know it's the ladies changing room but print everyone, male and female. Iain you can do it and get uniform to help."

"Peter and Roy, anything on James Dennis?" Shona continued.

"Roy here's a positive whizz kid when it comes to

108

computers," said Peter. "He's been showing me all sorts of ways to find information on our lawyer friend. He'll tell you as he came up with the goods." Peter sounded almost admiring.

"I've not got anything that will help us directly with our investigation," said Roy. "As the sergeant found earlier, there are a lot of suspicious transactions on his bank account, with several small amounts going out late in the evening, and the same with his credit cards. Despite earning over £3000 a month, he's broke. Several of the transactions lead back to some dodgy looking sites. It would seem Mr Dennis is in to porn in a big way. I think some are paedophile sites. Mr Dennis may be a lawyer but he's not the fine upstanding citizen he would appear to be."

Shona thought that they certainly couldn't call this case boring. There was no knowing where it would go next. She wasn't expecting that turn of events. It was true that if you looked under rocks bugs will always crawl out. They seemed to have caught themselves a one big juicy one.

Peter added, "We've also looked into the partner agreement that they'd drawn up and I was right. In the event of Megan's death, James Dennis gets the lot."

"Excellent. Maybe Megan found out about the porn and he killed her to keep her quiet. Or he could have wanted all the profits from the business. Hand the information we've got over to Child Protection and let them bring him in. There should be enough there to hold him for a couple of days and we can lean on him a bit further while we're at it."

"Right time to go home and see our nearest and dearest. Iain, tell your mum she makes a mean Dundee cake. We'll need to be early tomorrow to make sure everything's in place for the press conference. I'll see you at 0800 sharp. Roy, go via Child Protection and hand over what you've got."

There was a chorus of goodbyes accompanied by coat grabbing. As Nina headed to the door Shona noticed her handbag. She was sure it was Jimmy Choo. She couldn't work out where Nina was getting all the designer gear. Dundee wasn't exactly the haute couture capital of Europe.

She could hear Peter muttering. "Eight o'clock. It's getting earlier every day. Soon we'll no even bother going home. It'll no be worth it. How am I meant to get from Tayport to here by that time o' the morning?"

It would take him less time to get from Tayport than it would Shona from the Ferry. Still, Peter wouldn't be Peter if he didn't have something to moan about.

Shona still had a press statement to prepare before she went home. As she passed the Chief's door, she popped in to update him on the latest developments. Despite the lateness of the hour he was still there but putting his coat on. When he heard about James Dennis' activities he almost shouted "Throw the book at the despicable little toad. He has the cheek to rant and rave in here saying we're treating him badly and look what he's up to on the QT. What time have you called the press conference?"

"0900 hours. I'll have the press statement on your desk when you get in."

The Chief left, leaving Shona alone with a pile of work to do. She went into her office and whilst the computer fired up made herself a coffee. When she got back the computer was still going through its start-up routine. Shona often wondered how they were meant to do a decent job with prehistoric equipment. Shona mulled everything over in her head. What was she missing? The murders were too close together for them to be separate cases. Yet what could link the murders of three young women and an elderly man? The only thing thinking about that brought her was a headache.

Before going home Shona went up to the hospital to see Mrs O'Brien. They let her in for a few minutes and she handed over a box of chocolates she'd hurriedly purchased from the hospital shop. The amount she'd paid could have kept a family, in some countries, for a month. "How are you doing?" she asked.

"A lot better, dear, thank you. The nurses are looking after me. I'm still shaking after seeing poor Mr McKay like that. Him lying there so still and all that blood. I don't think I'll ever sleep again." Her eyes filled with tears. Shona made soothing noises. After a few minutes Mrs O'Brien composed herself. "That young policeman you sent to ask me questions was lovely. Such a nice, polite boy he reminds me of my grandson. I like his name Alasdair MacGregor. My ancestors were MacGregors a couple of generations back you know so I can wear the MacGregor tartan."

Although somewhat taken aback Shona smiled. "Thank you Mrs O'Brien. I'll tell him you said so. I am sure he will be pleased." Wishing the old lady well, she left her to the ministrations of the nurses. That was twice Roy had managed to surprise her in one day. Maybe he had something in him after all. Heading home she diverted via the Indian takeaway. Shakespeare wouldn't be impressed that it was Indian. He preferred Chinese. The fussy moggie would have to make do with Bhuna. She wasn't going to pander to the whims of a spoiled cat who was too fat anyway.

It was Guy Fawkes Night. Driving home Shona could see the iridescent flares of the fireworks as people set them off all over the city. Lochee Park was packed with children, holding tight to their parents hands, and gazing in wonder as the rockets and roman candles exploded in the night sky. The air smelled of cinder and smoke hung in the air, but no one seemed to mind. It lightened Shona's heart to see the children's unashamed joy. She hoped they didn't grow up to see, or experience, the evil she dealt with every day. Stay innocent little ones. Don't try to grow up too fast.

Having devoured her takeaway, comfortably seated on her favourite overstuffed sofa, she picked up the phone to ring her parents. A friendly voice was needed right about now. Her mother, as always, was cheerful.

"Shona lovely to hear from you. Your dad's out I'm afraid. His weekly get together with some of the other intellectuals to discuss matters of which I know nothing. How are you?"

No talk of murder, just everyday chatter. As her mother's soothing voice washed over her, Shona kicked off her shoes. With her feet up and Shakespeare cuddled up beside her, at last she was able to relax.

21

A jaunty spring in my step I walk through the now dark streets back to the place I am staying. With earphones in, I present a picture of just another commuter walking home listening to the latest hits after a long day at work. In reality there is no sound. I am listening only to that inner voice which is my mind. I am scanning all around me as I concentrate on the next planned steps. The fish supper filling my belly brings a feeling of comfort and warmth. Fish suppers are the one thing I had missed about Dundee. Crisp battered fish and thick, golden chips remind me of the only comfort I have ever known. Blending into the darkness, at one with the landscape I am alert. Making sure no one is around, or looking, I slip into my lair. There is no use taking chances at this stage of the game. Preparing for bed I am soon tucked up, warm and protected from the elements. Safe from the prying eyes of this nosy Scottish city. It has been said that Dundee is the largest village in the world. They are right. It's a place where everyone knows everyone's business. As far as I'm concerned despite this they still don't care.

Lying in the darkness I go through every part of the next part of my plan. I can't fail. Not at this stage. Every move is executed in my mind. Every possible complication imagined and dealt with. What will I do if… was as familiar as breathing. I know the life of my next victim as well as I know my own. The hours of research will be worth it. I smile as the blackness engulfs me, the muffled sounds of the nearby city lulling me to sleep. I dream of death.

22

November 2012

Shona decided to run to work the next morning, partly to combat the after effects of last night's curry. It would also give her energy for the day ahead. She ran through the misty early morning streets, with a fluid motion, gained through years of practice, breathing in the salty tang of the sea air. People were trudging to catch buses, too busy to notice anyone else. Something caught her eye. Another runner. Another fitness fanatic getting her daily fix. Shona was in awe of her speed, perfect pace and even breathing. It's a good job she wasn't the jealous type.

A shower was urgently needed before Shona faced the nation's press. She wanted to look less like a badly manicured highland cow than she had last time. Not that she was vain but credibility was next to Godliness in the eyes of the Dundee public. Shower over, she went to find the team.

"The press has arrived and the DI is dressed up like a dog's dinner. Posh frock, her hair a' up and a bit o' slap on," Peter said. A huge grin took the sting out of the words.

Nina added, "Looking good, Ma'am. Who are you out to impress?" This was accompanied by a few wolf whistles from the assembled officers.

Shona took it in good spirits. "Haven't you lot got anything better to do? Get back to work or have you all managed to forget we've a slew of murders on our hands. If the Chief sees you loafing you'll all be seconded to traffic control. I'm sure there are a few traffic jams down the ring road to occupy you for a couple of hours."

They turned back to work and she went into the Chief's Office. "Morning Sir. Is the press statement Okay?"

"Fine. I've changed a couple of bits so we don't give any more away but otherwise it's good. Are you ready?"

"Yes Sir." The Chief put on his jacket and they went to face the gathered press.

Entering the pressroom Shona took a step back and then stared. The room was packed. The nationals had picked it up and everyone was there, including the BBC. That's all she needed, the media following her around like a faithful lap dog. Hungry Rottweilers might actually be a more apt description. The whole sodding lot of them would be nipping at her heels. Blissfully oblivious to Shona's thoughts, the Chief stepped up to the podium, Shona by his side.

"Tayside Police can today report that two more murders have taken place in Dundee and the surrounding area. These happened over the weekend. This brings the total dead to four. We can tell you that these are three women and one man. The families, who are obviously extremely traumatised, have been notified; the latest victims have been named as Mrs Amanda Carter and Mr Stuart McKay. I would like to assure you at this time that the Police are doing everything in their power to catch the person, or persons, responsible. We are following a number of leads and several people are currently helping us with our enquiries. At this time we have no suspects. The police are appealing for information from anyone who may have seen anything out of place or any suspicious vehicles in the following two areas. Grange Road Monifieth between the hours of 5 and 6.30 pm on Sunday 4th November and Broughty Castle Bowling Club between the hours of 3 and 5 pm on Monday 5th November. If any member of the public has information which could lead to an arrest in this case, then please contact the Chief Investigation Officer, Detective Inspector McKenzie on 0300 572 8761."

This time the Chief stayed to answer questions.

"Hayden Greg, The Scotsman. What are the police doing to protect the women of Dundee?"

"I would like to emphasise that people should not panic. There are additional officers patrolling the streets and the police take public security seriously. However, we advise that everyone should take all reasonable precautions to protect themselves until this killer or killers are caught. No one should put themselves in any situation where they may be vulnerable."

"Becky Dunston, Press and Journal. What do we know about the victims? Is there any reason why someone would want to murder them?"

"This is the reason we are appealing for anyone, with any information, regarding motive to come forward and speak to us. We do not know why these murders have occurred. If anyone thinks they may have any answers as to why, no matter how inconsequential they think it may be, then it is important that they come forward."

"Matthew Simmonds, BBC Scotland. You said there were people helping you with your enquiries. Why are these people of interest?"

"These are routine enquires and I will emphasise that these people are not currently suspects."

"John Laird, Dundee Evening Telegraph. Given that three of these victims are women of a similar age, do the police still feel that this is unlikely to be a serial killer?"

"I am sure you would rather the police conducted a thorough investigation than resort to speculation. There will be no further questions. We will, of course, let you know immediately if there are any further developments."

Shona was impressed. She had observed an expert at work. She needed to watch him more closely in the future. Maybe he wasn't so daft after all. She knew press briefings were necessary but she always dreaded the questions which followed. The Chief had mastered the art of giving information without giving anything away. She thought about John Laird who was like a terrier with a rat. He couldn't seem to let go of the fact that this was a serial killer. She was beginning to think he might be right but that didn't let the weaselly git off the hook.

As they moved back to their offices the Chief asked her to join him for a moment. "Uniform is getting antsy. They say they don't have enough manpower to police the streets as they're all running around chasing after murders with your lot. Reg says the crime rates are climbing and it doesn't look good for him. We're going to have to free some of them up for their own duties."

"Sir, I need all the warm bodies I can get," Shona said. "We're never going to solve these murders with just my team. Uniform's crime rate might be rising but so is my murder rate. Can we ask Angus division for some help? One of the murders should have been theirs anyway."

"Keep three of the uniforms. Choose who you want. I'll get in touch with Angus and ask for some of theirs."

He turned to his computer and Shona was dismissed.

Shona knew it was time for some strategic thinking to justify her pay packet. Who had shown the most initiative amongst the uniforms? Soldier boy Jason Roberts was a definite yes. He was a bright officer and a hard worker. PC Morag Gibb had proven to be a quick learner with a steady head on her shoulders. PC Burns MacIntosh had shown an aptitude for CID. Feeling a bit more cheerful, she wandered down to her equivalent in uniformed to ask him.

"They're some of my best officers, but I know you've got a tough one so I'll say yes It's only temporary, mind. I know what you're like. I'll send them up to you."

"Thanks Mark, I owe you one." A cheery wave and she was off back to the murders.

A short time later the officers presented themselves in her office. "Get yourselves a drink, and me a coffee. You'll find some cakes as well. Bring it all back here."

Eagerness written all over their faces they hung onto her every word. "I'm really pleased to have you on board. We'll be busy until we solve this, remember and you'll have long hours. I'll demand a lot from you."

"I don't mind working hard." "Thanks for letting me be part of the team." "I've always wanted to come into CID so I don't mind what I have to do." The three spoke over each other.

Shona laughed. "We need to get you all to the same place as the rest of the team." A quick summary of events followed. Listening intently they took copious notes. No one had any questions until the end when Jason asked, "If it's only one killer Ma'am, why would they use four different weapons? What message are they trying to send out?"

"Both good questions Jason and the answer is, we don't know. But, it's our job to find out and, believe me, we will find out."

"I do believe you Ma'am. We'll do our best to help. Won't we?" There were nods all round.

"Morag go and find DC Barrows and help him fingerprint the bowling population of the Ferry. I'm sure some of the older women would appreciate a female. Jason and Burns I need you to do the rounds of the wine shops and find out if anyone has bought a bottle of La Croix de Beaucaillou 2007 St. Julien wine. It's an expensive bottle so not many of the shops round here will sell it. Start more upmarket. Get the descriptions of anyone who's bought a bottle and get credit or debit card details if they're available." That was unlikely given the apparent intelligence of the killer, Shona admitted to herself.

They went on their way full of boundless energy, which made Shona, feel a hundred years old. Saying that, she had done quite a good time on her run to work that morning so perhaps she wasn't that decrepit.

She went into the briefing room to look at the whiteboards, packed with information about the case. How could they have so much information and yet absolutely nothing to go on? All these murders were cluttering up an efficient investigation. Maybe that was the idea. She was beginning to think they were being played. Her resolve stiffened. She was going to solve these murders. Even the apparently loathsome Jennifer deserved that much.

Peter joined her. They bounced ideas off each other, each one becoming more bizarre. They were both hoping that some spark would be ignited that would set a fire blazing, leading them to the killer. All they got was a damp squib.

23

March 1998

I thought things couldn't get any worse. I couldn't be more wrong. This was worse than my imagination could have dreamt up. How they thought it up I don't know. My tormentors are evil. Increasingly evil. What kind of sick person could carry these things out? It just shows what human beings are capable of, given free rein. There had been extra study today as the exams were coming up. The school was quiet when they grabbed me and bundled me out of the door. No other pupils to see what was happening. Here I am tied to a hockey pole and left in a darkness so thick it smothered me. I am not going to cry. What's that warm feeling on my leg? No. Please no. I've wet myself. Will I be found like this in the morning? The thought chilled me even more than the cold. Is that movement? Yes. Someone's coming. I shout. "Help Me." My abject despair and shame is overcome by the thought of rescue. The figure approaches, the caretaker, coming to clear away the sports equipment. I call out again.

"Mr. Jenks. Help me please!"

"Heavens lassie you must be freezing. Let's get you out of here."

"Thanks." I stumble and Mr. Jenks catches my arm. He has to hold me upright. I don't think my frozen legs will hold me

"Will you be ok? Would you like me to call someone?"

"I'm fine. I'll be fine. Please, I want to leave."

My eyes fill but I still don't cry. I can't as my heart has turned to stone. Even the kindness of the caretaker cannot change that. It is too late.

24

November 2012

A feeling of impending doom engulfed Shona. Her first big case and she felt as if she was getting nowhere with it. She couldn't shake off the feeling everyone was watching her performance. Somehow she needed to get over this feeling. Bracing her shoulders she told herself she was ready for business. Message to the killer, whoever you are, we will get you.

Her reverie was interrupted by the sound of a ringing phone.

"Hi Shona, Murray Fraser here."

Murray was her equivalent in Fife constabulary. A fair man, and a good detective, he was always ready to lend a helping hand.

"Morning Murray. How can I help you?" she asked.

"It's not good news I'm afraid Shona. We've had a murder in Tayport. A young woman strangled in her bakery this morning. The customers couldn't get in and eventually one of them called round to the back door. Her name's Lizzie Struach and the bakers is Struachs on Castle Street. I've been keeping abreast of your murders now that we're all supposed to be one big happy family and sharing information. This one just might be part of your case."

"I'll be right over Murray. Thanks for the heads up." Shona went to find Peter. Living in a small town like Tayport he probably knew the family.

"Aye, but no' that well. Only because it's where

the wife buys her rolls and stuff."

"Would it be a conflict of interests?"

"Nah. As I say I only know them to see. I've not had much to do with them."

"Ok. I need your local knowledge. Grab your coat." She brought him up to speed as they drove.

Murray greeted them quite cheerily, given the reason for the visit. "Good to see you again Shona, Peter. Sorry it's under these circumstances."

"Likewise, Murray."

"Aye," was Peter's contribution to the conversation.

Moving towards the old fashioned bakery, Shona stopped at the door. She didn't want to disturb any evidence. This feat was inevitable given the state of the working bakery. A young woman lay on the flour-dusted floor. The tea towel wrapped around her neck, and her red bulging eyes, gave away the probable cause of death. Murray's team were efficiently processing the scene. There were a few footprints in the flour and some strange markings.

"Any clue as to what those marks could be?"

The Detective Sergeant who was processing the scene said "I would be willing to bet my next pay packet that the killer had tied something like plastic bags over his shoes to prevent leaving marks. With all this flour it's difficult to process the scene. We took some close up photos when we first got here. We've also photographed the shoes of the woman who found her, and the ones of some old bloke who also seemed to be strolling around in here."

"Why does everyone think they're free to wander round my crime scenes? These cases are awash with them. I'll go and have a word with the woman." She called to Peter, "Can you come and talk to her with me.

She might open up more to a local."

The woman, Angela Whitney, couldn't really tell them anything.

"I needed the rolls to make packed dinners for my kids at the primary school. I couldn't get in so I went round the back. Lizzie," her voice broke, "was just lying there. I couldn't stop screaming. Old Bert heard me and came in. He phoned the police."

"Och, Angie, I can understand you must be in a right state. Did you notice, was anything out o' place?"

"I don't really know. I've been in the back a couple of times but didn't take much notice."

"OK. Has anyone taken a statement from you?"

"Yes. That policewoman over there."

Returning to speak to Murray, Shona said, "I think you're right, it looks like it could be part of my case so we'll take it over. Could you send me all the info?" Murray agreed to get it over to them by that afternoon.

Just as she was leaving, the police surgeon arrived from Edinburgh, looking a trifle harried. "Bit of a nip in the air," he said, smiling. A bit of a nip in the air thought Shona. It was cold enough to freeze the gonads off a highland cow. The Scots, like most Brits, couldn't start a conversation without mentioning the weather.

Shona left Peter to sort out the final details, in a language she wouldn't be able to understand. "You can get a lift back from the Tayport bobbies. I'm sure they'll be up for a bit of a jolly with a pal." She wanted to see the post mortem on Stuart McKay. She could also pick Mary's brains. She might have an opinion on whether it was one or more killers.

When she arrived at the mortuary, Stuart's body was already lying on the slab. He'd been cleaned up a bit and Shona could see the puncture wound where the knife had entered his chest. Mary and her mortuary assistant were ready to start. "Good to have you here Shona. I'll get started if you've no questions." Shona nodded. Mary's soft Borders accent was clear as she vocalised every move for the benefit of both Shona and the recording equipment. She was both quick and thorough, her assistant efficient beside her. They were showing an impressive amount of respect for the body. It was obvious to Shona that she was watching true professionals.

Once finished Mary said, "Well I can tell you that Mr McKay here died from one stab wound to the chest which sliced both his aorta and the lung. He would have died by bleeding out fairly quickly."

"Thanks Mary, but how could one stab wound cause so much damage?"

"Whoever did this knew exactly what they were doing. They were after major blood vessels."

"Doesn't look like a random killing then?"

"That's your area of expertise but I'd say no."

"Could I have a chat with you for a few minutes?"

"Sure I could take a break before the next one needs my attention. Mind you my breaks are entirely dependent on the amount of bodies you send me."

"Talking of that," Shona said "Our next one will be on its way to you soon. It actually belongs to Fife but because it could be related to our cases they've passed it on to us."

"Another one. Do you not think I have my hands full enough without taking on Fife's cases as well? This is getting out of hand."

"I agree, that's why I need to talk to you."

Once they were settled, with the customary cup of coffee in hand Shona asked, "Do you think this could be the work of one killer?"

Mary thought about it for a few minutes. "I'm not entirely sure. The two knife wounds could be. They were both done by someone right handed and I'd say fairly tall. They would need some strength though. These stabbings have been carried out with great force. The gunshot could have been done by anyone who had firearms training. I've looked at the woman with the broken neck again and from the bruising I'd say possibly a karate kick, by someone with great speed and strength, and again fairly tall."

"OK. Thanks Mary. It's possible but not probable there's one killer. The similar ages of the women bother me too but I'm not sure where Stuart comes in. Maybe he was killed to put us off the scent, if we even had one. Or it could be nothing to do with the murder of the women." Shona sighed. She seemed to be doing a lot of that recently. Usually the eternal optimist, this case was turning her into a pessimist.

Shona headed back to the station and another meeting with the Chief. She was beginning to feel this was like Groundhog Day.

Peter was waiting for her when she got back. "Have you watched any of the news?" asked Shona.

"Nah. Too depressing. I'll nip out and get a *Dundee Telegraph* in a bit and we can see what they have to say. I'm sure they'll be the voice o' doom, striking fear into Dundonians everywhere." Shona didn't disagree.

The Chief took the news of the latest murder in his stride. "It will count towards Fife's murder rate and not mine. Keep me posted." His bent head dismissed her. The poor woman had only been dead a few hours and he's relieved that it didn't happen in his patch. God spare us all if that's what a life comes down to, Shona thought.

Angus Division had come up trumps and she now had another PC on her team. By way of introduction she called the whole team to the briefing room for a recap and update. As always where Peter went cakes followed. "Please tell me those cakes didn't come from Struachs Bakery, Peter."

"Aye they did. Lizzie Struach's dad told me to take them. He was worried about them all going to waste."

"Good grief Peter. I can't believe we're eating food from a murder scene. Couldn't they be evidence?"

"Whatever happened to Lizzie, Ma'am, I don't think it was because someone wanted to steal a cream cake. The POLSA from Fife took some too."

"Well I've seen and heard it all now. For goodness sakes let's move on."

Iain and Morag had fingerprinted everyone they could get hold of in the Ferry. A couple of the bowling club members were off on pre-Christmas jaunts, pensioners taking advantage of cheap deals. They were currently matching those they had to the ones from the crime scene. There was one interesting fact though. No, more than that, one mind blowing fact.

Iain said, "The swabs of the blood in the sink belonged to one of the previous victims, Mandy Carter."

"What! How the heck...? This has to have been done deliberately. The murderer's taunting us. This links one killer to Mandy and Stuart if not the others. Did you get any other samples from the blood?"

"Not a one."

"We're dealing with one cool customer here. Someone with a great deal of knowledge and expertise. Could our killer be in the medical field?" No one had an answer so they moved on.

Jason and Burns had come up with nothing on the wine. They had contacted every shop that sold alcohol in the Dundee area. Only three sold this particular bottle and none in the last six months. Jason said,

"Considering the Scottish Government are trying to cut down on the consumption of alcohol, there still seem to be an awful lot of places you can buy it around here."

Roy chipped in next. "Nothing about the case but Child Protection arrested James Dennis and seized his home and work computers. Turns out he *has* been accessing paedophile sites and they've now charged him. Dirty little sod. I hope he goes down for this. If nothing else, Ma'am, we've at least stopped that."

"That's one less law firm in Dundee then," Shona replied. "Good work Roy. Maybe you should transfer to Child Protection or cybercrimes. You seem to have a real aptitude for winkling out the bad guys in the darker reaches of theInternet."

"Oh no, Ma'am, I'd hate it if I left CID. I love it here."

Shona's open mouth said it all. From his attitude she had thought he hated CID. Roy never ceased to amaze her. She would hold on to him for the minute and see how he panned out. At least he was coming in useful. Not before time.

"We need a wee chat with James Dennis as well. I like him for Megan's murder. He could have killed her to get his hand on the practice to feed his habit. Or, as one of you already said, she could have found out and he killed her to keep her quiet."

Shona was determined that they weren't going to end the briefing until they came up with some ideas as to what might be going on. Batting ideas only proved frustrating. The only link they had was that each of the women had either been a student or a staff member at the university.

"This still doesn't give us any clues or a motive for murder." Shona said. "Take a break. Peter, you and I are off to Cybercrimes. I can see a stern chat in our Mr

Dennis's future."

Cybercrimes had James Dennis ensconced in a cell but they were happy to transfer him to an interview room. He looked none too happy. "Once more unto the breach and all that," said Shona. "I'm looking forward to this."

"Why do you lot keep interviewing me? I have done nothing. Have you thought about what this is doing to my business?"

"Sit down and shut up. You'll have the next ten years to think about your business when you're in Perth Prison. We, on the other hand, won't give it a second thought."

The recording preliminaries over, Shona took the lead. "Mr Dennis. I would like to say it is a pleasure to see you again but I'd be lying. It seems you're not quite as innocent as you make out."

"I'm innocent. It is obvious that the police have framed me."

"You had over ten thousand pornographic images on your computer. How the..."

She continued, "I was almost lost for words there. Tayside police have better things to do with their time than go around framing 'innocent' lawyers. I'm not here to talk about that. I want to talk about Megan Mackie."

"I've already told you everything I know about that. I had nothing to do with it."

"So you keep saying. One thing bothers me. It would appear that you are now the owner of the whole practice. Megan's death was quite lucrative for you."

"You're right. I inherited her half of the practice. However, are you lot too stupid to realise that one person gone means half the business?"

"Don't you speak like that to the DI. Ye'll do better to speak nicely."

"I'll speak any way I want. Someone speaking like you do would be better not to speak at all."

Yanking a furious Peter back into his chair Shona said, "We might be stupid but it doesn't take the brains of a halfwit lawyer to work out you could sell the other half. Did Megan know about your little kiddy fiddling addiction? Oh, sorry, alleged kiddy fiddling addiction."

"What... What... You can't say that. I told you I'm innocent."

"I'm sure. As sure as I am that Genghis Khan was nice to women and kids. Did Megan know? You see I have this theory. I think she knew and was about to report you to the police so you either killed her or had her killed."

"I want a lawyer. I'm not saying another word."

"Feel free. Peter take him to a phone. In the meantime I'm getting another warrant to search your apartment. Again."

"Can I have a cup of coffee while I'm out of my cell?"

"You'll get your coffee at the same time as the rest o' the prisoners. What makes you think you're special?"

"I'm sure you could rustle one up for me."

"I'm no your personal Teasmaid you ignorant sod."

Leaving Peter and the lawyer to debate the issue, Shona went to find the Chief again "Sir, did you have any joy with the research department at the University?"

"They wouldn't give up any information to me but the Super leaned on the University Principal and they opened up. This can't go in any official reports. It's highly sensitive. Mandy Carter was working on a new breakthrough treatment to prevent the growth of cancer cells. I think they gave me the simple version."

"Thanks Sir, I'll get Peter and we'll go and

interview the staff. There might have been something in the research that was worth killing over."

"You need to do this one alone Shona. Seemingly this breakthrough is mind-blowing and could revolutionise cancer treatment. It's probably worth a fortune to some people. The less our people know about it the better. It will save us bother should any leaks happen in the future."

"Right you are Sir. I'll make sure to record the interviews."

Phoning ahead, Shona was told that the department would make staff available if she came over now. "We would appreciate it if you didn't take too long as every minute counts. You must appreciate we have already suffered a huge setback with the death of one of our top researchers."

"I'm sure you will appreciate that every minute counts when investigating a murder too." One of their colleagues was dead and all they were worried about was the effect on their research. You'd have thought they would be a bit more upset.

Peter was fortifying himself with tea and cake when she got to the office. "I'm off to interview the staff at the University. Can you get a warrant and take the others to search our boy James's flat. Take as long as you like and do a thorough search. I'd love to keep James Dennis and his lawyer waiting. I've better things to do than pander to their sensitivities."

The research staff somewhat redeemed themselves on Shona's arrival at the Research Centre, providing her with a quiet room, a steaming mug of freshly brewed coffee and some top of the range chocolate biscuits. She interviewed Mandy's colleagues one by one. Unfortunately none of them could come up with a firm motive.

"It might have been someone from one of the drug companies. Our research would effectively render current drug treatment for cancer obsolete. That would have an impact on profits."

"Is it possible that one of the drug companies could have found out?"

"Virtually impossible. No one outside this department knows anything about it. We haven't even delivered papers on any part of it. It's that sensitive."

"Thank you for your time and your help. I'll be in touch if there's anything else."

This gave Shona something to think about. If the research was worth so much money perhaps one of the 'oh so innocent' researchers was going to sell it, and Mandy had found out. That meant Shona would have to look into the background of every researcher on the project.

The task had taken a very long and weary afternoon. Shona returned to a copy of the *Dundee Evening Telegraph,* aka the *Tele,* sitting on her desk.

"Serial Killer on the Loose in Dundee: Police Clueless."

She was livid. No one had, so far, said anything about a serial killer. Apart from her nemesis John Laird. This was pure sensationalism. If it was a lone serial killer then they now thought the police were on to them and would be covering their tracks more thoroughly. If that were even possible as they seemed to be doing a damn good job already.

Setting Roy and the Fife PC on to the task of checking the backgrounds of the university staff, Shona perched on Peter's desk after she'd cleared much of the debris littering it. The team's office had far too many people in it. Hers might be more like a cupboard but at least she was on her own.

"What did boyo's flat throw up Peter?"

"Absolutely nothing. If James Dennis murdered our lassie then he's pretty damn good at covering up his tracks. Iain went over every inch of the place and not a bloodstain anywhere. We brought back all his clothes to get them examined. Iain's elbow deep in the relevant disclosing solutions, as we speak. I can't see James Dennis being bright enough to cover everything up."

"I wish we'd found something that would put Mr Dennis in the frame." She sighed. "I suppose we'd better let the lawyer go until we've examined everything. Could you let him know he's a free man? The lawyer that is, not James Dennis. Oh, you know what I mean. There are far too many lawyers cluttering the place up."

"Thanks, Ma'am. That lawyer will no' be happy being cooped up here all day."

"He'll be as happy as a ferret down a rabbit hole, spending the day being paid exorbitant amounts of money for doing nothing. He'll have been supplied with endless cups of tea or coffee as well I have no doubt."

Shona returned to her office. It wasn't long before the jarring sound of her office phone interrupted her once again.

25

I was not going to take one more bit of their bullying any more. If the so-called authorities can't help me then I am going to help myself. Nothing else is going to harm me. I will not be hunted in this game of cat and mouse anymore. I need to find ways of staying inaccessible to these creatures.

Watching people's movements I worked out what they would do and when they would do it. I studied their every move, how they looked, every twitch, every gesture, the way they spoke and their detailed habits. I did this until I knew each one of them better than they knew themselves. The use of this knowledge gave me the ability to remain virtually invisible. I could keep completely away from them whilst keeping a very close eye on what they were up to. I, at last, am in the position of power.

Look at them. Furious at being foiled. Questioning why I am no longer within their cruel grasp. Having brains means I can put them to use in numerous different ways. This is almost fun, using it to plot and evade the enemy. I can take them down whenever I choose. I thought about different ways I could do this for a while. Should I put my brains to use playing them at their own game? No. I'm not going to jeopardise my escape route from this hellhole by being expelled. Still, an idea begins to form in my mind. As my emotions harden the idea grows stronger. Nothing and no one is going to hurt me again or ruin my future the way they have ruined my past. From this day forward, I will be the one in charge.

26

November 2012

Shona picked up the ringing phone.

"There's a woman called Rachel Davidson waiting to see you. She won't say what it's about and insists she'll only speak to you."

"Thanks. Get someone to bring her up to my office."

Whatever the woman wanted Shona hoped it wasn't any more bad news. She didn't think she could take another murder at the moment. She couldn't even seem to solve the ones she had.

Once the woman was settled in her office, Shona enquired, "How can I help you?"

Rachel took a nervous sip of the tea Roy had brought. She seemed to gather her courage and blurted out, "It's the murders. I didn't know whether to come or not. I've been reading about them in the paper. I know all the dead women. Mind you it could be coincidence."

Shona's pulse quickened. "Whatever you know could help us. How did you know them?"

"I was at school with them all. We were in the same year. Mr McKay was our headmaster."

Through an exploding brain and a suddenly dry mouth Shona said, "This could be really important. I would like to ask you a few questions. Come through to the interview room so we can record what's being said. I don't want to miss anything."

Sitting Rachel in the interview room Shona went to find

Peter. "We might have a lead. I want you in the interview."

"Nae bother Ma'am. That's the best news I've had all week."

"I know how you feel."

The usual preliminaries over, Shona asked. "For the benefit of the tape could you repeat what made you come to see us today?"

After doing so, Rachel added, "I really didn't know whether to come or not. When I heard about the first two murders I thought it was just a coincidence but when I read in the paper about the second two I thought I'd better come in. Why would anyone want to kill people from my school?"

"Which school did you go to?"

"Myercroft Academy."

"Can you think of anything that would link these women together other than being in the same school? Anything that might make someone want to kill them?"

She thought for a moment "No, not really. I think, but I'm not sure, they were all in the hockey team so I suppose they were friends. To be honest the schools aren't massive around here so most people are friends at some time or another. We were always falling in and out of favour as pals. All the dead women were extremely clever though. You would call them academically gifted now. There were even rumours they had IQs at genius level. Why..." she hesitated, "why would anyone kill them for that? Even in Dundee being clever isn't a crime. I'm a fire fighter. I know you're more likely to get killed for your mobile phone around here than your brain."

"Was there a girl called Lizzie Struach in your year at school?"

Rachel blanched. "Yes. Why are you asking? Is she dead as well?" her voice had risen several octaves.

"I'm sorry to have to tell you this, but yes. This hasn't been officially released yet so I need to ask you to keep it to yourself. Was she also one of the academically bright pupils?"

Rachel whispered, "Yes. Yes she was."

Although this new revelation was giving them something to go on, Peter saw the doubt and disappointment in Shona's eyes. He felt exactly the same. Questions hung between them as though they were telepathic. Why would anyone go around murdering a bunch of eggheads? Why kill the headmaster? Why now after 14 years? This still wasn't making any sense.

Shona asked, "Is there anyone you can think of that might have a reason for killing these women now?"

Looking pale, Rachel shook her head. "No. No I can't. They were all just teenagers doing what teenagers do. They probably worried about boys and make up and what university to go to. Nothing out of the ordinary. To be honest, I didn't actually know them that well. I wasn't particularly academically brilliant so was out of their league. I tended to keep out of their way." Her voice rose again as she said, "Do you think I'm in danger? What about the others?"

Rachel might be a roughy toughy fire fighter but she was, just like any other woman in the same situation, scared witless. Shona watched her fight back tears in eyes wide with fear. She had a right to be fearful. Who knew what this killer was capable of?

Shona had a sudden chilling thought. Had anyone spoken to Megan Mackie's parents to ask them if she knew any of the other women?

To give herself time, Shona said, "I need to go and speak to my team. It would be really helpful if you could write down any of the names of the girls who were in your year at school." Shona found a pen and paper and left her to it. This was more an exercise in calming Rachel down than in fact finding. They'd get all this information from the school records. She did have a point though. Who else was in danger? They needed to find names and contact details quickly. All staff and pupils from that year would need to be interviewed. They had a duty to protect the others. God help them if any more women turned up dead.

She went to find a glass of water to give herself a chance to think and to calm her roiling stomach. She wished the water would miraculously turn into a large glass of expensive single malt. She thought it was a shame it wasn't an option. If people have died because she hadn't asked the right questions she would never forgive herself. Taking some deep, calming breaths she reminded herself that she still had murders to solve. Maybe someone had asked and the answer was no. It was pointless worrying until she knew for sure.

Entering the office Shona asked the team, "Did anyone ask the Mackies if Megan knew the other two women?" Her answer was the blank stares. "Do I need to do everything myself around here?" she barked. "Can no one think for themselves?" She was asking herself why they hadn't followed it up sooner.

Shona knew self-flagellation would get her nowhere. She needed to save the self-recrimination for later. Taking it out on the rest of the team wouldn't help either. She needed to focus on what they could do now. "We're in for a long night. Get in touch with your nearest and dearest and let them know you won't be home any time soon. Nina, ring Myercroft Academy and get in touch with the head. Tell them we need urgent access to archived records. Jason, ring the Mackies and find out if the girls knew each other."

As she left the squad room Shona barged into the Procurator Fiscal. "What are you doing here?" she asked.

Douglas looked a bit taken aback but answered quite calmly, "I'm here to see you."

"I don't know why," said Shona. "There's not a dead body in sight that you need to concern yourself with. I'm sure Mary's got a few up the morgue she could let you see if you're desperate."

"No I'm actually here to see you. Have I done something to offend you?" he asked, his eyes full of questions.

"No. Not a thing. Now if you'll excuse me I've a witness to attend to," she said as she turned and stomped away.

Douglas watched her stiff back with interest. He thought this being left standing alone in hallways was getting to be a bit predictable. What on earth could be wrong? She seemed to like him, and now this sudden change. Maybe it was Rory and she didn't like the thought of kids. Mind you, she seemed to have really hit it off with Rory and Rory liked her. Women were a puzzle to him, especially this one, but he wasn't going to give up. She was the first woman he had been interested in for several years. Maybe that was why he didn't have a clue. He'd never understood his wife either.

Shona went to update the Chief on the latest development. She finished with "there might be a number of women who need protection." His silence said more than words. After swallowing a couple of times he spoke. "Are you trying to tell me we might need protection for about fifty women? How do you suggest we do that with barely enough officers as it is?"

"We're not sure of the exact numbers yet, Sir, or

even if anyone will need protecting but I wanted you to be prepared so you're not caught by surprise."

The Chief reverted to his usual sarcasm. "Well that's really good of you Shona. I'm glad to see you're working so hard to protect me. For goodness sake woman, get out there, find this killer and put an end to all this madness. You'll need to do it with the resources you've got. You could police New York City with the manpower I've given you."

What the...? She was doing her damnedest to solve the murders. The Chief shouting at her wasn't going to make it go any faster.

Returning to the interview room it was obvious that Rachel had not made much progress on the requested list. "I can't remember half the names of the pupils. It's been a long time. I'm sorry I'm not really helping."

"It's not a problem," Shona reassured her. "You've given us a few names so that will give us somewhere to start. It's possible we'll have to ask you some more questions later. Could you stay here for a while?" Rachel looked almost relieved.

Walking along a corridor, dingy with chipped paint, Peter said, "You're no' looking very happy Ma'am. Chief Inspector a bit uncooperative?"

"That's putting it mildly."

"We've got to nail this nutcase so you can stick it to the Chief Inspector."

"Nail him. I'll nail him all right. To a cross." With the Chief Inspector on the one on the right of him she added to herself.

Shona sent Jason off to the police canteen to get Rachel Davidson something to eat "Grab a load of sandwiches for the team as well" she added. "It's Doreen on tonight so tell her we want some fresh ones made up. She'll understand that things are bad enough without stale sarnies."

"They're not sarnies Ma'am. They're pieces around here."

"Call them whatever you like. Just get them. I'm a DI not a flaming linguist." Good grief it would be easier to learn Mandarin than all the nuances of the Scottish language. Why can't everybody in the British Isles speak the same language?

She gathered the team together for an update. Nina said she had managed to track down an address and phone number for the head teacher of the school. Shona phoned her and she was adamant that she would not be able to give them any access to confidential school records without a warrant.

"I'll get one now," said Shona. "You lot get ready to go over to the Myercroft."

Getting hold of the local sheriff proved easy.

"Of course you can Shona. I'm still in the office so send someone over to get it now." Shona had her warrant within the hour. Ringing the head teacher, they went to meet her at the school. Despite the lateness of the hour most of the team had a determined look. It was the first positive thing they had done.

At the sight of a warrant the Headmistress was much more amenable. "I've put all the files in a classroom. You can look at them in there. I'll be in my office if you need me." Shona was a tad surprised that she had left them alone. Still, it was an added bonus, as an anxious staff member, hovering like a dragon with his prey in sight, would slow things down.

The team worked in silence, making the odd note. Nothing seemed out of place to them. As Rachel said they just seemed like normal girls, occasionally in minor trouble but mostly well behaved. They were making headway through the pile of files when Shona said "I'm going to ask for the boys records as well. They might know something that could help so we need to get their names and addresses." The team groaned, but dug in and worked harder. It took a while for the folders to be retrieved from the archives and by then they had made serious headway into the girls' files.

It was several hours before they returned to the station. However, despite the lateness of the hour, the hard work was just beginning. "We need to find contact details for every name on the list. Prepare yourselves for a long night." The head teacher had managed to tell them where four of the ex-pupils were. One worked for the BBC in London as a radio presenter, one was an author living in Edinburgh, another was a teacher at the school and the last was now her GP. They would be easy enough to find but that still left forty two to track down.

"Start by sharing the notes you've made. Who's first?" Shona sounded more upbeat than she felt.

"One young lad, Simon Donovan, was caught selling cigarettes his parents had brought back from abroad," Peter replied. "He was told off and it stopped. I think I know what he's doing now. It might be him that owns the Donovan's chain of stores. Despite the fact his accounting might merit a bit of looking in to, I'm not sure why he'd start murdering over it."

Nina had found a couple of students who said they'd been bullied. "The headmaster investigated and it was no more than a couple of childish pranks. It must have stopped because neither girl complained again. To be honest it happens. I used to get called names at school because I was Indian but it stopped when they got to know me. I think everyone goes through it at some point."

There was also the usual skipping school but these

were bright pupils who were going to fly through their exams. It looked like they were well behaved. Probably because most of them were on the fast track to high paying jobs, and didn't want to ruin it by stirring up trouble.

For a couple of weary hours the team worked through the list, finding contact details and addresses. Numerous phone calls were made, some led to the information they needed. Some drew a blank. By the end, they had tracked down all but three. Shona said, "We need to call it a night. We can't drag people in to interview them at this hour. We'll have people from the Tay to the Sidlaw Hills shouting about police brutality."

Some of the young PCs were looking a bit jaded. CID wasn't the exciting place they had thought it would be. They were beginning to realise that it was 90% hard graft on long and tedious scut work. The other 10% was attending crime scenes and hoping they caught the perpetrator.

"Before you go,' Nina said. "You're all invited to my parents' Anniversary party tonight. Come as you are it's not a posh frock do."

"But it's getting…"

"You're coming as well Ma'am. My mum can't wait to meet you. My life will be a misery if she doesn't set eyes on you tonight. Everyone's coming. Including you lot from uniform."

Shona gave into the inevitable. "Let me at least put a bit of make up on and I'll be there."

As Shona walked through the door of Nina's parent's imposing house, a small whirlwind in an exquisite gold Sari enveloped her in a hug. Amid wafting scents of Chanel No 5, Nilima, Nina's mother said, "So it is you who is my daughter's boss. I have been wanting to meet you for some time. That Nina is a bad girl for not bringing you sooner. Come come. We have drink, food. All home made." A smiling Shona followed, offering no resistance. She could hear Nina laughing in the background. Shona felt the exotic music, bright colours and enticing smells surround her and soothe away her cares, if only for one brief moment.

27

It is night once again, the thick darkness my friend. I slip through the trees and out onto the quiet city streets. Acutely aware of everything around me, my eyes scan in every direction. Here a drunk stumbling home. There, teenagers jostling each other. The hunted now the hunter, senses on high alert. I know what to do and where to go. Every footstep reinforces my resolve to bring this plan to completion. I march to a drumbeat of – I'm almost there, I can do it, I will do it. The victor's banquet comes ever closer. I can see it in my sights. It will be all the sweeter for having been delayed so long.

In an unlit street is the house I am looking for. The security is a joke. Trained to get into any building and leave with no one knowing, this could not be simpler. I quickly disable the alarm, a piece of junk, which gives those inside a false sense of security. They'd been told, no doubt, that just seeing a security alarm would put most people off. The occupants were about to find out just how wrong this advice was. Slipping past the bedrooms of the soundly sleeping children I enter the final room. Without making a sound I pick up a pillow and place it over the sleeping woman's face. She starts to struggle. Waiting until the struggling stops, I hold the pillow for several seconds more. I need to be certain the job is done. Replacing the pillow I smooth the creases, make sure the woman is dead, and smile. I check on the children. Still sleeping. One of them cries out in her sleep. She looks to be about 1 year old. No more than a baby. My eye's softening, I gently brush her hair back from her face, my resolve softening. The blonde tendrils are soft in my hand. The action does as much to soothe me as it does her. I breathe in the fresh baby smells of baby bath and talc. For a few seconds I feel an unfamiliar emotion. Taking a moment to luxuriate in it, I then strengthen my resolve once more. I straighten, turn and walk out the door of the room. The children will be upset in the morning. They'll still be better off in the long run, without a mother who is rotten to the core. Every part of me knows this. Their suffering will be brief and their life will be happier in the end. With that the night swallows my lonely figure up once more.

28

November 2012

The next morning as Shona approached Bell Street she had to fight her way through a phalanx of reporters who had sniffed out the latest murder. Questions rang in her ears.

"Have there been any more deaths?"

"Are you any nearer to finding the killer?"

"No comment. As soon as we have anything, there will be a press conference."

John Laird, from the Dundee Evening Telegraph, couldn't seem to understand what she was saying. Maybe it was her English accent. Frickin idiot, she thought to herself.

"Is it true that all these women went to Myercroft Academy? What could this have to do with the murders? Do you now think this is a serial killer. What are you doing to protect others who may be in danger?"

If it was a serial killer Shona could be seriously tempted to enter into a contract with him to bump off John Laird.

"Do you not understand English? I've said I have nothing to say. Now move away from the station or I'll have you all arrested."

All she needed was potential witnesses trying to force their way through this lot. Snowballs chance they would run the gauntlet. They would bolt before they got through the door. Going to find the desk sergeant she snapped "Get that pack of rabid wolves off the doorstep of my nick. The minute they smell blood they're circling. If anyone coming in to talk to us is harassed, or even slightly annoyed by them, then I'm holding you personally responsible."

The desk sergeant thought it would be circumspect to say nothing. It was obviously a bad day for the DI already. He got up and lumbered off to find a couple of PCs to throw to the wolves.

Shona's mood had nosedived even further by the time she arrived in the squad room. Seeing everyone wrapping their molars around a pile of bacon butties from the canteen made it worse. "Anyone would think this was a café not a police station. Stop shovelling food down your throats and get on with some work. We'll meet in five minutes and divvy up the files. People could be dying whilst you're all sitting in here eating your breakfast." Shona turned and stomped out leaving her team with slack jaws. Peter thought the pressure must be getting to her. She was usually the first person to be devouring a filled roll. He'd kept her a nice sausage and egg one and now it was going to waste.

Right you lot, you heard the DI, get a move on," he barked, causing a flurry of activity accompanied by rapid chewing. It was going to be a long day. Peter prepared for it by picking up Shona's roll and taking a large bite.

Weeding out the former pupils, who no longer lived in the United Kingdom, reduced the list of forty two by ten people. This still left them with thirty two people to track down and interview. A further five now lived in England so would have to be interviewed by phone or by the police in their area. Three names were still unaccounted for, Michael Donovan, Mary Cabarelli and Laura Sands. "Roy, track down their current whereabouts," said Shona. "I don't care how you do it just get results."

"Cool beans." Roy scurried off.

"He's looking chirpy. What's with the transformation?"

"It's being given a job to do on the computer Ma'am. It always gets him a' excited."

"I'd better get him on there more often then."

They started the boring, yet essential, task of ringing people and asking them to come in and speak to them. Several were a bit annoyed, their general response being "I'm busy. I can't drop everything for no better reason than I was at school with a bunch of dead women." Shona, at the end of her tether, said, "You may not have time but I'm trying to solve a murder here. If you don't come in I'll send a police car to your place of work and bring you in. In handcuffs if I need to." Funnily enough they found they had time for an appointment after all.

Some of the women they contacted were, not surprisingly, worried and upset. They had already realised someone was targeting people from their school year, and wanted to know what the police were going to do to protect them. "We'll talk about that when you come in," Shona said, which roughly translated as, I don't have a clue.

Looking up, Shona saw the desk sergeant, looking quite cheerful for a change. "Yer favourite pal Auld Jock's here to see you. I've popped him in interview room two. My boys are sending up a nice strong cup of tea and a couple of bacon rolls for him, and a cup o' coffee for you. There are probably a few cakes from the squad room winging their way up there as well."

Shona groaned. Auld Jock was a homeless man who had taken a shine to her after he'd been in to the station a few times saying he was being harassed by youngsters. Strictly speaking there were no homeless in Dundee, the Council had it covered, but Auld Jock didn't want to move into a place. He was happy the way he was. One of Dundee's characters, everyone knew him and, on the whole, looked out for him. The lads at the station always made sure he got a decent feed if he came in. Ordinarily she didn't mind spending half an hour chatting to him but it just seemed a bit much to ask at the moment.

Reminding herself of her civic duty as an officer, she went to see him. "Hi Jock. How are you and how's Maggie?" Maggie was his wee Scottish Terrier who was named after his dead wife. "I'm good, thanks, Shona, and Maggie's out the back polishing off a lovely plate of sausages your boys brought her. I won't keep you long. I know you've got a lot on at the moment what with all these murders. I just wanted to make sure you were OK. I knew you'd have a break if I came in, as you're a kind lassie. You've been good to me through everything and I wanted to return the favour even though I can't do much."

Humbled by the kindness of this man who had nothing, Shona said "Jock you're a real gentleman. I don't know what to say." They ate in companionable silence for a few minutes until Shona stood up. "I really have to go now Jock but you can stay here in the warm until we need the room." She pushed the plate of cakes towards him. "You might as well take these with you. My lot are too fat anyway." Accompanied by Jock's laughter, she left him to his feast.

Returning to her office she found Peter waiting for her. He handed her a sheet of paper with a list of names and interview times. "The first ones will be here in an hour and then it's pretty full on after that. I wasn't sure who you'd want involved in the interviewing so I've left that for you. There are a lot of people. We haven't managed to get hold o' four o' them. Roy's still trying to track down the other three. So that's seven in total we're missing."

Thinking briefly, Shona replied, "The interviews will be done by you, Nina and me as the lead officers. Nina can take Iain as he's a bit more experienced, you take Jason and I'll take Morag. Burns can work with Roy to pin down the others and the Angus copper can be a runner as needed. Do you think any different? I don't want us to mess this up." Shona acknowledged his wealth of experience in dealing with such matters.

"No Ma'am, I'd have chosen that myself. Do you want me to tell the others and decide who we'll interview?"

"Yes, tell the others. No, to us doing the interviews on a rota. We'll just have to take turns with the interviews and keep them going. Some could take longer than others. Could someone make sure the interview rooms are ready and move Auld Jock along? Get that interview room aired before we get going. I'll tell the Chief what's happening so he can brief the super and the Lord Provost."

As people started arriving Shona took the first one. She noticed Jason with a bottle of Febreze, and a glade aerosol, at Interview Room 2 and smiled.

"Eileen, as you are no doubt aware from both the media coverage of the case, and our phone call to you this morning, we are currently investigating the murders of five people. They all worked at or attended Myercroft Academy at the same time as you."

The woman nodded.

"I need you to speak for the benefit of the recording."

"Yes," she replied, "they were all at school with

me."

"How well did you know the victims?"

"Not that well. I kept out of trouble so didn't have a lot to do with Mr McKay. The others were all in the top academic streams. I wasn't, so our paths never really crossed. Us plebs weren't in their orbit."

"Can you think of anything that happened at school that might have caused someone to kill them?"

"No not really. I remember Jennifer. Everyone will remember Jennifer. She was completely unpredictable and that's putting it mildly. Looking back I think she must have had some sort of personality disorder. She would be friends with people one minute, would use them, and stab them in the back the next. It wouldn't surprise me if someone wanted to kill *her* but why wait twelve years? I don't know why anyone would want to kill the others."

You and half the Dundee Police would like to know the answer to that Shona thought. "Were all these women good friends at school?"

"With Jennifer in the class friendships came and went. She was always a catalyst for change. A bit like a cyclone. No one stayed friends with her for very long."

"Was there anything else which linked them apart from them all being in the highest stream?"

"I think some of them were on the hockey team. I might be imagining that though."

Well that's not helping much. Even if a team had been beaten they wouldn't systematically pick off the winning players and certainly not twelve years later. Shona felt like she was mired in mud. Every step forward was slow and agonising.

Have you seen or heard from any of the victims since you left school?"

"No. I didn't pal about with them when I was at school so lost touch completely afterwards."

"Where were you on these dates and times?" A sheet of paper was passed across the table.

"Can I get my diary out?"

"Of course."

"I was working for three of them. I'm a nurse in the care home up at Ballumbie. I was out Christmas shopping with a friend for one of them and don't know what I was doing for the other one. Given the time probably getting ready for bed."

Shona made notes. "Thank you. Those are all the questions we have for you right now. I would like you to stay here, as we may have some more questions once we start speaking to others."

"Staying isn't a problem. In fact I'd rather stay. I'm terrified it could be me next." With that she burst into tears. Taking her to a waiting room Shona found the Angus PC to provide tea and TLC. She was hoping he was up to the TLC part as he might find out more just chatting.

Before she got a chance to start the next interview the desk sergeant was back. He looked a lot less cheerful than he had a couple of hours ago. "You're never going to believe this Ma'am. There's been another murder. A young woman by the name of Pauline Smith."

29

School has improved dramatically now that I've quietly wrestled control away from them. They're still searching everywhere for me but their game of cat and mouse has changed. One very clever mouse is now in charge. Ghost like I move through the beige halls and corridors of the school, knowing my enemies so well I can evade them easily. It's almost too easy. Their commander, and I do not use that term lightly, is growing more and more furious at her inability to carry out the torments she has devised. Hiding in plain sight, I can hear her shouting.

"Where is she? I'm telling you. You'd better find her. No one get's the better of me."

"I'm telling you I can't. She disappears the minute class is over."

"You'd better not be arguing with me. This isn't up for discussion. Find her and bring her to me."

"But..."

"Don't answer me back, just do it."

Her lackeys scurry every which way, looking in all the wrong places.

The more frustrated she is, the more stringent she becomes. Her tone venomous she barks out orders, and expects to be obeyed. No ordinary teenager this, but one who seems possessed.

I laugh to myself. A girl who manipulates all she surveys, this is probably the first time she has not got her own way. All I need to do is remain invisible until after the exams. My Chief tormentor isn't someone I can touch at the moment. I smile as I think, her time will come. I have already decided on my future career and a plan is starting to form in my mind. A previously unknown excitement buzzes through my body. I will get my own back. In my own time. In my own way. I, the hunted, will prevail.

30

November 2012

Shona's heart sank as she hurried to confirm that the name of the latest victim was on the list. It was one of the women Roy was trying to pin down. That made six murders in total, five of them classmates. This was now getting beyond urgent. They needed to get to the bottom of this pretty damn quick if they were to prevent any more murders. Pulling Peter and Nina from the interviews she said, "The body count's climbing. One of the women Roy was trying to find has been found dead. A single mother with four kids. They couldn't wake her this morning and eventually the oldest who's 8 went to knock on a neighbour's door. I don't know the cause of death so I suppose it could be natural causes. We're not taking any chances though. It's all too much of a coincidence. Peter, I need to stay here. You and Iain go and process the crime scene. Nina, you take Jason into the interviews with you."

"Lean on these people heavily and get some answers. There has to have been something going on at that school. The time is long past for being delicate. We need to find as many of the past and present staff as possible."

"Can we beat the info out of them, Ma'am," Nina said with a smile.

"I'll beat you in a minute. Go forth and interview and stop being so cheeky."

Heading towards the Chief's office Shona stopped beside Roy. "You can stop looking for Pauline Smith as she's dead. Peter and Iain are going to investigate now. Have you found any of the others?"

"I've managed to find addresses for a couple of them. Laura Sands seems to have disappeared off the face of the earth. We do have a current address for her mother but no phone numbers."

"When we get time we'll pay her a visit and see if she knows where her daughter is. One would assume she's safely out of harm's way if no one can find her."

"It's really strange though, Ma'am. Laura Sands has no online presence at all. Nada. Zilch. That's virtually unheard of in this day and age. It's like she's a ghost."

"I'm not asking for specifics here but have you used any unofficial means?"

"No Ma'am. I've kept it all hunky dory and above board."

"Perhaps it's time to go down into the depths."

"Are you sure?"

"All I'm saying is find Laura Sands, or anyone else who's missing, using any means possible. Do what you have to and I'll deal with the fallout."

"I'm on it." He turned back to staring at the keyboard and tapping keys like a madman on speed.

Pondering the wisdom of staying off the Internet, Shona went to ruin the Chief's day even further.

"Sir, there's been another death linked to the school. We're drowning here. We need to interview all the ex-pupils and all staff. If I don't get more people we'll never get through them. There's also the issue of protection. These women are terrified. How are we going to protect them until this murderer is caught?"

The Chief looked grey and haggard. He looks like he's not too far away from having a coronary Shona thought.

"Are you all right Sir? You look a bit unwell."

"I'm fine. Just a migraine. The tablets will kick in soon."

"Are you sure Sir?"

"I'm fine Shona. But, no wonder I've got a headache. There aren't enough officers to go around. Much as I would love to protect each and every one of these people, I can't. The best I can do is draft in some uniforms who can help with the interviews. Draw me up a list of questions they can use. Catching the murderer is the best protection I can give."

The reply wasn't entirely satisfactory but Shona was philosophical. At least she had more manpower, which was better than she'd hoped.

She now had an awful lot of people hanging around waiting for interviews and it was well past lunchtime. Ordering sandwiches and drinks for them all she managed to avoid thinking about the Chief's response to the bill. The food bill for this was going to be higher than the GDP of a small nation by the end of the investigation. Still it was better than having a shed load of angry and hungry Dundonians who were currently helping the police with their enquiries. Dundonians were known to be a feisty lot. She had enough on her plate without a riot in the station.

Going back to the interviews, Shona started putting pressure on people and asking ever more probing questions. There was a bit of a theme emerging about bullying and the name Laura Sands had come up a couple of times. Some of the teachers had arrived so Shona decided to interview them next.

Passing her office she found the Procurator Fiscal making himself comfortable. She was beginning to seriously wonder why this man could not take the hint. He had the thickest skin she had come across in a man and it took something to beat her ex-husband. Maybe she should just tell him straight to wrack off and stop bothering her.

Douglas smiled and Shona's heart beat faster. "Hi, I thought I'd come and see how the case was going. I hear there have been some new developments."

"It looks like the link goes back to their schooldays. Five pupils and the Headmaster murdered so far. We still don't know why. The latest one is today. A single mum found dead in one of those massive houses in Gowrie Park. Now, if you'll excuse me I need to go and carry on interviewing. Why aren't you over bothering my team at the latest murder anyway?"

His face clouded over as he leaned towards her and said, "I don't need to go to every murder scene. Look Shona, I don't know what I've done to offend you but you seem to be giving me the brush off. If you're not interested that's fine, but I like you and so does Rory. I thought we had something going?"

At that Shona really lost her cool. Her jaw clenched she spat out, "Something going? Something going?" Her voice was rising. "I don't go out with married men and if you think I would, you don't know me very well. I don't have time for this so go back to your wife and leave me alone." She left no room for any misunderstanding.

Douglas sat back in his chair slack jawed. Then he burst out laughing. "I think we've got our wires crossed here. I'm not married. My wife left me and moved to Australia with her "friend" when Alice was a year old. We'd been having problems anyway and she was never cut out to be a wife and mother. The only contact we've had with her since was the divorce papers. What on earth made you think I was married?"

Shona took a few seconds to reply. She had to get her emotions in check. With a red face, her voice moving up a quaver or two, she said, "Well you've got two kids. How was I meant to know there was no Mrs Lawson around?"

He smiled. "OK, it's a fair point but can we start again? I would really like to see you out of work when you get a spare minute. What type of food do you like?"

"What? I'm in the middle of the biggest murder case of my career and you're asking me out on a date and talking about food. But as your asking, I like anything really but Indian's my favourite," she managed to say in a voice now much steadier.

"Indian it is then the minute you're finished with this case. Bombay Joe's in the Ferry has a good reputation. That's if you want to go out with me?" he added.

Shona's smile was brighter than the ball of yellow in the sky that they weren't seeing much of at the moment. "That would be lovely but I really do need to go now. I'll keep you posted if we find anything new."

With a welcome lightness in her step, which was mirrored in her heart, Shona returned to the interviews. The case might be going nowhere but the sun was shining brightly in her world.

She beamed at Nina as she passed her in the long corridor.

"You seem to have cheered up. Either we've cracked this case or you've made it up with the procurator fiscal. I saw him mooching around. Which is it?"

"As a matter of fact Douglas has been in and things are a bit less chilly. Has anyone told you you're nosy?"

"Regularly, in fact nearly every day. So are you going on a date with him?"

"Will you shut up if I tell you?"

"Maybe."

"Ok. We're going for an Indian when this case is over."

"Awesome. Go Shona."

"We're at work. That's go Ma'am to you. Now shut up about my love life and find yourself someone to interview. You're meant to be knee deep in interrogating the good people of Dundee, not loafing in the corridor."

Shona forced herself to focus on the case. There was something about that school year which had now come back to haunt the pupils. She was getting ready to bet her granny that the teachers know what it was. She'd had enough. It was time to show them that the KGB could learn a trick or two from her when it came to interviewing. With a glint in her eyes that said she would take no prisoners, Shona went to meet the first teacher.

"Good afternoon. Thank you for coming in Mrs Blunt. I believe you were a teacher at Myercroft Academy in 1998?" When the teacher replied in the affirmative, Shona went on "I am sure you are aware that a number of pupils from that year have been murdered over the past few days. Can you remember anything happening in that year which could have led to what is happening today?"

"No nothing," The teacher replied. "I didn't really have a lot to do with the girls who have been murdered as I wasn't teaching sixth years then. The only thing that does come to mind is that most of the teachers hated teaching Jennifer Brown. I heard rumours she was quite a nasty human being even taking teenage hormones into account. I never taught her or even spoke to her though. I remember her because her father was the Lord Provost and he was always coming in to do things at the school."

Now that was interesting Shona thought. It would

seem Jennifer had a history of being hated. Not just hated, but almost feared. That could explain why she was killed but why the others? Why the headmaster? Were they a smoke screen? Questions screamed in Shona's head.

"Can you recall if Jennifer was friends with any of the other dead girls?"

"I don't know. I honestly didn't know any of them well. I was new to teaching then so had nothing to do with 6th years. The more experienced teachers taught them. Especially the boffin group as we called them."

As she finished the interview Shona thought she heard crying in the corridor. Unless these women were more anxious than she imagined, she thought she must be hallucinating. Opening her door she found the crying was real. Peter and Iain were standing in the corridor with four children aged between about one and eight years old. Peter was holding the one year old in his arms and was trying to comfort her. This case was turning in to a scene from Alice in Wonderland. Shona looked around for the Cheshire cat. He must be here somewhere.

Before she could say anything Peter chipped in, "These are Pauline Smith's kids. It would appear that nobody knows the father's whereabouts except he's in Thailand. It's a huge country and miles from Dundee. We couldn't find any other relatives and the social workers can't come and pick them up for three hours. We didnae know what else to do. We couldn't leave the poor wee bairns on their own." He shuffled from one foot to the other as he waited for the DI's response.

"Stop wittering, Peter. I get the gist. Haven't they got neighbours who could help?"

"We couldn't find anyone in. They live in one of those muckle great houses, the type where everyone round about is out working."

Shona kept her voice soft as she said, "Well kids let's see if we can find someone to look after you. I'm Shona and I'm sure one of my lovely police officer friends would like to spend some time with you." How she kept her voice so low and comforting she didn't know. What she actually wanted to do was scream. Here were four young children without a mother and she had been unable to do anything to prevent it. Plus they were currently running around her nick, which, now she thought about it, seemed to be permanently full of children these days. "Peter, why is my station always crawling with children? Maybe I'll open a crèche and let every waif and stray in Dundee bring his or her kids here for us to babysit. Heck, why stop at Dundee let's open it up to Tayside and Angus."

"Sorry Ma'am."

Turning to Iain she said, "Go and find one of the female uniforms, preferably one that likes kids, and ask her to meet me in the staff room. If the Inspector complains tell him our need is greater than his." Taking the children from Peter she led them all away to somewhere a little less daunting. They all looked bewildered. The youngest had stopped crying and was now dribbling down Shona's back. Shona patted the baby's back gently and made soothing noises. The oldest boy was clutching tightly to the hands of his two younger sisters. Shona's heart went out to them.

After she'd handed over her babysitting duties to a delighted PC she returned to the interviews. These continued in the same vein as before. She could tell that there was something a couple of the interviewees wanted to say but just couldn't bring themselves to vocalise it despite her questioning.

"It's really important that you tell us everything no

matter how trivial or even difficult. We need to know every tiny detail if we are to prevent more deaths."

Fear and apprehension flickered in their eyes but they remained adamant. "No, there's nothing." Even the thought that they could be the next victims wasn't loosening their tongues.

"If I find out you are holding anything back then you could be charged with interfering in the course of an investigation. You do realise that? I will have no qualms about arresting you and throwing you in a particularly unsavoury cell."

"There's nothing. I've told you everything I know."

Shona felt a mixture of anger and frustration. What on earth could have been going on at that school? What could be so bad that the teachers didn't want to say even 14 years later? Whatever it was she was going to get to the bottom of it.

31

November 2012

Tucked up in my lair I think about my next move and how it will play out. The thinking and planning always soothes my nerves. I feel like I'm in control. It's important that I'm the puppet master in this game. I picture the concrete façade of the police station in the centre of town. Inside it, my adversaries will be scurrying like ants. There's been a sudden burst of activity at the station so they must believe they have something to go on. I love watching the police scurry, trying to figure this out. It's almost as much fun as the killing itself. They might be actively looking for me soon, but I am the one with all the power. Years of practice in avoiding people will keep me right out of their way.

My thoughts move to my next victim. This was someone completely different and they will not be looking there. That's the beauty of my plan. I know what they are doing but no one knows what I am doing.

At the thought of this person my heart fills with loathing and hatred. This is someone whom I truly despise. I can picture them clearly but even the thought of killing them cannot remove the pain. My heart beats faster almost in full panic mode. Stop thinking about this. I force my mind to change the focus of my thoughts, just as I have been trained to do. It works. Thrilling inside at how anxious and worried so many women will now be, I take deep, calming breaths. There is no need to worry. This is the ultimate game, one in which I am now the master.

The sound of the rain, dripping from the trees, outside lulls me to a peaceful untroubled sleep.

32

Donna Douglas was a teacher who had worked at the school for forty years. She was about to retire.

Beginning the interview Shona asked, "Is there anything you know which might shed light on why these girls are being killed?"

"Yes, I think there probably is."

Shona tried to keep the excitement out of her voice. "Could you elaborate?"

"Some people may have told you that Jennifer Brown was a nasty piece of work. Well, that doesn't even give you a fraction of an inkling of what she was like. That girl was evil to the core. She could be as nice as ninepence one minute, and the next, could turn like a venomous snake. When she thought she was being noticed her smile could light up a room like sunshine in the spring. Turn away from her and her face would completely change, rivalling the prince of darkness at his worst. I've met many teenagers over the years but none who gave me chills like Jennifer. She would use people for a certain time and then drop them when she got bored with them. Every one of the murdered women was friends with her at some point if I remember rightly."

"But why would someone want to kill Jennifer and her sometime friends? Especially this many years after the event. It wouldn't be normal no matter how downright nasty she was."

"I can't answer that but I can tell you there was a

lot of bullying going on that year. Jennifer seemed to crave power like oxygen and light. The older she became the more evil the bullying became. She also coerced her friends into helping her. That is until they were discarded. There was always a new set waiting to be drawn into her special, albeit depraved, orbit. I'm not saying any of the murdered women were bullies but they were certainly on the periphery. It was seen as a real honour to be part of Jennifer's group. They'd do anything to impress her and keep her as a friend. Jennifer eventually latched on to some poor girl. I think her name was Laura something. She was the quietest girl I have ever met. Came from a dreadful background and was a bit of a loner. I don't know how bad the bullying of her was but it seemed to stop after a few months."

"There was nothing about this in any of the pupils' files," Shona said. "There was mention of a couple of minor cases but the notes said it was investigated and dealt with appropriately."

"No one could do anything to Jennifer because her father was George Brown. He was a bully too, but also the Lord Provost of Dundee at the time. He ruled Dundee with an iron fist so everyone was more terrified of him than of what was happening in the school. None of us wanted to lose our jobs so we kept quiet. The headmaster at the time, Stuart McKay, was a weak man. He was pretty much made headmaster because he would do whatever the School Board wanted. The Chair of the School Board was, of course, Jennifer's father. I tried to keep an eye out to stop anything too bad happening but I was too scared to speak out. As I say, it also appeared to die down. Laura was even quieter than before and you didn't see her unless she was in class or playing hockey, but she seemed OK. They sat their exams fairly soon afterwards and all moved on. We heaved a collective sigh of relief when Jennifer left."

Shona couldn't help herself. "So you're telling me that there was someone systematically bullying pupils at the school, and yet not one adult did anything about it?"

"To my eternal shame I am, yes. Sometimes it even seemed to be more torture than bullying. I dread to think what Jennifer would have dreamed up if she hadn't left school fairly quickly. Part of the problem was she that had the IQ of a genius and got easily bored. Unfortunately that boredom turned her to evil. We were all surprised when she went into medicine. I suppose it gave her even greater power. It sends shivers down my spine thinking what she could get up to in a profession like that. Going back to your question, you're right no one did anything to stop it. I will go to my grave regretting that."

If it turns out these murders are anything to do with it then you'll have nightmares day and night for the rest of your life thought Shona. The teacher was also going to be answering questions in court as to why she allowed the bullying to continue. Nightmares would be the least of her worries.

"You've been really helpful. Thank you. I would like you to wait in case I have any more questions."

Nina had also finished her interview.

"Grab us both a drink and ask the others to come to my office. It's time to take stock and compare notes."

What came out of it was, the common denominators seemed to be bullying, Jennifer Brown and Laura, who turned out to be Laura Sands. Some of the women and men interviewed, said they had been part of playing a couple of "tricks" on Laura. It was all meant to be childish fun of course. They were not sure if any of the dead women were involved, apart from Jennifer who was at the centre of everything. It would appear she was the leader and the others felt special to be a part of her exclusive circle. Most of them agreed that Laura was a bit strange, and quiet to the extent of mutism. They couldn't remember a great deal about her and said they'd heard nothing about her since leaving school. This woman seemed almost ethereal, a wisp that existed only in the imagination.

"We've got to speak to Laura Sands. Yesterday. I have a gut feeling that she holds the key to all of this," said Shona.

They seemed to be bogged down in a mud field of information, which was being churned ever more deeply the further into the investigation they went.

"This investigation gives new meaning to the expression as clear as mud. I feel, like a hippo, I'm wallowing in the stuff. I'm off. I need to ask Donna Douglas a few more questions. There could be something she's still not telling us."

Once Donna Douglas and Shona were settled in the Interview room she asked "I need you to tell me everything you can remember about Laura Sands? No one seems to know a thing about her, either back then or now. That's unusual for a group of classmates who go through six years of school together. It's as though she didn't really exist."

"Laura could have that effect on people. She was one of the quietest girls I taught. She would answer in class and could hold her own in any academic debate but that's as far as conversation went with her. She was probably the brightest student I ever came across by far. Her IQ was off the chart. Where she got it from I don't know as I also taught her mother and she barely had an IQ. Top place in any subject was always a toss-up between Jennifer and Laura, with Laura taking it most of the time. However, she appeared to have no friends and kept herself to herself. She was always clean, neat and a hard worker but apart from that I can tell you nothing about her. I have no clue as to her personality, her likes or dislikes or anything. Again that's unusual. As a teacher you pick things up; what type of music they like, if they've started going out with someone, that sort of thing. This just wasn't the case with Laura and it's probably why you feel her very existence should be disputed."

Shona had never heard such a sad tale. How could anyone go through six years of schooling without one person knowing the slightest thing about her? If the headmaster weren't already dead Shona would have him investigated and thrown into one of her dirtiest cells. With Auld Jock as a cellmate. On second thoughts she would strike that. It didn't seem very fair on Jock. She made a mental note that if she ever had any kids, to look carefully into any school they might be going to attend. This one sounded like something Stephen King would dream up, or a recreation of Dickens's Dotheboys Hall.

"I don't think I've any more questions for you just now so you can go. Just make sure to leave your mobile number so we can contact you if we need to."

Shona decided it was time to take a break from all the interviews and go and speak to Laura's mother. Perhaps she would give them a better idea of what happened at school. Mind you from the files and what the teachers said, it would appear she didn't go to the school and kick up a fuss. There was always the possibility of course that she had done so and nothing was recorded. The way that school was run it wouldn't surprise her.

"Come on Morag we're off to see Mrs Sands," she

said, reaching for her car keys. "She lives in Menzieshill near the hospital."

The area in which Mrs Sands lived was run down, but even that didn't prepare them for what lay inside. Her flat would be described in Dundee parlance as clorty or mingin'. It looked like it hadn't been cleaned – ever – and neither did Mrs Sands. There was a strong smell coming from the apartment and it certainly wasn't food. "What do you pair of f…."

Shona interrupted. "Mrs Sands?"

"I might be. What's it to you. I'm not interested in being a Jehovah's Witness, so bu…"

Shona shoved her foot in a rapidly closing door as she flashed her badge. "I'm Detective Inspector McKenzie and this is my colleague PC Gibbs. We…"

Mrs Sands interrupted "I've not done anything wrong and I'll no have the Polis saying otherwise. What are you trying to fit me for now?"

Shona said calmly "Nothing Mrs Sands we'd like to talk to you about Laura. May we come in?"

The woman held the door open and the smell increased. Morag gagged. She had the look of a woman who was about to part company with the pie and chips she'd scarfed down at lunchtime. Shona sent her a sharp look which clearly communicated lose the contents of your stomach and your career's ended. Morag swallowed a couple of times and tried to breathe through her mouth. Shona was busy swallowing herself. This was the worst she had come across in her career so far.

Behind closed doors, they had no idea that they were being watched. The killer noted down every little detail. She needed to know everything they did and how they did it. That way she could stay under their radar. This was an interesting development. Thinking how they would be feeling inside the filthy, stinking flat made her smile. Her first in many years.

33

March 1999

This training is breath and life to me. I find everything so easy. And exhilarating. Everyone else is finding it tough. It's designed to be tough. To wear down the weakest and let them drop out. Only the strongest will survive. I honed my skills long before arriving here. This place is nothing compared to the streets of Dundee. Compared to what I've already been through in my so far worthless life. As is my wont, I stay well away from trouble. To my astonishment, everyone is relying on me for help and support. Who would have guessed, that what I went through at school would have been such effective preparation for a career such as this? The running, even with a heavy pack on my back, is a breeze. Running everywhere as a child, backpack full of books, meant I was in peak physical condition even before I joined.

Avoiding the enemy had been injected into me out of necessity. This role, almost stamped in my DNA, is as natural as breathing. Being out in the cold, rain and snow, trying to keep warm and dry is a normal day for me. In fact it's easier now because I'm doing it wearing decent kit. Being dropped in the middle of nowhere and having to get back to base couldn't be easier. I watched everything and everywhere as we travel here. Every road, path, building, phone box, telephone pole and tree is imprinted on my brain. I can access the details at a moment's notice. The minute my feet touch the ground as we're thrown from the jeep I am moving.

"Back in under two hours. Every man for himself. Move it."

I hear the instructor's voice fade behind me as I run. My path is fast and true like the flight path of an arrow. I know all I need to know to get myself, not only back, but also in record time. I fly over different types of terrain but nothing bothers me or stops me. I am, of course, the first man back. I always am.

I'm not cocky though. I've learnt that cockiness can only bring you grief. Better to stay quiet and, sponge like, soak up every piece of information the instructors dish out. This means I know exactly what to do and when to do it. The hardest part is having to talk to the others and put on a pretence of normality. How they can make so much small talk is beyond me. The inanity of it all makes me want to scream. Nevertheless I go along with it, nodding and smiling in all the right places. It is a means to an end.

34

November 2012

If they thought the flat was a hovel from the hallway, they were even more shocked when they went into the living room.

"Sit down and stop hovering," the woman said.

Politeness dictated that they comply. However, as they perched on the very edge of the sofa, they were determined to get out of there as quickly as possible. Shona could see Morag staring at the room full of black bin bags, which were piled high. Every surface was covered by plates and mugs, which were green with mould. This carpet must have been clean at some point Shona thought. Now, every step left your shoes sticky with filth. With what, Shona didn't even want to imagine. Shona couldn't understand how anyone could live like this. They needed to report it to the Council. It must be some sort of a health hazard. God, I hope there aren't any rats. This was a heartfelt prayer. Panic quickened her breathing. She forced her breathing to steady telling herself it was unlikely.

"You asked about Laura. What's the useless little bitch been up to now? I always knew she'd end up in trouble with the Polis. She was never any use to anybody and certainly not to me."

"As far as we know she hasn't been up to anything. We just need to ask her a few questions. We need to know if she remembers about some things that happened when she was at school." Shona forced herself to keep her voice calm. If she got irate she'd breathe faster and that wasn't something she wanted to do in here. Swallowing rancid bile she added, "Do you know how we can get in touch with her?"

"No I don't. The minute she finished her exams she was out of here. She was an ungrateful little bitch seeing as though I'd brought her up and given her everything. Not that she was much missed. She never said a word when she was here and only cost me money in food and clothes. High and mighty Miss Laura always thought she was better than the rest of us."

The propensity of the human mind to fool itself, never ceased to amaze Shona. Given her everything she needed? If this flat was anything to go by then no wonder the girl had disappeared. Who in their right mind would ever want to be found by this woman? It was probably the first sensible thing the girl ever did. She had a certain amount of sympathy for Laura wherever she was.

Hiding her feelings she asked, "So you have no idea where she went Mrs Sands? Would her father know where she was?"

"I'm not a missus and I very much doubt her father knows where she is as I don't even know who her father was. I was a whoor working the docks then and it could have been anyone. Before you get any ideas about arresting me I gave up whoring years ago," she said.

Shona could see Morag's jaw dropping and her eyes go wide. She narrowed her eyes, signalling, "Keep professional or you're dead." Not that she blamed the young PC. That was the most jaw dropping statement she had ever heard. Who in the world would want to go anywhere near this woman never mind pay to sleep with her? Even with all her years on the force, human behaviour always managed to astound her.

"I can assure you, Miss Sands, that we have no

intention of arresting you for anything, but it is crucial we find Laura. She may have information that could help with a current case. Are you sure she didn't say what she planned on doing after school."

"She didnae say where she was going, in fact I didnae even know she was going. I came back one morning and her bags were packed and she was gone without a by your leave. Didn't even say cheerio. Not a peep since. The only thing I can think of was maybe she joined up. She probably did that to get away fae me. I don't know if she ever did though. It was just something she said during a row."

Thanking Miss Sands, Shona and Morag got up to leave. "If you do hear anything or think of anything can you let me know?" Shona said handing her a card. This was more out of duty than expectation. She knew they would never hear from this woman again.

The minute they were outside the block of flats Shona and Morag took some deep, cleansing breaths. "Can I go home for a shower and to change my clothes?" Morag pleaded. "I feel like I'm covered in vermin and I smell like a sewer."

"That's actually not a bad idea," said Shona. I'll drop you off and you've got till I return from my flat to be ready. No hanging about as I can shower and change in record time. The smell in that flat was the worst I've ever come across. I'll never complain about Auld Jock again. It makes him seem like he's drenched in Estee Lauder's most expensive."

When they returned to the nick everyone took the mickey out of them. "Typical women send them out to dae a job and they come back scrubbed up and wi clean claes on," said Peter. Scratching at what felt suspiciously like fleabites Shona said sourly "The next time we have to interview her you're going. You won't be quite so chirpy then and if you came back without a shower I'd personally send you to change."

Changing the subject she said "Morag get on to the Council and get them around to look at that flat. I can't believe the neighbours haven't complained before now. There has to be something in Scottish Law that prevents people living like that. I'm sure she's had a hard life but that doesn't stop her having a wash or occasionally cleaning her house."

"Peter if you're finished having fun at our expense go rally the troops. I need to speak to them and, of course, to you."

With a smile Peter said "Yes, General," saluted and turned on his heel. He's in a good mood she thought. I wonder why? She went to find the Chief to update him.

By the time she got back to the briefing room, Morag had rung the Council "They said it's too late to get anyone round there tonight. They've had several complaints already but haven't done anything about it. Seemingly the tenants around there are always complaining about something so they don't really pay much attention. Her rent and council tax are paid through benefits and that's all they're worried about. They're going to send someone around tomorrow."

"Good old Dundee Council. Always ready to help," responded Shona. "Right guys we still don't know where Laura Sands is. The best lead we've got is that she might have joined the Military. No clue which branch though. Roy I need you to work your magic online and see if having a bit more info can help us pin down Laura Sands whereabouts. Peter what's happening with the kids, have they been collected yet?"

"No Ma'am the Social Work Department says they're snowed under. They're trying to find some foster care for them and then they'll pick them up."

Shona was beginning to get to the end of a very short fuse "For goodness sake Peter, this is a nick not a playgroup. It's no place to be keeping kids especially ones who are upset. Get them back on and tell them, if the kids are not away from here in 30 minutes we're going to bring them and dump them on their doorstep. I need all the PCs I can get and one of them playing baby-sitter is not an option. Do not take no for an answer."

"Nina, you and I are going to go down to the Armed Forces Recruiting Office before they close to see if we can work out where Laura is through them," and with that she turned and strode away. However, the gods were most definitely conspiring against her as before she could get very far her mobile rang. It was a very nervous desk sergeant who said, "I hope you're sitting down Ma'am."

35

November 2012

What are the police doing here, swanning into my mother's house like they own the place? How did that complete bunch of wasters catch on so quickly? I can work round it though. I might not like it but the steps are in place to work around any such eventuality. The army has taught me to always be prepared. The cat in this game can conquer the mice and even the rats in any way she chooses. The control is mine no matter what anyone else tries to do. Everything I need is in my backpack. Always be prepared was one of the most important lessons I have learned in life. That and trust no one.

My upbringing has seen to that.

I take some deep breaths and run, hard and fast, towards Ballumbie. Anger radiates from every pounding footstep. I need to move more quickly. Finding a car in a quiet back street, I expertly hot-wire it and drive to Whitfield. There, I abandon it and continue my run. No one will miss it immediately and, by the time the police spare someone to find it, I'll be long gone.

I move from city streets to dreary country lanes without breaking stride. Day is turning to night. Arriving at the door of the isolated cottage I knock and step back. I don't have time to change and bloody clothes will be an inconvenience. The familiar feel of the cold steel of the gun in my hand is reassuring. The door opens, hesitantly at first, and then fully as she realises it's a woman. The woman I am here to see is framed in the bright light from the hallway.

"Hello. Can…"

I shoot, see the look of shock in the victims eyes; empty 5 more shots into her torso and head, and leave. Even if she isn't dead, she will be before anyone finds her. I feel nothing. Not until my thoughts turn to what I am going to do next. No need to delay things any more. I've been looking forward to the next murder for years. A warm feeling courses though me at the thought. It almost feels like happiness.

36

"Forget the preliminaries Sergeant. I don't have time. What's happened now?" said Shona.

"There's been another suspicious death Ma'am. This time it looks like a young woman was shot at point blank range in her hallway. Out of the way cottage, off the Kellas road so no one around to see or hear. They'd like you to go and take a look."

"If it's past the Kellas Rd isn't that Angus again? Can't they deal with their own murders?"

"I'm afraid not Ma'am it's just inside the Dundee boundary. She's definitely one of ours. Plus they seem to think it could be part of your case."

Shona hung up. "Change of plan Nina we're off to another murder. Go and find Iain, we'll need him. Jason can come too. Peter, could you ring the Recruiting Office and warn them that we need to speak to them first thing in the morning? Tell them what it's about and ask them to start looking to see if she joined up. She might have done it through them anyway."

Following a dreich day an inky darkness enveloped them as they drove to the isolated cottage. So close to the outskirts of Dundee, it was nevertheless too far for neighbours. The woman's father had called round to finish off some repairs and was expecting his daughter to be there. He didn't expect what he saw when he arrived.

Beyond the brightly painted wooden door the body

was lying on the hallway tiles. Dark, red blood lay in a pool around the woman. There were spatters of blood on the otherwise clean, obviously brand new pathway, and sprayed over the newly painted hallway. From the wounds it looked like she'd been shot – several times in the head and chest. Whoever killed her meant business. By the number of bullets Shona thought that this woman's killer was angry about something. That was seven murders all on her watch. There was no way Shona was letting this crime spree go down in the annals of station history. The killer was a marked man, or woman, as the case may be.

"Does she look pregnant to you?" she asked Nina.

"Yep, although not too far on. Not that I'm any great expert."

"Me neither. Right Iain, work your magic."

Nina and Iain set to work processing and photographing the crime scene. A man was standing just outside the doorway, crying. This was in direct opposition to the normally stoic Dundonian men. "Is that the victim's father?" One of the PC's nodded that it was.

Shona walked up to him "Sir, I'm sorry for your loss. I'm told your daughter's name was Marian Ellis. Was she married?"

"Yes, with a wee boy called Duncan who's only twelve. He's out with his father today, fishing. Then they were going out for tea to give my daughter a break. She's pregnant and gets tired easily." He started weeping again.

The total was now eight murders.

"What was Marian's maiden name?"

"Macintyre. She was Marian Macintyre."

"Would you like us to ring her husband and tell him about Marian's death?" she enquired.

"No, I'll do it. It'll be hard enough for him but it

might be better coming from me."

"Thank you. Could you ask him to come straight here?"

She went to find Nina. "Was there a Marian Macintyre on the list from Myercroft Academy?"

"Yes. She was one of the first people I interviewed this morning. I thought she looked familiar but I've seen so many people today I wasn't sure. Do you think the murderer knows what we're doing?"

"I'm certain the murderer knows exactly what we're doing and it pains me to say it but, whoever it is, they are playing us."

They finished processing the body in record time, practice having, if not proved perfect, at least improved their efficiency. The police surgeon arrived to pronounce the body dead.

"It won't come as any surprise that this looks like gunshot to me Shona, but it's up to Mary to decide. And your forensic team as well of course. Mary's not going to be happy having another body flung her way. I heard tell she was asking for help from Edinburgh to get through the backlog. Don't take this personally but I really hope I don't see you again anytime soon."

Guilt seized Shona like a vice but she dismissed it. She wasn't the one bumping off the natives at a rapid rate of knots. She wasn't exactly keeping up herself so Mary would just have to man up and get on with it like the rest of them. Shona was exhausted and rapidly losing sympathy for anyone else involved in the case.

On the way out of the cottage she saw Mr Macintyre, just outside the crime scene tape, speaking to a middle aged man and a sobbing boy. He'd had the presence of mind to stop them before they could actually see Marian's body. Moving over to the group she said, "DI McKenzie."

The dazed man replied, "Robert Ellis, I'm Marian's

husband." He faltered. "Was her husband? I don't know how you say it."

"I'm sorry for your loss Mr Ellis. We'll need to ask you some questions. Are you all right with that?"

"Yes. Yes. Anything to help."

"We'll sit in my car. It's freezing out here. Mr MacIntyre can you and Duncan go and sit in my Sergeant's car. It will be warmer for you both."

Once they were settled Shona said, "What time did you leave this morning Mr Ellis?"

"Duncan and I left this morning at about 8 am. We wanted to get a full day in."

"Was your wife expecting anyone?"

"No. It's been a bit of a difficult pregnancy. She was just going to rest. That's why I took Duncan out for the day. To give her peace."

"Did your wife keep up with any of her old school friends?"

"A couple of them, but only saw them occasionally."

"Does the name Laura Sands mean anything to you?"

"Not that I can think of. It doesn't ring any bells."

"Thank you Mr Ellis. Is there somewhere you and Duncan can go. You won't be able to stay here," she said as gently as she could.

"Marian's dad will take us to his house."

"If you could give my officer the address and phone number before you go, in case we need to get in touch with you."

Driving back, she phoned Peter and asked him to get a Chinese delivered for them all. The wonders of hands free systems in cars. Hopefully the food would arrive at the same time as she did. She prayed it might restore both her energy and her sympathy. Mind you, this linking murders to food and dates was getting to be somewhat weird.

After she'd ploughed her way through most of the foodstuff on offer, especially a tasty lemon duck, Shona felt a hundred times better. "How did you get on with the Recruiting Office?" she asked Peter.

"They said they'd start looking tonight and get back to me if they found anything. Nothing so far and they're shut up tight for the night now. They said we could go and see them at 8.30 tomorrow morning. I said you and Jason would go as they wanted names. I thought soldier boy might know the right things to say to get them on side."

"Good idea. I'll meet him there first thing. Roy, what about you? Have you come up with anything new?"

"To be honest, Ma'am, I'm totally baffled. I've drawn a complete blank. It's as if the woman doesn't exist. Obviously I can't get into military computers but on every other channel there's absolutely nothing. I can't even find a bank account. That's a first. There aren't many people who have a zero online footprint. That in itself sets off warning bells as it's generally accepted these days that you need an online presence to exist. It's suspicious to be totally absent online. I could hack into the military computers if you want."

"Much as I appreciate the offer Roy, no. Not a chance. We've a good relationship with the MOD and I don't want you jeopardising that. That's apart from the fact it's completely illegal even for us."

All this digging and they were still no further forward.

Despite the lateness of the hour Shona thought she might still be able to get hold of Mary at the mortuary. She felt guilty at not having spoken to her and wanted to at least catch up. Mary was indeed still hard at work and sounded as exhausted as Shona felt.

"Shona, what's happening? I no sooner clear one body than you send me another. I'm prioritising yours but I've got Ninewells and Perth Royal Infirmary breathing down my neck. For goodness sake, woman, solve your blasted case so we can all get a bit of rest."

"I know you're having it tough, Mary, and I really do appreciate all the work you're doing. Has the latest body arrived yet?"

"Yes, but I've no chance of getting to it until tomorrow. I'll email through the most recent results to you and then do the same with this one tomorrow. Do you still think it's different killers?"

"No, we're leaning towards one killer with a grudge against women who were in 5th year at Myercroft Academy in 1998."

"That's some grudge if they're being bumped off with a time lag of 14 years. Whatever it was it must have been bad. Either that or one of them has gone crazy."

"I don't get the impression our killer is crazy. Psychopathic maybe. Sociopathic most likely. Everything he or she does appears calculated and well planned out. We think we have a lead on someone, a woman named Laura Sands. Thanks for everything you're doing to help us. I'd better let you get on."

"Great that you've got at least one lead. I'll be praying it pans out for you. Bye now."

Shona hung up and returned to dismiss the team for the night. There was nothing more they could do until the morning. She found all the younger officers looking out of the window.

"What's so interesting?"

Roy said, "Have you seen PC Brian Gevers's new Scooter? It's the only red Piaggio scooter in Dundee and the only one in Scotland that's DiMaggio fly type three. It's boss."

"A scooter! You're all riled up about a scooter?"

"It's not just any scooter, Ma'am. It's unique."

Rolling her eyes Shona said, "I can just about imagine the guys drooling over a lump of metal but what's your excuse, Nina?"

"I love bikes. My boyfriend's a biker."

"A biker! I never had you down as a biker chick."

"Only since I met Andros. He's gorgeous. Really tall, dressed head to toe in tattoos and has a lovely pair of …"

"Nina, that's enough."

"Sunglasses. I was going to say sunglasses."

"Yeah right. Remember we're friends. Hang on, who's Andros. I thought your boyfriend was called Don."

"No he's old hat. Get with the programme, Ma'am."

"Your love life has more plot changes than an episode of Coronation Street. How am I expected to keep up? Right, I'm off home. You lot can stay and stare at scooters all night if you want. Me, I've got a life to lead."

Shona's flat was cold and not particularly inviting. It was all very well living alone and having the freedom to do what she wanted but on days like this she missed having someone to talk things over with. Her ex might have been generally worthless but he did have some uses. He was a great cook for a start and would have had a meal ready for her. This turned her thoughts to Douglas and she realised he hadn't come to today's murder. She wondered if anyone let him know. She'd better ring to make sure.

Douglas was pleased to hear from her despite the lateness of the hour.

"Did anyone ring you about our latest victim?" she asked.

"They did but I wasn't able to get there. I'd no one to look after the kids. My parents are on a cruise in the Med and my sister's gone to Florida with her husband and kids. I've been left home alone looking after all three houses." The warmth in his voice made her feel better. The picture in her mind of the way his smile translated to his eyes gave her shivers. Marvellous, Shona thought. The middle of a murder investigation and here she was getting all doe eyed and mooning over a man.

Giving him a quick update, she asked how Rory was. Douglas laughed. "He's as precocious as ever. He wants to come back and visit you at your office. Another nine years and he'll be applying for your job. He's told Alice all about you and she keeps asking when is Shona coming?"

"How old is Alice?" Shona asked.

"She's five and even more precocious than Rory if that's possible."

"I'd love to meet her. Maybe not in the office though or the pair of them might have me out of there and themselves ensconced before I can blink."

"They certainly would. Alice would order you out of your chair and you'd find yourself standing on the other side of the desk without asking why. She'll be Chief Constable one day. Maybe when this mayhem is over we can all get together and do something. I'll warn you, though, you're in for a tough time with my two."

"If Rory's anything to go by I can well imagine, but I'll look forward to it."

Shona yawned. "Sorry it's been a long day."

"I think you had better go get some sleep. I'll see you soon."

Shona went to find Shakespeare who was

remarkably quiet considering she'd been out all day. Going into her spare room she found out why. Shakespeare was lying comfortably on a pillow from the spare bed, surrounded by four kittens and looking remarkably pleased with himself. Or herself I suppose, thought Shona. "Well, Shakespeare, you never cease to amaze me." She'd noticed he'd been getting plump but she had attributed it to age. Some detective she was. "I might be an older single lady, puss cat, but that doesn't mean you have to provide me with a crazy cat lady starter kit." Giving Shakespeare a stroke and gently tickling the kittens, she went to fire up the computer and find out what the heck one did with a nursing cat.

37

November 2012

I need to rest and recharge. The army has taught me that an exhausted soldier is no use to anyone. I am taught to push myself to the very edge of human endurance and then some, but to take time out whenever possible. I need a small hiatus in my obsessive, if entirely necessary, killing routine. The enemy will still be there when I return tomorrow with renewed strength and greater determination.

I return to my bedroom and, lying on the bed, force myself to relax. This proves difficult for me. My brain is always on overdrive, but I know I need to shut it down. I force my mind to focus on something other than the mission. I take some deep breaths and think of my future. Used to living on nothing, I have barely touched my wages since I joined up. My only luxuries have been some decent clothes and a love of good wine. I had brought a bottle with me and thought of opening it. No. This is not the time. I let my mind drift forward to the future. I have saved enough money that I could retire right now. Move somewhere cheap. Live my own life with nothing and no one to bother me. But no, that's not an option. I would miss the thrill of the hunt. The excitement of putting the bad guys out of action. The way I can use my mind to outfox everyone. I will return to the Army and no one will be any the wiser. I'll continue to climb the ranks at a meteoritic rate. It's a given that I will reach the top in my chosen career. I am too clever not to.

Pulling out my iPod, I plug in the earphones, and let Beethoven's Piano Sonatas wash away my cares. A small interlude, not only for me, but for everyone involved in this deadly game of tag. Some of them don't yet know they will be tagged.

38

November 2012

Shona went for a run in the pouring rain the next morning after checking on a very content Shakespeare and her four kittens. She needed to blow away the cobwebs and leave her with some energy. Not only was the rain torrential, it was freezing. Shona remembered from her criminology course at university that violence is more prevalent in hotter climates. Whoever came up with that one had obviously never been to Dundee. It was probably the coldest, wettest place on the planet, yet it had enough murders at the moment to make even the hottest of nations jealous. On the way back she called into the corner shop to get a box. She was going to have to find another name for Shakespeare. The present one didn't quite cut it for a female. Returning to the flat she tried out the name Agatha but Shakespeare didn't look impressed. She looked at Shona and then the kittens as if to say, welcome to the world of humans. They're all nuts. Oh well, did it really matter what she was called? She could keep the name. "You win Shakespeare." She knocked on her neighbours' door. Thankfully Mrs Gordon was an early riser and she loved the cat. She was delighted about the kittens and readily agreed to look after all five of the animals whilst Shona was at work. "Could I have one of the kittens when they're old enough? I've been thinking about getting a wee cat."

"Of course you can." She made a mental note to buy Mrs Gordon a present.

She had arranged to pick Jason up and they would go to the Recruiting Office together.

"Jason you look like crap. You're not ill are you?"

"No Ma'am. I just didn't get much sleep last night thinking about this case. I don't mean to be rude but you're not looking so hot yourself."

"I was in the same boat as you but with knobs on."

They were met by a friendly, and willing, Warrant Officer. He shook their hands and introduced himself.

"WO2 Henry McVicar. I was in the Military Police myself for a few years, before I transferred to the Physical Training Corps, so I know what you guys are going through. I've been following it all in the papers. I think you've got as many deaths here in a week as we had in my whole tour of Afghanistan. At least you expect it in Afghanistan but not here in Dundee. You must be going crazy trying to figure it out. Now what can I get you to drink?"

"I'm DI Shona McKenzie and this is my colleague PC Jason Roberts. He used to be in the Infantry. I'd love a coffee with just milk." She looked at Jason.

"Coffee for me as well. NATO standard."

"Ah, A fellow soldier. Two coffee's coming up."

When Henry returned, his colleagues, from the other services, accompanied him. "This is CPO Chalkie White from the Royal Navy and Flight Sergeant Dinger Bell from the RAF. We've all looked through our recruiting records and Laura Sands definitely didn't join up through this office. Do you know whether she would have joined as an Officer or as a Junior Rank?"

"We've no idea, or even if she actually joined up. She didn't come from a very good background, which would probably indicate Junior Rank. On the other hand her IQ was at genius level so she may be an officer."

"We're going to make a few phone calls to see what we can find out. Could you hang about in case we have any questions? It might make things go more quickly if we have you on hand. Have you any details on her other than her name." Shona gave him a copy of the sheet from Laura's school file.

"Thanks, that should help. We'll leave you here. Feel free to help yourself to drinks and make use of the phone. I know you must have a lot to do." With that they were left alone.

Shona thought she'd better ring the Chief and the team and let them know that they could be some time. The Chief was already in a bad mood and it was only 9 o'clock. "That's great; you sit and have a wee tea break with Her Majesty's best whilst we're all left here to do your work. The minute you get back I need to speak to you. The Lord Provost's been on the phone. Jennifer's dad has heard rumours that people are bad mouthing his daughter and he wants it to stop."

An astonished Shona responded, "Sir, no one at the station has been bad mouthing anyone but it looks like Jennifer was a nasty piece of work and her behaviour could be right slap bang in the middle of this. We need to look into it as part of the investigation."

"I'm not discussing this on the phone. The minute you're in I want you in my office. Don't even bother going anywhere else first or you'll be looking for a new job." With that he slammed the phone down. Shona wondered what had got the Chief so excitable. It wasn't like him to bow to pressure so easily. There must be something serious going on. She didn't really care what the pressure was. She was going to investigate this case properly regardless of who was getting their knickers in a twist. If they thought they could scare her then they had another think coming.

Next she phoned Peter. "The Chief's on the

warpath so keep out of his way. If he finds you lot stuffing sandwiches, instead of working, we'll all be drawing Job Seekers Allowance. Either that or we'll be mollifying him for months. Shona was beginning to think that this management lark was not all it was cracked up to be. Who needed it? She thought she might find out if Tesco were hiring.

She took out her laptop and began to review the case. It didn't take long. What they had so far were an awful lot of murders and just one lead, and the lead wasn't exactly getting them very far. "Jason, have you got any insights that might help us?"

"Not a one Ma'am. This CID malarkey makes the TA look like a walk in the park. A tour in Afghanistan for a wee holiday looks inviting."

After about an hour, the RN and RAF lads came back. They said that Laura had definitely not joined either of these Services. Shona thanked them and asked if they knew how Henry was getting on. They said they weren't sure but it would be a bigger task for him as his was the largest Service.

Just as Shona was beginning to get impatient Henry returned.

"It's good news and bad news I'm afraid. The good news is she definitely joined the Army. The bad news is I can't seem to find where she's currently posted. I am going to dig deeper but it may take longer than I thought so I would suggest you go, and I'll ring you when I find out. Have you got a mobile number?"

Shona gave him her number and she and Jason drove through torrential rain back to the station. "It wouldn't surprise me if there were floods," Jason observed. "That should keep Traffic busy."

Yes, and fewer personnel for us thought Shona glumly. What else could distract them from this investigation?

The team were even more frustrated and impatient than Shona. They had done everything they could but the case seemed to have stalled. The interviews had turned up nothing new – just the same endless litany about Jennifer being a nasty piece of work who needed to hurt people to keep herself amused. To relieve the boredom they had put on a Christmas CD and the sound of "I wish it could be Christmas every day" was filling the room.

"What's with all the Christmas jollity?" said Shona. "Isn't it a bit early?"

Peter looked up from his *Courier*. "You remind me of one o' those literary characters."

"Who would that be?"

"Scrooge."

"Let me see if I've got this right. We're in the middle of a murder investigation with more dead bodies than we know what to do with, and you want me to be all mistletoe and good cheer?"

In the space of a heartbeat Nina said, "I bet you wouldn't mind the mistletoe if the Procurator Fiscal was here."

"Don't be so cheeky. Get some work done you lot, or I'll swap the whole bally lot of you for a new team."

Leaving them to it she went to see the Chief. She had put it off as long as she could. He certainly hadn't recovered his good humour by the time she saw him. If anything, it had worsened. "This has to stop Shona. Ex-Lord Provost George Brown is on the warpath. He says there are rumours flying around about his daughter and if this office doesn't stop them he'll insist we're investigated. He says this is making his mental anguish worse."

"Sir, we've interviewed nearly a hundred people

during this investigation. This has obviously brought up a lot of memories for some of them and they are going to talk. It's impossible for me to stop them. The last thing on my mind at the moment is George Brown's mental anguish." Shona was indignant.

Shona was dumbfounded when the Chief's voice softened "I know, Shona, but you've not lived in Dundee most of your life. This man is poison. He controls a large chunk of the City and has his fingers in an awful lot of unscrupulous pies. He could make things very uncomfortable for us and that's an understatement. We've got to be seen to be doing something. Not that I believe we are doing anything wrong at all. It's just that any investigation of this department will stop us doing our job. Oh, and by the way, we need to send out a statement to the press to stop them camping on our doorstep. Could you do that but run it by me first?"

Stop the press. Shona couldn't believe the Chief had just confided in her. Things must be worse than she thought. "I'll do my best to sort things out Sir."

She returned to the squad room. "You lot can keep yourself occupied by ringing round everyone and telling them to keep quiet. Explain it could jeopardise the success of the investigation."

"Most o' the good and the great citizens of Dundee are not going to be happy. I can just hear them protesting about freedom of speech."

"Tough. Tell them our murder investigation trumps their right to gossip. Divvy them up and get on with it."

39

July 2003

The sunlight bounces off the dusty roads as our convoy travels towards Fallujah. Although fairly safe inside our vehicle we are constantly alert for roadside bombs or attacks from Iraqi insurgents. Emotions run high, and adrenalin pumps through taut veins, as we slowly travel towards battle. I am quiet as I scan the surrounding terrain. Every one of my senses is on high alert for a sign of the enemy, or anything which looks out of place. Yet inside I am exulting. This is what I have trained for. This is part of my destiny. I have no fear. What is there to fear? When your life has little meaning, why would you fear death?

No one is talking. Everyone immersed in his or her own thoughts. Focussed on what lies ahead yet still subsumed by loved ones left so many miles away. It didn't do to think about that. It made your fear greater. Would you ever see your wife, children, parents again? I am thankful that I don't have that problem. There is no one waiting for me or worrying about me. I am certainly not worried for myself. I'm not even worrying about the men and women under my command. I have to rely on them, and trust them in battle, but that is as far as it goes. I don't want to see them as people. They are merely pawns in a much bigger game. As am I. The truck goes over a bump spooking every strung out passenger who is startled from his thoughts. As a man they reach for their rifles. It could just as easily have been a roadside bomb.

"Steady. Nothing to worry about." I calm them. The last thing I need is this lot accidently firing off rounds. "Steady and stay focussed. Thoughts on the mission. Your family and friends have no right to be here in Iraq." There were a few murmured grumbles but the men seemed more interested in the job in hand. Good job too. Emotion is worthless and has no place in a battleground.

I return to my thoughts. The battle ahead is all that matters. My mind runs over all the endless possibilities that could happen. I have studied the maps of Fallujah till I know the streets and structures almost as well as I know my home city. Wherever we go, whatever we have to do, whatever building we have to capture, I am ready. The endless permutations of what the enemy might do and where they might attack plays in my mind like a multitude of scenes from an endlessly repeating movie. It is so real I can almost smell the exotic scents of the Arabian city out here in the desert. I have a plan in my head to combat every eventuality and we will not fail. As the noise and smell of battle draw ever nearer I feel every one of my nerve endings thrill with anticipation and excitement. I was born for such a day as this.

40

November 2012

Having spent the intervening time talking to a bunch of irate, anxious or upset Dundonians, Shona was glad to hear from Henry at the Recruiting Office. It still wasn't particularly good news. "Her file's locked down tighter than the Bank of England's vaults. Usually this means the soldier is SAS but she's a woman and there are no women in the SAS. She's not showing up in the Special Reconnaissance Regiment either and I can't get anyone higher up to open up. In fact I've been ordered to back off. I'm so sorry Shona I can't go any further. Whatever this woman is doing in the Army it's something special and extremely hush hush."

Thanking him for the amount of time and effort he had put in, Shona hung up.

Yet again she went to explain what was happening to the Chief.

"Leave it with me. I'll talk to the higher ups and we'll get access to that information. Never you fear. Might be one for the big boss himself. We'll make him work for his money."

"We need to hurry Sir. I'm worried that the more we stall, the more dead bodies will turn up. I have a real feeling in my gut that this woman is our culprit. We don't have time to waste."

The Chief agreed but was cautious. "I'm well aware of that, Shona, but I need to go through the proper channels. I'll make sure everyone knows the urgency but they can only do what they can do. It might take time to get the Chief Superintendent to act. I'm sure you can find something worthwhile to occupy your team while you wait. If not, I can find a few duties for them and I'm sure they won't like them."

Gathering the team together Shona broke the news that they were still somewhat stalled and that the Chief had better find them gainfully occupied or he'd have them all doing endless paperwork. They, to a man, groaned.

"We've got a couple of cases which have been put on the back burner due to the pressure of this one. See what you can do with them." One was a twenty one year old man who had disappeared during his final year at university, along with his girlfriend. His family, in England, were worried, as he didn't usually do rash things and it wasn't like him to disappear without telling anyone. Because of his age and the fact that someone else had gone with him, they hadn't looked into it too seriously. Also the girlfriend's family weren't too worried as they said she was very impulsive. It would keep them occupied and if they found out his whereabouts then it would put his family's mind at rest. He had now been missing for two weeks so there could be foul play involved.

Shona took five minutes to grab a coffee and then turned her thoughts back to the investigation. She hated having her hands tied, having to sit and wait for someone else to get information, but there was nothing she could do. Someone much higher up the food chain than her would have to sort this one out. She shuddered to think how high up both the Military and Police command this would have to go before they got results. Unfortunately that could take more time than they had. Sighing, she started the press report she suddenly remembered agreeing to write. When it was completed she went to ask the Chief for his stamp of approval.

"Good work Shona. Get it out to everyone with my name at the bottom. We need to let the nation know we are taking this seriously."

Thankful she didn't have to rewrite it, she never the less thought that it was a blasted cheek, the Chief taking the credit for all her hard work. Still, it didn't really matter whose name it went out under. The press would do exactly what they wanted with it anyway. She could only imagine the lurid headlines, which would appear in Scotland's newspapers tomorrow. It was probably too late for tonight's editions.

She went to review the file of the young man who had disappeared. He was a popular student both with his peers and professors, hardworking, articulate and extremely bright. What was it with all these bright pupils Shona thought? They all seemed to end up in bother. Mind you she wasn't entirely sure he was in trouble. He just hadn't turned up for lectures one day and that situation had continued. After a few days his parents had phoned the local police and filled out a report. His father had telephoned several times since, to check progress, but they hadn't had the manpower to deal with it. They were all tied up with the murders. Also he had probably gone somewhere with the unpredictable girlfriend. Being young and in love was a heady combination but not a crime. Even Shona, with her chequered history, could remember that.

She went to find out if the team had discovered anything. It turned out this disappearance was easier to solve than the murders. A strange religious sect had set up home in an old farmhouse up in the Sidlaw Hills – The Church of Perpetual and Only Truth. The missing young man's friends said he had become more and more involved with them and spent a lot of time up there. It looked like the pair of them had finally gone to join them for good.

"They're calling themselves CPOT for short. Sounds like it should really be bampot to me. They all sound like a right bunch of nutters," said Peter.

"I'm sure you're right Peter. Nina and Iain go and check the place out. Confirm if the lad's there. You've nothing better to do at the moment. These cults can be a bit odd so don't leave until you've clapped eyes on the pair of them."

At least they had almost closed one case today. Hopefully that would bode well for the murders too.

Shona returned to her office to catch up with some admin. She hadn't been there long when the Chief Constable himself knocked and came in. Shona jumped up from behind the scarred wooden desk.

"What can I do for you Sir?"

"It's more what I can do for you," he said. "I have a name and address for Major Laura Sands Commanding Officer." He placed a sheet of paper on the desk along with some plane tickets. "You don't want to know what I had to go through to get this. He has agreed to cooperate fully with us and give us any information we need. The only stipulations are that you need to go and meet with him face to face, and that all information remains strictly confidential. He won't talk otherwise."

Shona looked at the address and the tickets and asked "Would you like myself and DS Johnston to go to Hereford and interview him?"

"Of course I do Shona. Your names are on the tickets. Your plane leaves from Dundee in an hour. The CO has agreed to send a car to meet you in Birmingham. You'll return on the last plane this evening, which should give you plenty of time. Get all the information you need because we only have one crack at this. I'm trusting you here."

No pressure thought Shona. "Thank you Sir. I'll make sure we do a good job."

As the Chief Constable left she followed him to go and break the news to Peter that they were off on a jaunt.

41

November 2012

This is not going to be hurried but slow, oh so slow, and painful. I want my latest victim, who happens to be my mother, to be to be fully aware of every single, preordained cut I make on her body. My time has come. I am going to inflict the maximum amount of pain as payback for every painful minute I went through in the 'so-called' care of this woman. I have all the time in the world as no one ever visits this worthless heap of rags masquerading as a woman. I start to laugh, as I think of what I am going to do, and then knock on the door. My mother answers. I give her time to register who I am and then push her inside and slam the door. Showing her the knife I am holding I say, "one word and you'll feel the edge of this blade." There is bewilderment in my mother's eyes, followed by fear. She speaks, "What are you…" but stops abruptly as the tip of the knife nicks the skin at her throat.

"I said don't speak." The fear turns to terror.

My mother looks worse than she ever had. I didn't think that was possible. Years of prostitution and alcohol abuse had taken their toll. The rank smell doesn't bother me. I'm trained not to react to such stimuli. Show no fear, no emotion, and no response. I've been in worse places than this. I lower the knife to get a roll of duct tape from my backpack. She moves suddenly to grab the knife and I slam my elbow into her mouth. Weighing virtually nothing, she falls, bleeding.

"Why? I'm your mother," she mumbles through a

mouthful of broken, rotting teeth. Tears are pouring down her face.

I almost laugh. Being my mother is an argument for, not an argument against, what I am doing. "I told you not to speak. You can add don't move to that." I begin by taping her mouth. I don't want some interfering neighbour getting involved because they'd heard a noise. Not that that was likely around here. The neighbours weren't interested in anyone else. Only getting their next drug fix. Tying the woman's hands behind her back with rope completes the first stage of the procedure.

Settling down to enjoy every last unhurried minute of this I make myself comfortable. The squalor doesn't bother me. I've seen worse on operational tours. This is just another tour of duty, if a very different and personal one. I want to watch her, to see the horror deepen on her face as the minutes tick by. I can see the realisation of what is about to happen widen her eyes in shock. Little does she know just how bad the remaining hours of her life are going to be.

I refuse to think of this creature as my mother. I could never have come from someone like this? We cannot be related. The others meant little to me, as they were merely pawns in a much bigger game. Apart from Jennifer, that is. She was also personal. The others were a means to an end to get my own back and rid the world of evil. Isn't that what I'm meant to do as a good soldier? Take out the enemy. Although this was personal, this woman was also the enemy. A mother was meant to love and care for her child. This bitch had done none of this. Her way of showing love was to abuse me at every opportunity. So now it was payback. The revenge, served as cold as fourteen years would allow, was going to be very sweet indeed.

Examining the knife in my hand I pause, wondering

where to start. I need to make the first cut count. My eyes roam over her body. I contemplate this for a moment and then decide. As the knife heads towards her face, the woman's eyes widen in fear and horror. She knows what is coming and I can see, by the look on her face, that she knows what her fate will be. The steel, sharpened to perfection, moves towards the woman's skin. Slow, caressing, it travels down her cheek, blood slowly trickling in its wake. She jerks and attempts to scream through the tape. If she had managed there was no one here to hear them. It was almost a pity I thought as I apply the next cut. My artistry is perfect. So begins a torture session, which defies description. This woman is going to suffer unimaginable horrors.

42

November 2012

Shona and Peter gathered what they needed and jumped into a squad car, which drove them to the airport, Siren screaming. Missing this flight would mean missing their one chance to pin Laura Sands down.

"She's on leave at the moment but the Army has agreed to bring her in for questioning. I've a feeling in my gut she's the killer. It's a good job the Army keeps quite a close choke hold on their personnel."

Shona stopped talking and lapsed into deep thought. So far there was nothing which tied Laura Sands to the killings, apart from the fact that she was at school with all the women who had died. Yet every one of Shona's instincts told her that Laura Sands was their killer. Unfortunately Shona's deeper feelings wouldn't go down well in a court of law, and were certainly not going to convince the Army to part with one of their officers. They needed to prove this beyond all reasonable doubt. She wasn't entirely sure how they were going to do that. Laura Sands, if she was the killer, was one cool customer.

Once on the plane Peter started his usual moaning. "I'm starving. Why is there nothing but peanuts to eat on here?"

Shona, on the verge of telling him to wrack off, merely took a gulp of scalding coffee. They were both on edge and arguing wasn't going to make the situation any better. Plus Peter's main coping mechanism was moaning. She could just tune him out.

Met at Birmingham Airport by the Military Police they were blue lighted to the Unit in Hereford, where they were met by a fit looking Corporal. "The Commanding Officer thought it would be quicker if I picked you up. He almost ran them to the car. Shona and Peter looked at each other. What was all the rush? If Laura Sands was being returned to the fold then surely everyone could relax a bit.

Within the hour they were through the gates of the Unit and in the CO's office where drinks, sandwiches and biscuits were waiting for them. This put a smile on Peter's face and allowed Shona to relax a little. She was awed by the delicacy of the bone china plates and cups, and the silver tea and coffee pots. This was a far cry from the canteen in the nick. She thought that maybe, just maybe, she ought to join the MPs. The Army certainly knew how to do things in style. It was a pity that all this refinement couldn't soften the news that the CO was about to deliver.

"I'm Col Jeremy Forbes-Ratcliffe. Welcome to my Unit." He was posh, clipped and succinct. "I know time is short so I'll get right to it. It would appear that Major Sands is not at the address she put on her leave pass. I got the local MPs to call round and the address doesn't exist. So we have no idea where she is. Knowing Major Sands, as I do, she could well be anywhere, including Dundee, carrying out your murders."

Shona registered Peter's astonished look and glared at him. All she needed was for him to start on the Colonel and they'd never get any information. They had to get, and keep, this man on their side. Mind you she could understand Peter's astonishment. How could the Army manage to lose one of its officers? Shona thought they had a tight rein on everyone and knew exactly where they were at any given moment. It didn't seem very efficient to her.

Before Peter could draw breath to speak, Shona interjected to give the Colonel a brief overview of the case so he knew the enormity of what they faced.

"Could you tell us a little more about Major Sands please? We've been unable to gather much information about her. She remains a bit of an enigma as far as our investigation is concerned."

"It's difficult to know where to start. Laura Sands is possibly the most interesting and unusual officer the Army has ever produced. So much so that she almost defies description. Given her background, she would, under ordinary circumstances, have joined as a junior rank. However she has the single highest IQ of anyone who has ever applied to join one of the Services. She passed every aptitude test in record time and was first in every ranked task, without exception. This continued throughout her time at Sandhurst where she received the Sword of Honour. She had regiments falling over themselves to recruit her."

"So you're saying she's the Army's greatest asset? If that's so then why would she be risking her career to murder people she hasn't seen for fourteen years?" Shona asked.

"In some ways she is the Army's greatest asset. She is way beyond, even the wildest imaginations of her peers when it comes to all things strategic and tactical. However, when it comes to socialising she is the complete opposite. To our knowledge she has no friends and has not built up a rapport with any of her fellow officers. She does what she needs to do in terms of socialising, in that, she'll make small talk at functions, but that's as far as it goes. She's a complete loner. If she wasn't so brilliant in a military sense then I don't think she would have risen as far or even remained in the Army. Being an officer is more than preparing for and fighting wars. There's a certain element of camaraderie that goes along with it. Her team trust her militarily as she has uncanny instincts, but they don't trust her otherwise. That's because they know nothing about her."

This confirmed everything they had heard from both her classmates and teachers thought Shona. This woman had a serious problem relating to other people. Which would make it all the harder for them to find her. There would be no friends or contacts to help track her down. There was a madwoman loose in her City and she didn't have a clue where to start looking.

"What I'm puzzled about is why everything about Major Sands is so secretive. Why is everything locked down tight as a ducks derriere? There can't be many women in the Army with their own file stamped TOP SECRET."

Jeremy looked uncomfortable. "I've been told to tell you everything by the top brass, but it goes against every military instinct in my body. Do I have your promise that this will all remain completely confidential?"

Both Shona and Peter assured him that was indeed the case.

"This is an SAS unit," he continued, "so you'll understand the secrecy. However in Major Sands case it is even more important that anonymity is maintained. As far as the world and 99.99% of the Army is concerned there are no women in the SAS. She shouldn't actually be here. She's an experiment. You will find no information about her in the public domain or in the big Army. It's as though she doesn't exist. As I say the only reason you're getting to know anything about her now is because of orders from the top brass."

Shona, to coin a phrase, was gobsmacked. This

wasn't exactly what she was expecting to hear. When she finally discovered her voice again Shona asked, "So how on earth are we going to find this woman if she's been able to drop off the Army's radar?"

"That's the million dollar question. It's going to be virtually impossible if she doesn't want to be found. You're not dealing with an ordinary woman here. Let me give you just a glimpse of what she is like. Major Sands is one of the most brilliant strategists the Army has seen, and that includes Monty in the Second World War. You would probably need to go back to Alexander the Great to see her equal. She has an originality of mind that is quite startling. She can blend chameleon like into any background. In terms of her personality she appears to be able to dissociate quite readily, which makes her fearless in the field. She appears to have no regard for life, either her own, or others. I would say she has absolutely no feelings or emotions whatsoever."

Shona was incredulous. "Are you sure she's not a machine. She doesn't sound human."

"I've often thought that myself." He paused to allow this to sink in. "In terms of your investigation," continued Colonel Forbes-Ratcliffe, "what I am about to tell you now is even more concerning, if that were possible. Laura Sands, as I say, is a brilliant strategist. What makes her so is that she watches and processes everything. She will know every move you make before you even think of it yourself. She is an Army sharpshooter and was headhunted to shoot for Great Britain in the Olympics, but turned it down. She is also an expert in hand-to-hand combat and can beat any of her male peers without breaking a sweat. She achieved her black belt in both Karate and Judo and got there in record-breaking time. She runs everywhere and her times for her Basic Fitness Test and Combat Fitness Test are off the chart. But that's not all. The really worrying part for you is that she is an expert in escape and evasion. Even *my* guys can't find her if she doesn't want to be found. That's the reason she is in my Unit. No other Unit knows what to do with her. Add all that together and mix with a previously unheard of dose of ruthlessness and you get a small glimpse of who, and what, you are dealing with."

Shona felt sick. "I know I don't know much about the SAS, but I thought I heard somewhere, that all the members of the team had to agree in order for someone to be transferred to the Unit. If that's the case then how did Laura Sands manage to get in?"

"Ordinarily that is the case but when the order to take her comes directly from the Chief of the Defence Staff then you are in no position to refuse. I, in turn, ordered my personnel to accept her and keep their mouths shut about the fact she was here. No one in the SAS would ever refuse an order. Except Major Sands it would seem. So the result is that she's here and, to be honest, on the whole she's been a real asset. All the men are in awe of her because she can beat them hands down at everything. A couple of the officers are a bit jealous but a sharp talking to from me has kept them quiet. It helps that she doesn't really want to mix with anyone and keeps herself to herself."

Taking all this in Shona said, "I know she would have access to guns, but what about taking them off camp?'

"Major Sands has a gun collection of her own. As I say she is an Army sharp shooter and there is no law against the military shooting in gun clubs. I've checked and there are no guns missing from camp. However, if she was planning this she could have got some on the black market. It's not unheard of."

Shona sighed and then a thought popped into her head. "As an officer would she have access to expensive wine in the Officer's Mess?"

The CO didn't seem phased by the abrupt change in direction. "Yes, we have an extensive cellar here. Is there a particular bottle you were thinking of? I could get my Mess Manager to look into it."

Shona checked her notebook for the name. A wine drinker she may be but not to the extent she could remember that particular wine. "A bottle of La Croix de Beaucaillou 2007 St. Julien has cropped up as possible evidence in the case. Could it be one of yours?"

"Give me a minute and I'll check," he said as he picked up the phone. After a few minutes he turned back to them "I can confirm that wine is sold in the mess. Also Laura Sands bought a bottle before she left to go on holiday. No one thought anything of it as good wine seems to be Major Sands only pleasure."

"It's beginning to look like your Major Sands is our killer," said Shona. "Have you got any idea where we could start looking for her or any tips on tracking her down."

"None whatsoever I'm afraid," the Colonel replied. "If Laura Sands doesn't want to be found then you're not going to find her. If I were to hazard a guess I'd say she's probably hiding in plain sight. That's what most of us would do. I would suggest searching in out of the way places such as abandoned buildings, countryside, woodland etc. You also need to have a word with the Military Police. They will obviously be interested in what's going on and will be keen to join forces with you to bring her in. You can't tell them she's SAS though. Even they don't know. As I said this particular experiment is extremely hush hush and if leaked would have heavy consequences for the Army."

"Have you got a recent photo of Major Sands?" Shona asked.

The CO had prepared for this question. He handed

her a colour photograph of a striking young woman with long auburn hair, which was tied up in a bun. "How tall is she?" asked Shona.

"Five foot ten inches."

Well at least she had a physical description, which would help. Shona looked at the photograph again and had the odd feeling she'd seen her somewhere before. She told herself not to be daft. This case was getting to her. She was imagining things.

Shona thanked the CO for his help and hospitality and then she and Peter went to find the waiting staff car, which would take them back to the airport.

Sitting in the car they had a chance to talk. Shona was confident that the SAS soldier driving them would not be blabbing their business about all over the place. "What are your thoughts Peter?"

"I'm glad I'm not married to her," Peter said. "Joking aside, though, she's not a woman to tangle with. Goodness knows how we'll catch her. My honest opinion is that we're stuffed and we should all hand our resignations in now."

Despite feeling glum and secretly agreeing with him Shona refused to give in to Peter's despondency.

"Does she look familiar to you?"

"Never seen her in my life before."

"I feel like I've seen her before. Maybe not." Silence fell, then, "There must be something in there we can use."

Batting ideas between them all the way back to the airport got them nowhere. They still had no clue as to how they were going to proceed. Their chances of catching the killer seemed to be receding with every passing minute. As they mounted the steps of the plane Shona said, "I wonder what we'll face back at the station. Despite the bad news, this has been a welcome break from the chaos."

Shoulders drooping, Peter trudged into the plane.

43

November 2012

As the last of the blood trickles from the woman's body I stare down at her dispassionately. Her body is covered with thousands of cuts, blood pooling around it like a puddle of dark red jelly. No fast flowing river for this one, just congealing blood, evidence of the unhurried torture she had endured. Over the four hours it took my mother to die, I had made sure that each slice of the knife had counted. Each cut was accompanied by a telling of something she had done to wound me. As I cut deep into her belly and eviscerated her I told her that this was payback for her ignoring my abuse. Any normal mother would have been up to the school complaining vociferously. Not this one. All I got was a further beating for ruining my clothes, or my schoolbag or anything else she could think to throw at me. The abuse would then carry on at the fists of her latest 'partner'. As I chopped each finger from her hands I made it clear that this was in payback for the abuse, rather than comfort, her hands had dealt out. Cruel, rather than gentle hands.

There was no mistaking what this was about. I expected to feel better once the woman was dead but this hasn't happened. I still felt nothing. My feelings had long turned to ice. Nothing seemed to be able to unfreeze them. Searching for a suitable finale, I carefully sharpen the blade of my knife. Then drawing back my hand I plunge the knife deep into the dead woman's chest and leave it there. I don't want to be associated with anything that has been inside this house. Changing my clothes and shoes I stash them in a plastic bag which I would toss later. On second thoughts, I will leave the bag here. No one will notice. The police would have to go through everything in this house. God help them. I even feel slightly sorry for them. Still, I decide not to discard the bag so close. I won't leave anything but the knife behind. They will never trace me by the knife. I had brought it back from my travels and it couldn't be traced. There would be nothing to incriminate me. Most people have probably long forgotten that this woman ever had a child. Apart from the police of course, who somehow have worked this out. With that thought I make my way back to my lair to make preparations for the next part of my plan. Everything is going smoothly. I am almost finished and I will soon be able to leave the garbage of my past behind. A bright, less painful, future beckons just beyond my immediate grasp.

44

Everyone was still in harness when they returned, and about to depart for another murder scene. Nina's grim face said it all. "Laura Sands' mother has been found dead – murdered, by the sound of things. The Council didn't manage to get round to her until 6 o'clock this evening. The chaps from the Council took one look at her and reported it to uniform. We were just about to go and clap eyes on it. Seemingly it's not a pretty sight."

"How could it be worse than the previous murders?" Her heart sank at the prospect.

"I would agree, but seemingly it is. The cop who called it in to us mentioned it specifically."

"God spare us. We'll all go to this one," she said. "The more minds focussing on this the better."

Grabbing coats, they all filed out the door.

The smell of blood, combined with the general decay, hit them as they entered the flat. The cop was right, it was even worse than before. Shona heaved. Mrs Sands was covered in so many cuts that her skin hung off her body in flaps. Congealed blood surrounded her body, which was crawling with flies. A seething mass covered her face rendering it unrecognisable. Their high-pitched buzz surrounded them and invaded the room adding to the general idea of squalor. Her fingers were discarded beside her hands. Embedded deep in her chest was a knife. The murder weapon Shona supposed. The killer is getting arrogant Shona thought. It felt like she were taunting them with her confidence.

Catching a glimpse of the PCs who had recently joined the team she barked, "Get your peelly wally faces outside now. I'll not have the contents of your stomach contaminating my crime scene. It smells bad enough in here already."

Nina said, "You're getting to be right Dundonian Ma'am. Peely wally. I love it."

Shona ignored her. As she listened to half the team part with their steak pie dinners outside, she thought, in fairness to them it wasn't the best place to see your first dead body. This would sort the men from the boys. Shona could have quite cheerfully joined them.

She scanned the scene, searching for any clues that might indicate the killer's current state of mind other than the state of the body. It was hard to tell if anything had been disturbed since their previous visit. This murder, in particular, looked like revenge. It also looked personal. Laura Sands was paying everyone back in full for all the slights, real or imagined, that she had experienced in her youth or childhood. Every cut on her mother's body would have corresponded, in Laura's mind at least, to some deep festering memory.

"I would like to imagine that Laura Sands is deranged but we all know that's not true. Every move is cold, calculated and executed according to some plan that makes sense only to her."

She was quiet for a second and then said, "Iain, what are your thoughts on the scene?"

Unusually for him Iain looked gloomy. "No disrespect, Ma'am, but are you having a laugh. What do I think? I'm thinking it looks like the four horsemen of the apocalypse have waged a war in here. It's going to take us weeks to sort this out."

"That was my thought exactly." They both stared at it for a few minutes, thinking deeply. Shona shook herself from her reverie and said, "You stay on it with Morag and one of the PCs. Give them explicit instructions as to what you want."

"No bother Ma'am. Consider it done. Could I not have a couple more people though?"

"You can keep the Angus PC and Burns but that's it. I need everyone concentrating on trying to find the ever-elusive Laura Sands. I'll see if uniform can give you anyone."

"OK Ma'am." He turned to the three PC's "Don't touch anything until I tell you to. We need to do everything systematically or we're lost."

"I'll send a van over for you to start bringing items to the nick. We'll use the forensics garage as it's the biggest space we've got. Has Jennifer Brown's car been moved out yet?"

"Thanks Ma'am. It's still there, but we've finished with it, so it could go outside. "

Leaving the crime scene in Iain's more than capable hands, they all returned to the station. As they gathered in the briefing room, Shona distributed copies of the photograph given to them by Colonel Forbes-Ratcliffe in Hereford.

"You're holding a current photo of Laura Sands. A couple of the Royal Military Police's best are on their way to join us. They're flying into Leuchars and the RAF's blue lighting them here. Should be with us in about an hour. Use them wisely. Seemingly they're a crack team with a lot of experience. They should be a real asset."

Shona related what she and Peter had learned in Hereford, leaving out the SAS connection. There was stunned silence. Even Roy didn't have a stupid remark.

"Knowing what we do about her, it is likely that Laura is hiding out in woodland or an abandoned building."

A collective gloom descended.

Roy beat the others to it by a nanosecond. "How on earth are we supposed to find her Ma'am? Even if we do, how are we supposed to catch her if she's some sort of modern day Amazonian?" Dundee was a small city but it was surrounded on most sides by woods and open countryside. Abandoned buildings were a bit less of a problem given that most of them were current building sites. There was too much activity there to stay hidden for long.

Before Shona could reply Peter said, "Aye, you're right lad but there's one thing we need to bear in mind. Laura Sands is possibly doing everything on foot as she doesn't appear to have any transport, which means she can't be living too far outside the City limits. Naebody's mentioned a car unless she hired one, and that would be difficult if she disnae exist."

"Peter, speak English."

"If she's got a car then she's been wiped from DVLA's records. She's not showing up there. I looked," said Roy.

"How did you...? Never mind, I don't want to know. Peter you're a genius. You should be doing the Chief Inspector's job. You've hit the nail on the head. Let's stop thinking that this is an impossible task and focus our thoughts on, what we already know, and what we can do. I've a load of maps here," she said pointing to the table. "Split into pairs, take one and identify possible areas where she could be hiding. If we know that then we have somewhere to start our search."

She walked to the door and then tuned round adding, "Jason. You must have had some escape and evasion training in the TA's?"

"I've done the basic course Ma'am. Did it in the Brecon Beacons. Other than that my time serving was in Afghanistan which is a far cry from the highways and byways of Dundee."

"That may be, however, from what I've heard the Brecon Beacons are pretty much like Scotland just less inhabited and a lot more sheep. You take charge as you've got the most expertise."

Shona went to see the Chief. She knocked and entered without waiting for his usual permission. The Chief looked irritated. What do you want now Shona?" he snapped. "What's happened?"

"Laura Sands has killed her mother in a seriously brutal way. It looks like she's escalating," Shona said with a determined edge to her voice. "She's on a one woman revenge spree. We need to catch her pronto. I require every spare man or woman on this until we do. If we don't there will be further blood on our hands."

"Stop being so dramatic. You sound like something out of a Shakespeare play. *You* might want every man in the Scottish Police to be reassigned to your investigation but it doesn't work like that." The Chief was stony.

"I'm sorry Sir, I'm just a bit harried. Let me explain." She filled him in on what they had learnt in Hereford. "So, as you can see, Sir, once we manage to narrow it down to a number of areas, where she might be hiding, we need the manpower to carry out the search. If we don't catch her it's more than likely she will go on killing."

"You make a good case Shona, but that doesn't change the fact that we simply don't have enough officers to go around. Go back to the team and narrow it down to a couple of areas we might cover. In the meantime I'll see what I can do."

Having achieved the best that she could hope for Shona thanked him and returned to the briefing room.

Everyone was deep in conversation whilst poring over the maps. Looking at the areas they had identified, Shona's heart sank. There were more than they could ever hope to cover. "Good work guys but unless the Chief pulls a rabbit out of the hat in the shape of extra officers then we need to narrow it down further."

There was a knock on the door and the Duty Sergeant entered with the two recently arrived Military Police Sergeants. After introductions were made, Shona took them back to her office to brief them over coffee and biscuits. "I'm glad to see that the civvy police are as partial to biscuits as we are," one of the MP's said, smiling. Shona laughed and said, "If there were a biscuit or cake shortage, then all the police forces in Scotland would grind to a halt. We can't work without them. Now, to more serious matters." She gave them a brief outline of the case so far. There was a heartbeat of silence and then one of them said "Blimey! This Officer sounds like a one woman war machine. How on earth has she managed to continue in the Services? Anyone, be they Junior Rank or Officer, who carried on like that would usually have been up before us and booted out long ago."

Shona said only, "They must think she's worth hanging on to or I'm sure she would be gone."

Sending the MPs to join the others, she returned to the Chief's office to see if he'd managed to come up with the goods in the way of manpower.

"I've managed to get you fifty extra coppers for a few days and then that's it. You have three days or you need to pull back as this case is going nowhere. I've told them to be here at 8 am. It's far too late to start any effective search tonight."

No pressure then, Shona thought, but said, "Thank you Sir. That will make a big difference."

She returned to the briefing room, to find the team

had written a list of place names on the whiteboard.

"We're going to brainstorm likely hiding places," said Peter.

Shona nodded her agreement. One by one they listed the pros and cons of each area. Some, such as the Sidlaw hills, were a bit far out. They were in agreement that it was unlikely she would be there unless she'd suddenly decided to join the same cult as the young students. There was a heated debate on whether she could be camping out on the Law hill. One side argued that every inch of the area had been searched after the first murder. The other side, that it would be the perfect place to hide out once the cops had left.

Nina finally said, "I think it's a bit too public to hide out for long," and the others agreed. It was deleted from the list.

Their final list consisted of Templeton Woods, Camperdown Park, the woodland just behind Ballumbie, Blackmuir Woods, and St Port Wood in Tayport. Camperdown Park was a bit of an outside chance as it was a really public park but it covered several acres and had a number of very out of the way places.

The team had also noted down a few disused and somewhat derelict factories that might bear looking at.

"Peter, you know Dundee better than the rest of us put together. Are there any factories in particular you think we should search?"

"He probably saw them all being built at his advanced age," quipped Roy.

Through gales of nervous laughter Peter said, "Cheeky beggar. Keep your smart remarks to yourself. Pitalpin works is the only one I can think of. It's abandoned, and tucked out of the way. It would make a great hiding place for someone like our suspect. There are no' many people around there."

"Let's go. We'll search there tonight. There should be enough of us for an effective search without uniform being involved. We don't want to make a grand entrance anyway. Softly, softly is better in my experience. Grab torches and sign out guns. Stab vests as well."

"Did you know stab vests were invented by women," said Peter.

"Peter, you're a fount of all knowledge. I'm sure we'd love to listen to your useful facts but another time might be better. Grief man. We're hunting a killer here."

The graffiti covered, stone building was a sad monument to days long gone, a dislocated skeleton of its former Victorian grandeur. Split into two teams, they moved up the dark, narrow lanes, which bordered the building. Hugging the walls they moved with stealth. Blackness enveloped them. No street lights here. A forsaken area of dereliction, left to the ravages of time. No one left to care. Even the poor would not come here. Smashed windows, rising as high as the attic, provided a perfect vantage point for anyone waiting above them. The eyes of each team member moved, scanning the area under their feet, up above, and all around. Shona could almost smell the pent up nervousness, tinged with determination. It radiated from every pore.

The doors of the building had long been boarded up, all but one, where torn away boards had been left to rot.

Shona whispered, "The wood looks too rotten to have been wrenched off recently."

Nina agreed. "That doesn't mean our killer hasn't taken advantage of the work done by local kids." Shona pushed the remainder of the wood, which fell away with a dull thump. They froze, listening. Was that a sound? Shona strained her ears. Hearing nothing further, she motioned them on, and in, with her torch.

In a low voice Shona said, "Jason, you stay and guard the entrance. This seems to be the only way out. You've a gun. Use it if you need to."

"OK."

The torchlight illuminated a rubble and glass strewn floor. Discarded crisp bags and papers from the chippy down the road indicated some level of occupation. Was it recent?

They moved forward making the minimum of noise. A muffled expletive from one of the team, "Ssh," said Shona, her voice low.

"I twisted my ankle a bit." Iain's voice was equally low.

"Shut up or get out."

They moved forward. At each tiny crunch of broken glass they stopped and listened. Were they stirring their suspect or was she lying in wait for the perfect time to shoot?

Peter's voice rang out from higher up on the other side of the building. "Stop right there. Don't move." Shona hurried towards the sound as fast as safety would allow, Nina, and Iain close behind her.

A dirty young man cowered in the corner illuminated by the light from Peter's torch.

"I hivnae done anything. I came in here to get out of the rain. I've no place to sleep."

Not Laura, but one of the city's rough sleepers.

"What's your name?"

"Stuart Donaldson. Please, I swear I've no' done nothing."

"Ye can't sleep in here. It's not safe. Get yourself down to the sally bash. They'll find you a bed."

The man scurried off. He was probably relieved

that he wasn't being arrested. Shona thought for a minute. If he had been arrested he would at least have a dry bed and some food.

"Iain. Take one of the cars and make sure the Salvation Army have a bed for him. If they don't, bring him back to the station and we'll put him in a cell overnight. Charge him with trespass." She turned to the others. "If Laura Sands was here she'll be long gone now. We'll search and see if there's any sign of habitation." There was none.

Returning to the station they met Iain minus his charge. "I left him wrapping his molars around a huge plate of sausage and mash and eyeing up a large slice of apple pie. He'll be all right for tonight at least."

"Thanks Iain.' It's too late to do any effective searching of woodland so you're free for the day once you've checked in the guns. I want you here at 0700 so I can have a word with you before the others arrive."

"I'm off for a pint. Anyone want to join me?" asked Roy. Most of the youngsters said they would go for one but Shona and Peter declined.

"I don't know where they get their energy from," Peter said.

"Me neither. See you bright and early tomorrow. Although bright isn't exactly the way we'll be describing that lot after a night down the pub."

Back at her flat Shona found a very discontented Shakespeare. Her frantic meowing left Shona in no doubt that she and the kittens had been left alone all day, starving and what was she going to do about it.

"You're a fraud Shakespeare. I know for a fact that Mrs Gordon has been making a fuss of you all day." Never the less she topped up the food and water bowls. There was enough strife in her life without upsetting a family of cats. "Now keep it quiet Shakespeare, the kittens and I want a decent night's kip." Shakespeare's meow seemed to say, me too, you think you're exhausted .Try looking after my lot.

A heaven sent aroma led Shona to a slow cooker full of chicken casserole, thick with steaming pieces of chicken and huge chunks of warming potato and vegetable. A note accompanied it. "I knew you would be tired and would enjoy this. Ida Gordon." Shona thought she might nominate her neighbour for sainthood. After crawling around in a freezing, damp, factory she was ready for something hot. Later, replete, she fell into bed and an exhausted sleep.

45

April 2012

Despite no one knowing what to do with me, my Army career has been meteoric. I'm the best at every single aspect of my job, which, as I find everything so easy, isn't that surprising. No one has as much experience as me at observing for, and dealing with, potential conflict.

I know unerringly whether to engage or avoid. My soldiers trust me because I'm so smart, although they are also wary. My fellow officers work with me, using my knowledge and experience, but otherwise they keep right out of my way. That's how I prefer it. Not for me all the false camaraderie and bonhomie that goes on in Her Majesty's Forces. This aspect of army life makes me want to be physically sick. All the other officers are a bunch of idiots who are only interested in having a good time. Unless they're on an operational tour of course when it's all serious and missing their loved ones. Hypocrites to a man, as most of them are having affairs with each other.

Despite this I'm exalting in every minute of my tour in Afghanistan. This is what being in the Army is all about and what I am meant to be doing. It is almost as if I had been born to this life. In a Landrover with several of my men, no one is talking. Each one is focussed on the mission ahead. Our task is to go into a local village, and intercept and bring back, a member of the Taliban who is believed to be in hiding there. The American Special Forces are going in from the other side. Communication between us has to be kept to a minimum. We leave the Landrover hidden on the edge of the village and silently make our way on foot. There isn't a soul around. This makes me somewhat uneasy, as I am positive the Taliban must have lookouts. How did we manage to get this far without being attacked? I scan the roofs and windows, but nothing. Still my gut tells me that something isn't right. My brain rapidly goes over every permutation of what could be making me feel this way. The place should be crawling with Taliban so where are they? Is there a landmine or two waiting for us?

Highly trained, we merge into the background, hugging buildings, and moving with caution, until we reach the target building where the Taliban leader is supposedly hiding. It appears to be a school, but if the Taliban are there then the teachers and children must be long gone. Probably gone from the village as well, if the silence is anything to go by. I give a moment's thought as to whether the building could be rigged with bombs, and then dismiss the thought. We need to go in. I give the signal and, as one, we kick open the doors and throw in smoke bombs. Guns blazing we storm the building to get to the target. A beautifully executed manoeuvre. However, it is then I realise how wrong I have been. The villagers haven't gone. There must be a hundred children and adults crammed into the school. The whole village seems to be here. Despite this I give the order to continue. My men's eyes widen in shock but, nevertheless they carry on. Trained to obey, they will never willingly disobey an order given by someone senior to them. We have to continue. This is too important. We have to bring back our target. I am employing the rule of the greatest good for the greatest number. What are a few civilians when considering the greater good of peace in Afghanistan, and a halt in the chain of terrorism in the West?

By the time we have finished everyone in the building is dead. There are also casualties in my team. The medic deals with the wounded and we gently place them in the back of the Rover along with their dead colleagues. Slinging the dead body of our target in beside them I order the driver to take us back to base. It is then I know for certain what I suspected all along. Life is cheap and only the mission matters. Nothing else. Even the dead members of my team are merely collateral damage. Despite the wounded and dead, I thrill at a job well done. Death is merely a means to an end, nothing more.

46

Up at 5 a.m. Shona decided to forego her usual run, as she would be on her feet all day during the search. She needed to save her energy for survival in this weather. With temperatures below zero it was baltic out there. What had possessed her to leave the relatively balmy south of England? She wondered if it was too late to get a transfer back. Right about now would be good.

Arriving at work by 6 a.m. she set out a plan for the search. It needed to be tight, with all the t's crossed and i's dotted, before the others arrived. All those extra officers were a gift straight from heaven, but both they, and the search, needed to be carefully managed. Drawing up a set of watertight parameters, she was certain they would all be hurtling down the same path. Not literally of course. Too many Bobbies, with big feet, crashing around in the undergrowth, meant less chance of finding this woman. To be honest she found herself in a bit of a dilemma. On the one hand they needed to get the area searched quickly. On the other too many personnel in the area would alert Laura Sands that they were on to her and on their way. She would disappear before they could find her. Net result – more murders.

She glanced down at the front page of the *Courier* she had bought on her way to work.

Dundee Murders: What are the police doing? ask the public.

Following several more deaths in the City of Dundee the general public are, quite rightly, worried. Many, but especially young women are terrified that they are going to be next. However, what worries them most is that the police are floundering. It would seem they are no closer to solving the murders than they were a week ago. Yet they are still doing nothing to protect the public. The Courier has spoken to a number of women over the past couple of days, all of whom have the same questions. Why have the police not solved these murders? Why are the police not doing more to protect us from this monster stalking our streets? The Courier agrees that these questions need to be asked, as there appear to be fewer police on the streets rather than more. As the body count continues to rise, the Courier suggests, citizens need to know that the police are going to act. They need reassurance they can go about their normal lives free from fear that they could be killed at any time. When questioned, a police spokesman said "We are doing everything in our power to catch this killer. Extra personnel have been drafted in and we believe we are close to a completion of this case. The public will, of course, be informed immediately the killer is caught."

The Courier would suggest that this is not good enough. The police are obviously not doing everything in their power, or this evil monster would be safely behind bars. The public are suggesting that extra police be brought in from other forces to help with the search and, the Courier would have to agree, that this would be a sensible answer to the problem. Yet this has not been done. If there are any more deaths then Tayside Police will have blood on their hands.

The article went on in the same vein for several more paragraphs. Basically, the police are a bunch of numpties and couldn't solve a crime, even if the killer stood on their doorstep, with a bloody knife in his hand, confessing guilt. Shona, never a great lover of the local press, was even more irritated by this latest attack on the force. What did the flaming public expect? How in heaven's name were the police meant to look for a murderer and put more police on the streets at the same time? Trained police officers didn't grow on trees. Of course it would be a great idea to deplete the entire expanse of the Scottish Police and divert them all to Dundee. That would do a lot for crime everywhere else. She lobbed the rag at the wastepaper basket. It would be more productive to concentrate on catching Laura Sands than reading this rubbish.

By the time everyone arrived, she had everything organised. They all squeezed into the largest incident room they had.

"You'll be split into teams, each headed up by one of the officers from CID. Go and get some food from the canteen and you can eat whilst I brief you."

They all needed some decent food inside them if they were to search freezing temperatures. As everyone returned, bacon rolls in hand, the desk Sergeant showed up. "Auld Jock's here to speak to you."

"Oh For goodness sake man, can't you see I'm busy? I've better things to do today than have cosy chats with the City's homeless."

The Sergeant was terse. "I realize, that, Ma'am, but he says he has important information about the case."

"How on earth could an old tramp have information which could help us catch a serial killer?" asked an incredulous Shona. "Why don't we just let every stray soul in the city join us in our job. I suppose I'd better come and see him but this had better be quick."

Her mood deteriorating, she went to find Jock who was ensconced in an interview room, with a couple of rolls, a plate of cakes, and a mug of steaming tea. Shona fumed and muttered under her breath, "I've flaming well got better things to do with my time than take tea and stickies with the station's resident tramp." Entering the room, she made herself speak quietly. "Hi Jock, I believe you have information for us. I don't mean to be rude, but I need to get out on a search, so could you keep to the point and make it quick please."

"Aye lassie I know. You know I used to be in the Army?" Shona nodded, wondering where this was going, but forced herself to be patient. "Well, I've been up in Camperdown Park the past couple of days as I've got places I can shelter there. There's a couple o' bra outhouses that belonged to the old farm. They're no' used now."

"Is this going somewhere Jock? I'm in a hurry."

"Aye. Sorry. Someone's set up a bivvy shelter right up against the wall right next to the Muirhead road. It looks like it's been there a while and it's barely noticeable. I wouldn't have found it myself but I've done my time kipping out and hiding my whereabouts. It's a perfect spot. Not too far away from the paths but far enough out of the way that no one goes up there. It might be nothing, but I thought I would let you know. You've been kind to me so I wanted to help if I could."

"Jock I could kiss you. In fact I will." She carried out the deed to the amazement of a now red-faced Jock. "I've got to go, but sit there for a while. I'll get them to keep up an endless supply of tea and cakes. Then a squad car will take you up to the Friary for their free lunch. We might as well treat you."

Jock was beaming like a toddler with an ice cream. "Thanks lassie. I appreciate it. It's a bit cold even for me out there. It would be good to sit in the warm for a while and, you know me, I'll never turn down the offer of a cake."

Feeling decidedly more optimistic and cheerful, Shona went, to order the requisite tea and cakes and, to tell the waiting search teams about Jock's discovery. The mood lightened almost immediately as chatter broke out.

"Who'd have thought Auld Jock wid come in useful? There's always something comes along to amaze me every day," said Peter, at her side.

"Listen up," shouted Shona. "That wasn't an excuse for everyone to take their attention off the task in hand. The bivvy might not belong to Laura Sands but it does give us somewhere to start. The woman we are looking for is no ordinary woman," and she went on to tell them what, or rather who, they were up against.

"Sounds just like my missus. Can you arrest her?" one of the uniforms shouted out, to the instant sound of laughter.

Shona grinned. "Much as we'd love to arrest your wife we might need to leave it until we've caught Laura Sands. Now remember, Major Sands is extremely dangerous. She has a gun, possibly several, and will not hesitate to kill anyone who gets in her way. We will all be armed, so go and get guns and ammo, and meet me out back for transport to Camperdown. I've got a list of teams here so could the Team Leaders gather their officers together. There will be another briefing on the bus."

Shona may have sounded confident but in reality she was far from it. Camperdown Park was an extremely popular area and a large number of people used it daily. She only hoped that the weather would keep most people away and it would be fairly empty. She didn't want to be responsible for putting members of the public at risk. Imagine the backlash if some innocent bystander was killed with nearly 100 members of the police in the park at the time. The papers would have a field day and whip the fine upstanding citizens of Dundee into a frenzy of hatred against the force. Never mind that they were trying to protect said upstanding citizens. Things were bad enough already without adding fuel to the fire.

On the coach to the park the tension was palpable. Each officer was given a picture of the subject and a specific area of the park to search. She didn't want the plods shooting each other in the pursuit. Friendly fire wasn't taken lightly in the force, for good reason.

"I know several of you may be thinking it's a waste of time searching the whole park when we know vaguely where the bivvy might be. But we're leaving nothing to chance here. This woman is cleverer than we could ever imagine and that camp could be an old one or even a decoy. Do not underestimate her intelligence and cunning. Stay alert and keep your eyes and ears sharp. Most of all look out for yourself and the others in your team. Make sure you've got each other's backs covered?"

"If necessary can we shoot to kill?"

"Were you not listening at the briefing? I said shoot to warn or disable, but if necessary, and only if necessary, then shoot to kill. I'm sure the Army wouldn't take kindly to us killing one of their officers no matter how unstable she may be. Into teams and go."

A stream of officers poured off the bus and headed quietly into the park through a barely used gate. Fortunately, Camperdown, originally the estate of the

Viscount of Camperdown, has many out of the way entrances. They needed every advantage they could get.

47

November 2012

Despite the freezing day I'm feeling quite snug inside my sleeping bag, hidden away from prying eyes by the almost invisible bivvy I have built. I'm confident no one can find this place amongst the trees. If the Taliban couldn't find me then these idiots, employed by Tayside Police, will never manage. I smile to myself at the thought of them all running around in circles, not knowing which way to turn to end this chase. They will never work out who is carrying out these murders because, as far as the world is concerned, I don't exist. If I don't exist, then how can I be on a killing spree, and how can the police track me down? Yes they've spoken to my mother, but they've spoken to everyone from the school. None of them, including my mother, knows where I am. Therefore, the fact that they have spoken with my mother is of no consequence. She won't be telling them anything now anyway.

Could it be that my confidence is entirely misplaced? That is not something I am used to.

This is the last day of my plan and then I will be gone, back to the protection of my unit, back to killing officially. Still, despite the fact I am on leave, I am only doing what I have been trained to do. The world is better off without every one of the dead women and one hateful man and. like any good soldier, I am just making sure the world is a safer and better place. The last, and most exciting, part of my plan will happen later today. It will be like pouring boiling water down an anthill and watching them scurry. This is my grand finale. A deed such as no one in this miserable, God forsaken city will be able to ignore. Everyone will see immediately how terrifying I can be. Until then, I can lie here snug and warm, taking a well earned rest, and go over every move of the deed which lies ahead. I play it out on the stage of my mind. My thoughts then turn to what I have already accomplished. A sense of achievement and excitement bubbles up inside me. No one has ever been so successful in executing a plan. I am the master, no longer the downtrodden underclass. No one will ever conquer me.

My reverie is interrupted. My ears, trained through the years to take note of anything out of the ordinary, hear a sound. There are people moving through the crisp leaves littering the ground. The sound is distant, nowhere near me. It doesn't sound like a casual walker but a systematic search. For an instant I feel numb. What is going on? Immediately I make myself calm down. I focus on my breathing whilst still listening. I relax my muscles but I am coiled, like a snake, ready to strike. They could be looking for anything such as a child who has gone missing. With my breathing now calm I make silent preparations to leave. I know deep down in my soul that they are on the hunt for me.

48

November 2012

Shona had Roy and three of the uniforms in her team. Moving stealthily, looking and listening with every step, they covered the ground inch by cautious inch. The only sound was that of birdsong and the occasional crunch of feet on frost. The crackling frost was an added worry, alerting anyone to their movements. Every few steps they stood and listened. Anything out of the ordinary was noted and communicated without sound – hand and eye signals and jotted notes would suffice. All five were ready to pull their gun and kill if necessary. This was not a suspect to mess with and hesitation could mean death.

Shona, outwardly calm, felt her heart hammering in her chest. She stopped, took a couple of deep breaths and steadied her heartbeat. This was no time to be running scared. It was her chance to catch Laura Sands and to put a stop to the blood running in Dundee's streets. The others stopped too as they gathered themselves and took stock of what was around them. Frozen trees painted an eerie backdrop to their chase. Undergrowth, crisp with frost, was treacherous underfoot.

The clock slowly ticking down through the seconds, they moved forward in agreed formation, acting as one. Inch by measured inch, they crept across the rotting, leaf covered, terrain. Tension whipped between them, an almost physical presence. When Roy signalled he had heard something, they stopped, looking around intently. When they realised it was just a plastic bag, flapping in the branches of a tree, there was a collective, slow, exhalation of breath. Shona smiled to reassure them and signalled them on. Jittery to a man, they jumped at the piercing shriek of a cawing crow. Nerve ends tingled as they moved over the frozen ground.

Roy was enjoying every minute of the chase. This was why he had joined the CID. To catch the bad guys, and get them off the streets. Never in his wildest dreams did he think it would be an insane woman he would be chasing. After three years in the police he knew women could be worse than men but this one makes Freddie Kreuger look like someone you'd trust your baby with. One thing he wasn't enjoying was the cold. He couldn't feel his fingers and toes, and was increasingly convinced he would lose them all to frostbite. Every step was agony as he put one foot in front of the other. Despite everything, he was not going to give up. Not in front of the Detective Inspector. He knew she didn't think much of him. This was his chance to prove himself to her.

Shona signaled the group to stop. Her voice low she said, "Eat some protein bars." They needed calories to carry on in this limb-numbing cold. They opened the packages carefully, not giving their presence away by the crackling of paper. All her senses on high alert, Shona could hear the soft wind soughing through the trees amidst the creak of waving boughs. There was nothing out of the ordinary. She wondered how much of the park they had actually covered. Not much she estimated. This seemed no more than a tense wild goose chase that could go on all day.

They moved forward again making little sound. A fox darted out of the trees. Shona fought back a scream as it passed, inches from her feet. Roy banged in to her back as she stopped abruptly.

She jumped, whipped round quietly and said, "Roy?"

"Sorry Ma'am."

"Don't worry. Just watch where you're going."

Shona stood even more still, the others frozen behind her, listening intently. Her heart was doing a staccato beat in her chest. Something was out of place. A slight crunch as though there was footfall on the frosty ground. She signalled everyone to hold his or her position, and waited. Roy pointed to someone in the distance. Shona peered ahead and realised it was an unsuspecting member of the public doing nothing more sinister than walking her dog. Shona willed her to hurry up and leave. They were too far away to warn her. The drumbeat in Shona's chest grew stronger and faster. She held her breath. That was all she needed, the search turning into a hostage situation. There would be no reasoning with Laura Sands, and she would kill anyone in her way.

They watched, wondering what to do next. Shona's eyes took in everything as she listened for any abnormal sounds. What would be the best course of action to keep this woman safe? The dog walker made the decision for them. She threw a ball and moved in the direction of the car park. Shona offered up a prayer of thanks. Some higher authority must be looking out for them.

Collecting themselves, they moved at Shona's signal. Every Officer knew that this was their one and only chance to catch the killer and didn't want to be the one who let her get away. This focused their minds, hearts, and souls on the chase. There was no room for extraneous thoughts.

Shona saw another figure in the distance. This time every nerve in her body told her that they had found

Laura Sands. Thoughts flew through her head as she decided what move to make. She signaled for the others to stay where they were and she would move forward. They were to cover her from behind. She moved quickly, and as quietly as the rough ground would allow, intent on catching the killer unawares.

Suddenly Laura Sands started running. Shona realised that the Major knew she was being chased. It was then she realised how she knew this woman. She was the runner she had passed on her way to work one morning. She had been so close to their killer and hadn't known. Snatching her gun from its holster, but keeping it pointing downwards and forwards, Shona set off in hot pursuit. She didn't need an accidental discharge, or to literally shoot herself in the foot. With the speed this woman could get, even through frosty terrain, Shona would have to use every single bit of effort she had to keep up with, never mind catch her. The two women matched each other for speed, as branches caught at clothes and they stumbled on foliage and roots. However, Laura's larger pace covered the ground more effectively. Shona, vaguely aware of other sounds in the background, was too intent on the chase to work out what they were. Shona forced herself to focus.

"Stop. Police," she shouted.

When Laura didn't stop she fired a shot. It missed its mark completely. It was more of a warning shot, into the air - even the best of shooters couldn't fire and run at the same time. That only happened in bad movies or British soap operas. However, Laura Sands did not stop. Why would she? She had probably faced much worse than this in the Army. A small city copper, waving a tiddly little pistol, wasn't going to faze her.

Suddenly, Laura disappeared. Shona was puzzled but continued to move forward, fast but with caution, her senses alert to everything around her. Stopping to breathe she heard the nearby snap of a twig. She turned. It was then she found herself staring down the barrel of that Browning pistol.

In that moment it seemed as if everything stopped, even the birdsong. Shona held her breath and then let it out slowly. Fear tingled down every nerve ending. She wondered why she was not already dead? In the stillness the only movement was their breath, which curled up into the icy air. This should not be happening in this place, on this day. These woods were a place of refuge from the nearby city. People came here to enjoy both beauty and peace. Not today. The beauty of the area belied the current macabre dance being played out beneath its branches. Standing underneath the ancient trees clothed in their glittering winter splendour, Shona sensed nothing but evil. It was a cold, malign presence, mocking her dreams and freezing the life breath in her lungs, surrounding her as though seeped into the very cold itself. In this snapshot in time beauty and evil existed in perfect balance, with evil a hair trigger from winning.

As the seconds ticked by, Laura eventually spoke, in a measured tone, totally devoid of any feeling. Matching the icy air around them in icy coldness.

"I take it you're the Detective Inspector they mentioned in the paper?"

Shona responded, "Yes. Detective Inspector McKenzie." This conversation was bizarre. She was, more than likely, about to die and here she was exchanging pleasantries with a trained killer, as though they were at a cocktail party. Her last words on this earth were going to be something incredibly stupid. They wouldn't make the best of epitaphs.

"I have to say you must have more brains than I gave you credit for. I didn't think you'd ever find me.

That's as far as it goes though because we both know this is the end of the road, and you are not going to be taking me in."

Shona, wondering how she could remain so calm, given the circumstances, said, "If it's the end of the road then you've nothing to lose. So tell me. Why have you done all this? After leaving everything behind and doing so well in your career why kill all these people?"

A look of evil, so pure it almost froze the blood in Shona's veins, flashed across Laura's face. She spat out, "People? They weren't people. They were inhuman. Each one of them made my life a living hell. They stole my childhood and took every ounce of self-respect away from me. They deserved to die. The world is better off without them. I'm a soldier and that's what soldiers do. We rid the world of evil."

Shona was looking into the eyes of the devil himself.

A shot rang out. As Shona contemplated meeting her maker, Laura suddenly grabbed her shoulder and dropped her gun. As Shona kicked it out of the way she felt a sudden pain in her abdomen. It took her breath away. The karate kick that Laura had delivered dropped her to her knees but she managed to raise her gun. "Freeze." That didn't last long as another kick from Laura knocked it from Shona's hand. Crying from the pain, Shona heard another shot which missed its target. Roy appeared from the trees with his three colleagues from Uniform in hot pursuit. By this time Laura had picked up both guns and, despite her injuries, was running again. Shona thought, does this woman not feel any pain?

The team stopped to help Shona. "Never mind about me you fools. Catch the suspect," she managed to gasp out before vomiting. Roy hesitated and then, leaving one of the PC's to protect Shona, ordered the other ones on. How on earth had Roy managed to step up to the plate so well, Shona wondered? Suddenly he was in charge.

Roy had no idea where Laura might have gone. Instinct told him she would keep to the cover of the trees. The time for caution past, they all ran at breakneck speed, propelled by fear and adrenaline. But which way had she gone? By Roy's count Laura had two guns and ten bullets. She could do a lot of damage with that before they could catch her. If they caught her.

Laura ran through the woods as though the hounds of hell were snarling at her heels. She could feel a dull pain in her shoulder, where the bullet had entered, but it didn't slow her down. She knew she could outrun these slow-witted goons, even with a gunshot wound. Her whole life she had been in training for this. She could run further and faster than anyone and she would not be caught.

She felt a sharp pain in her thigh and fell to the ground. Looking at her leg, she was incredulous. She'd been shot. How could that have happened? There was no one within pistol range. They couldn't have anything more lethal than a pistol here. It was too public.

Out of the corner of her eye she could see an officer approaching. Keeping him in sight she let off a shot the minute he came close enough. Using her left arm, the shot was slightly wide of the mark but it still managed to wing him. He cried out and dropped his gun.

Suddenly officers surrounded her. "Police! Put down your gun."

She threw down the gun. Lying still until one of officers approached, she pulled out the other pistol and shot him, and three of his colleagues, before any of them could respond.

As the officers lay bleeding around her she turned the gun on herself. "What the f...?" She felt a sharp pain in her arm. The gun fell.

Peter ran over and kicked the gun out of her way. Then he and a number of other officers unceremoniously jumped on her, cuffing her hands and feet. This was no easy feat. Despite her injuries Major Sands did not give up without a struggle.

"You bitch." Nina grabbed her head as Laura kicked her.

"Keep still or you'll find my knee landing just where your wound is," Peter said.

In reply she spat in his face. Then screamed.

"Sorry. You're moving that much I didn't know where I was putting my knee."

"That's classed as police brutality. You can't do that to me. You are a dead man."

"It was an accident. I've several officers who will back me up in that. Hold still and it'll not happen again."

"Do you think it was an accident?" he spoke to Nina.

Nina agreed. "Yep, she was struggling and you slipped. It was unfortunate you fell just where her wound is."

Laura stared at them coldly. A look so evil it could freeze liquid gold.

Shona staggered up holding her arm, her face so white it blended in with the frosty surroundings. Looking at the injured officers, all of whom were being given first aid by their colleagues, she asked, "What happened? How did you catch her?"

Peter looked bewildered. "I don't know, Ma'am. A shot seemed to come from nowhere and she dropped. It wasn't us that's for sure. Sounded like a rifle shot".

"Oh for goodness sake, here we go again with the rifles. This case seems to be awash with bally rifles. I'm not in the mood for this Peter. Find out what happened and make it quick."

Turning from Peter, she barked out "Someone phone an ambulance. These guys need medical attention, and," indicating Laura Sands, she said, "much as I'd love to leave this basket case to bleed to death, the powers that be would take a dim view of that so we'd better get her seen too."

"Already done Ma'am. There's several on the way," Morag replied.

"Make sure the officers are seen to first. I'm sure they're the most seriously injured. Our prisoner…"

She could see Laura Sands mouth opening. Before she could protest Shona said, "Laura Sands I am placing you under arrest for the murders of Megan Mackie, Jennifer Brown, Amanda Carter, Stuart McKay, Lizzie Struach, Pauline Smith, your mother Miss Lena Sands, Marian MacIntyre and unborn baby MacIntyre. Now, as I was saying, our prisoner looks like the least injured of the troop so she can wait till last for help and assistance from the medics."

Just then PC Roberts strolled up jauntily swinging a rifle. "What the …?" Shona was lost for words.

"What in heaven's name are you doing with a rifle? Was it you who shot her?"

Jason's grin was wide. "Yes Ma'am. It was luck really. I got up on the wall to see if I could catch a glimpse of her. I had my rifle ready just in case and she happened to run past. I was a sniper in the Army".

"Well I'm glad you got her but where the…" She caught herself, "Where did that blasted rifle come from? I gave orders to issue pistols."

"Ma'am the person who issues weapons is a pal of

mine. We were in the TA together for a couple of months. He knows I'm good with a rifle and gave me one. It's not his fault Ma'am. I take full responsibility"

"You'll *both* have to answer questions," Shona said wearily. "I'll deal with you later. How did you get a rifle past me on the bus?"

Jason opened his mouth to speak, "I..."

"Never mind. On second thoughts I don't want to know. I'm telling you now, you are never getting near a gun again as long as I'm in charge of CID."

She looked around for a second and then said, "Roy."

"Yes, Ma'am."

"You're in charge of getting everyone back to the station. That is, the ones who aren't going to be in Ninewells getting treatment."

"No bother Ma'am. I'll sort it out."

"Ok. You've surprised me today. Good job."

She could see Roy's chest swelling and he seemed to stand taller. His face flushed. She must compliment him more often.

The ambulances arrived. "I'm riding in the one with the prisoner. I don't want her going all Houdini on us."

"You're in no fit state, Ma'am. You get fixed up. Nina and I are on it. We'll see you at Ninewells." said Peter. Shona, remonstrated with them for a minute, then, in too much pain to argue, gave in gratefully.

49

Later, once the A&E department had finished with her, Shona went to look in on Laura Sands. She was handcuffed to a trolley with both hands despite the wounds in her arms. She must be in agony. Shona hoped so. She was long past the stage of sympathy, her own wrist being plastered and in a sling. Several officers were under the Surgeon's knife as she spoke. Thank goodness none of them had died. Peter had already interviewed the murderer and she had made a full confession. Only God, or the devil, would know why she had suddenly decided to spill her guts. It seemed they were right. It was revenge. Some revenge spree this turned out to be. Despite everything Laura sounded upbeat and almost cheerful. It was probably the effect of the pain medication.

The two MPs were guarding Laura. "Hi. I need to have a word with her."

"Of course Ma'am …"

A nurse interrupted. "You can't come in here and bother her. She needs to go to theatre."

"And I need to speak to her and get some answers. It will go much more quickly if you leave me to it. Then you can give her all the medical treatment she deserves." Which was none as far as Shona was concerned.

"I'm going to get the Doctor. You can't talk to me like that." The nurse hurried off, back straight and bristling. The nurse was lucky that was all Shona had said. She knew the nurse was only doing her job but she could shove off. Shona had had a gutful today with people interfering.

"There's no way the Army is going to let you keep me. I know too much and could cause them serious damage. They'll take me back and let me carry on regardless. If I talked I could cause a lot of trouble for the Military, and they know it so I'm free. You will not be able to touch me." Her face, as always, was devoid of any emotion as she delivered the words.

Shona was furious but had more sense than to argue with her. It was pointless. The sad thing was that what she said was probably true. This epitome of Satan on a bad day was going to get away with it. This was confirmed when Shona's phone rang.

"Shona, it's the Chief Inspector here."

"Sir?"

"There's an ambulance, some Lieutenant Colonel and more MPs on their way. They will be escorting Major Sands back to her unit. She will be operated on by Military surgeons and looked after by Military nurses."

"But Sir…"

"No arguments. It's a done deal, come down from on high by people with much larger pay packets than you or I. You will sign over the prisoner to the Army and do it with good grace, and politeness. Do I make myself clear?"

"Yes Sir." She turned and walked away. Shona couldn't bear the look in the prisoner's eyes.

She didn't get very far. Nina came running after her. "Ma'am we have another problem. You need to come back and speak to Laura Sands."

"Why? We're finished with her. The Army's taking over. I never want to speak to her, or even hear about her, again."

"No we're not. She's now said that she had planned to set off explosives in Myercroft Academy. I heard her bragging to the MPs that this was going to be her final act of revenge."

Shona's blood ran cold as she thought about that scenario. "Did she actually set the explosives?" Her mind was running over all the possible solutions.

"I don't know. I thought it would be better to get you."

Shona ran along the corridor back to Laura's room.

"You had better not be serious. Is this some sort of joke?"

"Do I look like I'm cracking a joke?" Laura's soulless eyes gave Shona her answer.

"Have the bombs been set?"

"Why should I tell you? What will you give me in return?"

"The Army's dealing with you. I've nothing to barter."

"You could speak to the Army for me. Ask for a measure of clemency."

"Fine. I'll do it. Now have the bombs been set?"

"Of course. You should know by now I'm serious. Deadly serious."

"What time?"

"You've had your one piece of information. What I will say is you're too late. As a bonus I'll add that there are several bombs."

Shona flew from the room almost in a panic. Pulling her mobile phone out of her pocket she said, "Nina, find every Officer in the hospital. Get them here. Peter, phone the head teacher at The Myercroft. Tell her there is a credible bomb threat. She has to evacuate the building immediately. Ring Roy or Iain and get the team to report to the Myercroft."

She dialled the Chief's number. "Sir. There has

been a development. Can you call in the Army Bomb Disposal Unit for The Myercroft? Laura Sands says she's set explosives."

Next she rang her contemporary in Uniform. "Mike, we need all the roads around The Myercroft closed to vehicles and pedestrians." She explained the situation.

"I'm on it," and he hung up.

A suited and booted Senior Army officer approached Shona. "I'm told you are Detective Inspector McKenzie."

"Yes. Shona."

"Lt. Col James Redburn-Smith. I would say it's a pleasure to meet you, but given the circumstances..."

Shona wondered if you had to have to have a double-barrelled name to be one of Her Majesty's finest officers?

"We can dispense with the preliminaries. I've not got time. You're here to pick up Major Sands?"

"Correct. We'll also need full details of what has happened."

"I'll send through a report. Give your contact details to one of my Officers. I'm sorry to be so abrupt but your prisoner has set a bomb in a school."

Shona led the shocked officer to the prisoner and left him to it. Looking at her made Shona want to commit GBH. The Army were welcome to her.

As she left she could hear Laura Sands shouting after her. "You need to speak to the Colonel and ask for clemency."

Shona ran back to Laura Sand's cubicle, as fast as her current pain levels would allow, and said to the officer, "Throw the book at her. If there is still a statute on the books for the death penalty in the Army then use it. You'll have my full support to write up a case."

Flying from the room she heard Major Sands say,

"You bastard." It was the first bit of emotion Shona had seen from her. Shona shouted back, "Now, now Major there's no need to swear," and then smiled despite the severity of the current situation. Revenge is sweet.

Returning to the casualty waiting area, she found Nina, Peter, and a couple of Uniforms. "One of the ambulances is going to take us to the Myercroft. They're going there anyway. The Chief has called a major incident. I'll brief you en route."

50

When they arrived at the school the whole area was cordoned off. In the gloom, the flickering blue lights of the emergency vehicles softly bathed the area making it look surreal. There were hundreds of chattering, shivering, school uniform clad teenagers watching everything closely.

Shona found the head teacher. "Isn't there somewhere else they can go? Surely they can at least be parked in the halls of other local schools. If an explosive device does go off we don't want them injured."

"I agree. I'm waiting for buses to come and move the whole school. They're going up to St John's. They can stay in the hall until their parents collect them."

Are you sure all the pupils are out?"

"I'm waiting for the final registers to come in, but they're all accounted for so far."

"Good. We'll need you to stay in case we have any questions about the layout."

"Of course. I've given the Bomb Disposal Unit our major incident file. It has a map of the school. This building seems to be cursed. It doesn't seem that long ago we had a major fire. It would be less trouble managing a prison."

Shona went to speak to the officer in charge of the Bomb Disposal Unit. "What can we do?"

"Just keep everyone out of the way. We don't know exactly where the explosives are, and there could be more than one. Seemingly Major Sands is keeping shtum. Our MPs have questioned her but she hasn't said one word."

"How can one woman cause so much devastation?"

"Beats me. Especially since she's meant to be trained to obey orders."

"Trust me, you've never come up against anyone like her before, and you never want to. I think Satan himself takes hints from her."

His radio crackled, "Excuse me." He listened, said "over," and turned back to Shona.

"They've disabled one device. It was in the hall where the kids would have been having their dinner. They're carrying on the search."

Shona felt like she was in some sort of vacuum as the minutes ticked by.

Peter said, "You'd think they would have found something by now."

"For goodness sake, man, let them do their job and stop mithering."

"I'm only saying."

"Well, don't say." Everyone was tense and nervy. Shona was also in a lot of pain which wasn't helping her patience.

"You're looking a bit pale. Are you OK?" said Nina. Shona swallowed and nodded. Truth be told she was far from OK. Nina handed her a couple of paracetamol and a bottle of water, which she'd cadged from one of the firefighters. As popular as ever she suddenly seemed to be chums with most of them. Shona accepted gratefully.

"How can you be chatting up firemen in the midst of this, Nina, even if they are good looking?"

Nina smiled but even that was a bit subdued. "I'm surprised you noticed given your current infatuation with the handsome Procurator Fiscal."

"This is no time to be discussing my love life, or lack of it."

Silence fell. They all waited. There was no more talking, each engrossed in his or her own troubled thoughts.

A few minutes later there was an explosion. There was hushed silence as the dust settled and then the onlookers started to talk. Murmurings led to shouting and reached a crescendo of sound. The Army officer said in Shona's ear, "That wasn't a controlled explosion."

"We need to go in." Shona's voice was loud to be heard above the hubbub.

"No. Leave it to us. We need to make sure the area's clear."

"What about your men?"

"I don't know but we can't worry about that. We have to clear and stabilise the area."

His radio crackled. He listened and then turned to Shona.

"They're OK. Well, mainly OK. Seems like one of them has a crushed leg. His oppos are bringing him out for the medics to deal with. No fatalities" Shona let out the breath she didn't know she had been holding. "Thank you, God."

Some hours later they all returned to the station. The OIC of the Bomb Disposal Unit had assured them the area was safe. The fire crews had taken over responsibility for the bomb site, and were being ably assisted by Uniform and a handful of soldiers the Army had left behind.

"I don't know about you lot but I need something to eat and a pint with a whisky chaser," said Peter.

"Nothing for me. I don't think I'll ever eat again. What a day. I know you're exhausted guys and gals but there are reports to be written. As the saying goes, a policeman's lot is often not a happy one."

51

November 2012

Much as she wanted to go home and lick her wounds Shona had to brief the Chief and complete a mountain of paperwork. Weapons had been fired, and officers injured, so there were reports to be filed explaining the circumstances.

Going to speak to the Chief she outlined the morning's events.

"Well at least you managed to catch the killer but I would have preferred if you had done so without injuring any PCs. My equivalent in uniform branch is not a happy man. You're likely to be out of action for weeks as well so what am I going to do? You'll be filling in paperwork for months. Oh, also you'd better send out a press briefing and let them know what's happened."

Shona knew that would be the extent of any thanks she would get. She returned to her office, coffee in hand. It was true a prophet was never welcome in his own hometown. The Chief could have been a tad more effusive after the day they'd all had. Even after all this he couldn't find it in his heart to give them a word of praise.

Reluctant to make a start on the paperwork, Shona rang Douglas. She needed to hear a friendly voice.

"Shona it's good to hear from you. How are you? Caught the killer yet?"

"Yep caught, arrested, and stolen by the Army."

"What?"

"It's a long story. I'll explain later. Could you pick me up and take me home. I've broken my arm."

"How on earth did you break your arm? Never mind, tell me later. Of course I can pick you up. When would you like me to come? I'll chauffeur you to the Ferry personally and make sure you're settled and comfy."

The sound of his voice made her feel warm and reassured. Her woes faded into the distance.

"Thanks. It will be good to see you."

A couple of hours later Shona was finished, and waiting for Douglas to arrive, when the phone rang.

"DI McKenzie."

"DI McKenzie, it's Colonel Jeremy Forbes-Ratcliffe here. I'm afraid there has been a fatal accident. Major Laura Sands is dead."

I knew that one of the players in this game of cat and mouse would be dead before the day was out. I was right.

Laura Sands was also right. The Army did look after its own.

<<◇>>

WENDY H. JONES

Wendy H. Jones lives in Dundee, Scotland, and her police procedural series featuring Detective Inspector Shona McKenzie is set in Dundee.

Wendy, who is a committed Christian, has led a varied and adventurous life. Her love for adventure led to her joining the Royal Navy to undertake nurse training. After six years in the Navy she joined the Army where she served as an Officer for a further 17 years. This took her all over the world including the Middle East and the Far East. Much of her spare time is now spent travelling around the UK, and lands much further afield.

As well as nursing Wendy also worked for many years in Academia. This led to publication in academic textbooks and journals. Killer's Countdown is the first book in the Shona McKenzie series.

FIND OUT MORE

Website: http://www.wendyhjones.com

Full list of links: http://about.me/WendyHJones

Twitter: https://twitter.com/WendyHJones

Pinterest: http://www.pinterest.com/wjones64/

Photographs of the places mentioned in the book can be found at: http://www.pinterest.com/wjones64/my-dundee/

Printed in Great Britain
by Amazon